L

Berith

and the Plight of the Lions

Anne,

Thank you so much,
I hope you enjoy it,

Paul Petrone

Contact Paul Petrone at: DanBerithLions@gmail.com

ISBN-10: 1-523-88509-2
ISBN-13: 978-1-52388-509-1

Printed by CreateSpace
an Amazon.com company

CONTENTS

DEDICATION

This book is dedicated to the United States of America. A country which has given me so much, and to which I've given so little.

To show my appreciation, a percentage of the proceeds of this book will be donated to charitable organizations that serve our nation's veterans. It's not enough, but it's something.

Part I: It Happened So Fast

"I'm gonna live till I die."
– Frank Sinatra

All she wanted was a deviation.

Ashley Morris, 28, had done all the right things. Straight A's in high school, 3.8 GPA at Emerson. Sure, she had that brief slipup that one semester where she fell in love with that one guy, but other than that, she was the prototypical student.

Prepared. Kind. Kept her mouth shut. Raised her hand when she knew the answer, but not every time she knew the answer. Just enough so she was seen as engaged, without seeming arrogant.

Her career began with four years in the capitol city, Hartford, working for an insurance company. Doing email marketing for customers to decrease churn and hopefully upsell them. And she produced.

Her email open rate was 43 percent, one of the highest in the industry for opt-in users. Her click-through rate was 23 percent, exceptionally high. Churn in her target group reduced by 14 percent. And her targets – single-payer auto insurers in the U.S. – were one of the quickest in the company to adopt new products. Her biggest success was selling a new line of motorcycle collision insurance.

Then came the offer from Pfizer six months ago. To start, $84,000 a year, to run email campaigns for their hospital buyers. It was a new initiative for the pharmaceutical company, as primarily they used outside sales to drive new business. This was the first time they'd use marketing automation to both drive new prescription drug sales and retain acute care providers, and it was completely her domain.

Three now worked under her, a graphic designer, a copywriter and a marketing automation specialist. She was going from a place where she often felt her voice was never heard, where the good ol' boy philosophy of doing it the same old way was the only way, to an innovative new project where she would have real responsibilities and real control. Hell, she was even managing her own budget now.

"What a great opportunity," her mother said when Ashley received her official offer. "I'm so proud of you."

Ashley always called her mother daily, often twice daily, and especially when she had big news like a new job as marketing and relationship manager at Pfizer. She told her mom just about everything: the movies she watched, the exercise classes she was into and even the dates she went on.

But not the date tonight. No, it was a rarity for Ashley to keep anything from her mother, especially something as exciting and anxiety-inducing as a first date. But she didn't call her mother at all that day, just texting her around 5 that she was tired and was just going to watch some Netflix, so her mother wouldn't be worried.

She didn't want her mother to know, fearing she'd talk her out of it. Preying on her guilt, which was high enough already. But Ashley needed this, she knew she needed it, and she knew if she talked to her mother she wouldn't go through with it.

Ashley had been in a relationship for three years with David Payne. They went to high school together – Ledyard High, Class of 2002 – and rekindled their friendship at Sarah Jacobson's beach house party in 2008. Well, more than just rekindled their friendship, as David kissed her that night for the first time.

It was the most aggressive move Payne ever made. He spent the entirety of their relationship at the same job doing inside sales for a media company. And he wasn't particularly good at it, making his calls each day and facing rejection after rejection after rejection.

The sex was rare after the first year and David was traditional. Too traditional. Just missionary he enjoyed, and God forbid he go down on Ashley. She suggested handcuffs one time, costumes another, but David just laughed both off.

That was the secret Ashley kept from everyone, most of all her mother. She told her mom she decided to break up with David three months before because she didn't think he was ambitious enough and that the "relationship just wasn't going anywhere." That might or might not have been true, but that wasn't why she broke up with him.

It was because of the sex. David sucked at sex – he'd last about 15 pumps and then curl in a ball and fall asleep. And his tastes were so vanilla.

Ashley's tastes were chocolate. And strawberry. And double-fudge caramel. And every other ice cream flavor there was, complete with threesomes and role-playing and whips and any other steamy, freaky thing you could think of. Her biggest fantasy was she wanted to be tied up and pounded, submitting completely to a man's will.

Those thoughts were ones David never had, or at least never acted on. And she couldn't imagine having that same boring sex for the rest of her life.

Her hope was that tonight that would change. Two weeks ago, a 36-year-old man named Mike messaged her on Match – she had signed up a month before, with her mother's blessing – asking her if she "wanted to hang out

4

sometime." Mike, at least in his profile, was different from the guys she dated before. He was muscular, but she'd dated muscular guys before. That wasn't it. And he had tattoos, which she didn't find particularly attractive anyway.

He had a beard, tightly cropped, and short dark hair, styled up. He was classically handsome, with the square jaw and chiseled features, and had pictures of himself driving a motorcycle and playing with his two dogs.

But it wasn't even his looks that made Ashley want him, although she found him very attractive. It was something else – his confidence, his swagger – that oozed off the photos. She knew, just from looking at that two-dimensional photo of him in her iPad in her bed, that Mike would give her the sex she wanted.

The sex she craved.

She masturbated to him the night he messaged her. It isn't as if she'd never masturbated before, she did it about twice a week, even had her own vibrator. But she never had an experience like that.

It felt like Mike was there. It felt like he was penetrating her. It was the best orgasm she ever gave herself.

A day later, she messaged him back. Three days, three painful days, she heard nothing. On the inside, she was dying, but she never told a soul of her plight, not even her closest friends.

Secretly, she liked the pain.

On the fourth, he finally responded. Short, brief, to the point. A man of few words, she thought to herself.

He wanted to meet her for drinks at Rosanne's in Noank. Rosanne's was a middle-class coastline bar parading as an upper-class bar, a place where the waitress would read off all the white wines a person could order, with the patrons politely nodding as if they knew what a single one was, and then just picked the second-cheapest one.

Tonight was the night, tonight at 7:30. Did he mean to buy her food? Seven-thirty was on the edge of dinner and drinks or just drinks. Maybe she would eat a small meal before, and if he asked her if she was hungry, they could share an appetizer.

That would be cute.

6:41 p.m.

What should she wear? Ashley was never blessed with large breasts, her A cups a source of lifelong disappointment. But she was fit enough and had a nice ass – David would always rave about her ass, her shapely white ass – so she figured she could show that off.

It was fall, so she wore a white sweater over a tight pink blouse, her straight brown hair coming down to her shoulders. Her pants were tight and intentionally ripped and faded, the pants David always said made her ass look best.

"I'm going to get laid tonight," she told the mirror. "For the first time in my life, I'm going to get laid. Real, passionate sex. Doggie style, cowgirl, whatever he wants, I'll do. Heck, if he wants to tie me up, he can tie me up. And I'm going to enjoy it."

Ashley never had a one-night stand before. She made her boyfriend in college wait three months, David two. Mike, she would give herself to Mike within a few hours, if he proved to be the man she was so desperately hoping for.

Noank, Connecticut

7:40 p.m.

She drove herself in her 2011 Audi to Roseanne's, fashionably late. Walked into the restaurant and saw Mike talking with the bartender, a less-attractive version of himself.

She could tell right then, by the way he moved his arms, the perfectly fitting black shirt he wore and the smile on his face, that her instinct was pinpoint. He was unconditionally confident – arrogant even – and that's exactly what she wanted.

"Hello," she said, smiling, extending her hand. Mike never even got out of his seat, shaking her hand in his bar stool as she took the one next to him.

"Watch out for this guy," the bartender said, smile on his face. "He's a heartbreaker."

Ashley smiled seductively at Mike, a hand going to her face to brush away some of her brown hair. "Is that true?" she asked.

"Oh, I'm not so sure about that," Mike said, smiling. His voice was deep, masculine. She melted the first time she heard him use it.

8:46 p.m.

They'd spent about an hour there, sharing an appetizer about 30 minutes in, with Ashley doing most of the talking. Mike was like a conductor, steering the conversation whichever way he wanted it to go, with Ashley acting as the pistons, doing all the actual work.

She told him about Pfizer, her mother, her friends, how

she likes to travel, even her car. He laughed occasionally, rarely broke eye contact and kept a smile on his face – the perfect listener.

He's a better man than expected, Ashley thought. Maybe I misjudged him, maybe he's more than just a one-night stand, she thought.

For Mike, meanwhile, this was his eighth date off of Match in the three months since he joined. Four of the previous seven ended in the bedroom.

Ashley was in the middle of talking about her new job. Mike had no real idea what she was talking about – he ran a successful AutoZone in Montville, and knew or cared little about modern content marketing – but sat in his stool, smiling, nodding at all the right times.

"You see, my boss Jim wants to keep our efforts strictly to the Northeast so we work directly with our own outside sales team to close deals," Ashley explained, partially worrying she was talking too much about work but partially thrilled that someone (aside from her mother) would allow her to talk about work for this long of a time, uninterrupted. "But I told him that's the whole point of this strategy, it's scalable. And we need more data points than just a five- or six-state region. I mean, that's only about 73 acute care units – sounds like a lot, but generally you want campaigns to have thousands of potential buyers to..."

Bang!

It took only a millisecond, but Ashley heard the bullet fly out of the chamber, enter the right side of Mike's forehead and exit out the back end, taking most of his brain with it.

You always think in those moments you are going to

do the exact right thing – in this case, duck behind the bar and call 911 on your cellphone. But even though the world slows down to the point that you can watch a bullet enter a person's head and come out the backside frame-by-frame, a sense of matter-of-fact inevitability tends to take over the situation.

Ashley knew the bullet had killed Mike. She turned in slow motion and saw the next bullet coming for her own head. She knew that bullet was going to kill her too, forever ending every thought she would ever have again about marketing or her mother or the fuck she always wanted but never really got.

Looking back, if she could look back, she wished her brain could have told her head to move. Or at least scream. Something. Anything. But instead, in that split second, despite knowing the bullet was headed straight toward her head and would kill her, she was static.

In that moment, she accepted her death.

The bullet did exactly what it was intended to do, flying into her brain at 2,500 feet per second, barely slowing down as it whizzed out the back of her skull. It killed her instantly, her body dropping on the hardwood floor.

What happened next is anyone's guess. Did Ashley's soul hover over her body, saying goodbye for one last moment, before it rushed up to heaven?

Did her entire life flash before her eyes, and then was some part of her sucked down to a place so unimaginably terrible, words could never do it justice?

Or was there just nothingness, her mutilated body no different than one of a squirrel after an unsuccessful attempt to cross Main Street during rush hour? Perhaps Ashley's life, her dreams, her relationships were all over, her existence forgotten completely a few years after her passing, less than a blip on the trillion-year history of the multiverse.

The only people who know for sure aren't around to talk about it.

Meanwhile, the shooting raged on, with ululations and gunfire canceling out screams of the 40 or so people who ate inside. By the end, not a single one survived, all sharing the same unknown fate Ashley encountered.

The man, once the deed was done, moved on. So far, he'd done a good job of accomplishing his main objective: chaos.

Part II: Glass Houses

"The mass of men lead lives of quiet desperation."
– Henry David Thoreau

New London, Connecticut
Tuesday, May 15, 2012; 6:48 p.m.

Tick. Tock. Tick. Tock.

The seconds passed by on the oversized clock in my living room.

Tick. Tock. Tick. Tock.

Despite my best efforts to block them out, I still heard each movement of the hands.

Tick. Tock.

Another night.

By then I'd showered and eaten and was lying on the red couch in my living room, watching my 48-inch flat-screen TV. The goddamn thing cost me $500, figured I might as well get my money's worth.

On it was the last 12 minutes of an old sitcom. A funny show, at least.

My living room was a rectangle of light blue walls – robin egg, to be exact – lined with framed comic book covers and pictures of sports heroes. My favorite shot is the one of Tyree in the air, grabbing that wayward throw.

Brings me back. What a great day that was.

Over the next 12 minutes, I laughed once out loud at the show. That's impressive, honestly – rarely do I laugh aloud when I'm just lying around, watching TV by myself. During the commercials for prescription drugs, a new romance movie and beer, I checked my phone.

No new phone calls. No new text messages. One email advertising a two-day sale for DVDs.

I unsubscribed from the email. Still, I thought about buying a DVD for a minute, but figured I could just stream the movies instead and save some money.

The only reason to buy DVDs is to decorate the bookcase. It doesn't make any sense, I know, but for some reason that appeals to me. Just not enough for me to part with $8.

7:22 p.m.

I was still watching TV. It was another rerun of the same show, and I hadn't laughed once at it. I grabbed my crotch in boredom.

7:38 p.m.

I was on my bed, my computer to my side, temporarily content. The typical position of myself right after I'm done doing the thing men do all too often when they're alone, yet never talk about.

My bed wasn't made, so I was lying partially on the rumpled green sheets and partially on the blue comforter, which was folded over on itself. The room was off-white and the walls barren, the only room in the house I hadn't painted and "decorated" since I bought the damn thing four years ago.

That's not true; the whole upstairs isn't done, where the tenants live. But you know what I mean, the part I live in.

I stared at the ceiling, not really wanting to move.

7:58 p.m.

I had made my way back to the couch in my living room, where I texted my buddy Ryan, asking him if we were still getting wings on Thursday at that new bar on Main Street. Ryan texted back four minutes later, confirming the appointment.

I responded, "cool man."

End of conversation.

8:22 p.m.

I was watching the Celtics play. It's the playoffs, but it sucks – the Celtics have no shot of going anywhere. Good news, though, as on the TV's channel guide I saw a movie I like was playing at 9.

I thought about making popcorn, but figured I probably shouldn't. It isn't healthy for me and I'd been eating like crap lately.

Plus, I didn't really feel like getting up anyway.

8:34 p.m.

I was on Facebook, computer on my lap, although nothing really interesting had been updated on the site since the last time I checked on my phone, 30 minutes earlier. In reality, nothing interesting is ever on there, yet it doesn't stop me from checking a dozen times a day.

Why? I don't know. I've always noticed that: We always have higher expectations for things than what we should, so we are almost always disappointed. No matter how many years of disappointment we have, we keep making unrealistically high expectations.

Why? Part of me thinks it stops us from going insane, part of me thinks it makes us insane in the first place.

Deep, right? Ah, fuck you, not everyone can be fucking Descartes.

I checked Facebook chat and saw Alexandra was on. That's exciting, I supposed, in a creepy sort of way.

The last time I had seen Alexandra was 10 days before. She was out with two girls – both of whom I knew, all three went to high school with me – at this overrated Irish bar on State Street.

I had seen on Facebook that Alexandra broke up with her boyfriend a few months before and was posting a lot on there, a telltale sign she was lonely and looking for some new guy. And I knew the two girls she was with that night – Julianne Hopkins and Erica Lindros – both had boyfriends.

That had to make her feel even lonelier, ripe for the pickings, I figured. I'm a sleazy fuckhead, I figured.

That night, I was with my buddy Jack, who was pretty good friends with Julianne's boyfriend so, by proxy, he spends a lot of time with Julianne. The two of us went over to talk to the three girls, Jack leading the way and yours truly left talking to Erica and Alexandra.

Alexandra was somewhat attractive – brown hair, brown eyes, thin, not much of a body and an okay face. That was good, I figured. She wasn't too hot where she wouldn't give me a chance but she wasn't too ugly where I'd be embarrassed to introduce her to my dad or anything.

The guys who get the hot girls, they probably don't think like I think. They probably think they deserve the hottest girls in the room. But, what the hell, I'm not wired that way, so I'll just play with the cards I was dealt, thank you very much.

That night, I talked to her and Erica for about eight

minutes, made them laugh a few times. I said I lived close by and Alexandra said, "We should all hang out sometime," so I figured that might be an opening.

Truth be told, I didn't see it as an opening in the moment. Only later that night, when I was alone, right before I went to bed, did it come to me. That's the way it goes – the further removed I am from talking with a girl, the more I think they want to bang me.

Just like I said, humans are the kings of jacking up expectations.

Anyway, after we talked to the trio and returned to our seats at the bar, Jack and I agreed Erica was probably the hottest one, but she seems like a drama queen. The kind of girl who would throw a drink on you in a crowded bar if you wouldn't un-friend your ex-girlfriend on Facebook, we agreed.

Julianne was cool, Jack said. He didn't comment on her looks because she was his boy's girlfriend. If you ask me, I'd say she was pretty hot too. But then again, no one asked me, least of all Julianne.

All Jack said about Alexandra was that "she's cool" as well, probably because she's the least attractive one of the three and he didn't want to go out on a limb and say she was attractive. I followed up with "I'd bang her," and we both laughed.

Goddamn, why do I talk about girls the way I do? Is that what all guys do? Am I any more or less sleazy than the rest?

Done exploring life's deeper issues, I stared at Facebook, wondering if I should chat up Alexandra. And all I'm thinking about is, why can't getting girls be like framing a house? Framing a house, you know exactly what to do. You frame the house just like people have been framing houses forever.

If you want to frame the house quicker, you work longer, harder hours and the house gets framed faster.

It's simple, straightforward stuff.

But girls aren't like that. If you try harder, they get turned off. Instead, you're left trying to play this impossible-to-figure-out game where you are not sure when to nail, when to cut and when to not do a damn thing.

I don't want to come across as some sleazy creeper. Truth is, I hate those types who just do what they do and never talk to the girl again. I'd love a girlfriend. That way I'd never have to figure out this impossible-to-figure-out game ever again, where I'm stuck trying to figure out on some random Tuesday night if I should Facebook-message this girl or not.

Worst of all, she isn't even that hot.

Overwhelmed with my own thoughts, I got up and walked through my "office" – my favorite room in the house – and into the kitchen. The kitchen was painted brown, decorated with just a few pictures from my trip with Tom to Alaska and an ornate clock hung on the wall, slowly ticking away.

Tick. Tock. Tick. Tock.

I reached into his fridge – the fridge was a mess, overdue for a cleaning – and grabbed a brew. Good news was I still had four left from Saturday night, when Tom came over and we pregamed at my house.

Well, make it three now.

I turned around, took two steps forward, reached up

and opened a cabinet to get the popcorn. The cabinets are ugly: overly finished wood with gold knobs that don't fit in with my 113-year-old house. At all.

That's the new saying, by the way, in case you hadn't heard. Every 22-year-old girl says "at all" at the end of declarations to make them particularly emphatic. You know, when they aren't too busy retaking photos of themselves with their phones.

The countertops in the kitchen were ugly too: brown, speckled laminate. I would love all-white cabinets with brass knobs and blue granite countertops, but that probably isn't happening anytime soon.

I grabbed the popcorn, threw it in the microwave and uncapped the beer – the diet would start tomorrow, apparently. Meanwhile, Alexandra and her ordinary face and pencil body were running through my head, as I tried to figure out if I should message her or not.

Maybe the beer will help me figure it out.

8:52 p.m.

I was sitting in my red armchair in my living room with my computer open, looking at the green dot next to Alexandra's name in Facebook chat, indicating she's available to chat.

Suddenly, the green dot disappeared and was replaced by a phone icon, indicating she was away. Guess that saying was right, he who hesitates is lost.

I downed the rest of my beer and went into the kitchen to grab one more.

Going to start eating real healthy tomorrow, I promised

myself. I just need one last binge, I promised myself.

9:43 p.m.

I'd been watching this action movie since 9. But I've already seen it, and honestly it isn't really that great, so I'm getting bored.

Maybe I'll check Facebook to see if Alexandra is on.

10:23 p.m.

I was bored, pacing in my kitchen, debating if I should drink a beer or not. I knew I didn't want to go bed — that's like giving up on the night — but I didn't really have anything fun to do, either.

I went back to the couch and had just started flicking through channels. Nothing really that interesting on, as I'd given up on that movie, no fun watching the same movie again.

I guess I could message Alexandra, but that doesn't even sound that exciting, I thought. Honestly, I figured she's nothing really that special and she's not really that hot. And what was I even going to say to her anyway?

10:47 p.m.

I messaged Alexandra.

It was three minutes ago — 10:44 p.m. exactly. I wrote the very romantic "Hey."

She just wrote back: "Hey Dan, what's up?"

Shit. I had no idea what to write next.

I figured I could make casual conversation. I could ask her out. I could profess my love for her ordinary face and pencil body. No matter what, I should probably write something.

"What's up!?" I wrote.

Geez, what am I, a 14-year-old girl? What's with the explanation point?

Chill, Dan, focus, I thought to myself. I grabbed a beer in the kitchen quick and ran back to the computer.

"Oh, not much just watching TV," I found as I returned to my red armchair.

10:53 p.m.

I could recant the rest of my conversation with Alexandra, but it was so pedestrian, so uninspiring, it's almost too embarrassing to do so.

Basically, I told her I was watching that movie – even though I wasn't – and she said her brother loved that movie and made her watch it and she thought it was pretty cool, and I said that was cool, so few girls have seen that movie.

And then she said she wasn't like other girls and watched action movies, and I felt that was a little trite, but whatever, I guess that's cool, and then I wrote back pretending like I thought that was really cool because I knew she wanted to hear that – even though I don't think it is really that cool and she's probably just saying that to look cool, which definitely isn't cool.

Then, she told me it was cool to see Jack and I the other weekend and she thinks that bar is pretty cool – even though I think it is overrated – but I was like, yeah, it's pretty cool and it was really cool to see you. And then she made some generic comment about hoping to run into us – key word us, not me – again, and I said that would be really cool, it would be so cool to see you again.

Bottom line, a lot of things were cool. Even though I didn't really think any of them were really cool.

And then she said she was going to bed and "it was great talking with you" and I said bye. That was it.

I spent the whole night drinking beer and worrying about having the most boring, generic, sterile conversation possible in human history. Aside from that, my other accomplishment for the night was kinda sorta watching a movie I'd already seen.

Exciting night for me. Wish I could say I was being sarcastic.

11:11 p.m.

I was in bed. About to sleep.

I reflected on the night and became mad at myself for eating the popcorn and drinking the beer – I'm supposed to be eating better.

I didn't even really think about my conversation with Alexandra because the whole thing was so overblown in my own mind and was so terribly uninteresting in real life that I couldn't even bring myself to have an opinion on it, and I have an opinion on just about everything.

Hell, I'd rather have bombed completely than did what I did, which was basically nothing. At least it would have been interesting.

11:23 p.m.

I couldn't sleep so I checked my phone to see if Alexandra was on chat. She was. She didn't go to bed.

Whatever, she has a pencil body anyway and her face is plain-mother-F-er-Jane, if you ask me.

1:15 a.m.

I awoke in the middle of a dream about framing the house I framed earlier that day. Golly, even my goddamn dreams were boring.

I rolled over and tried to go back to bed, but I could hear that goddamn clock all the way in the living room.

Tick. Tock. Tick. Tock.

Couldn't get that noise out of my head.

Guantanamo Bay, Cuba
Date: unknown

"Hello."

John Dempsey walked into my desolate white cell carrying a chair, frowning, his soft blue eyes looking like he was the gentlest man in the world. I was handcuffed.

"How are you today?" he asked.

I stared at the corner, ignoring the American.

"Not very forthcoming, are you Akil?"

Silence.

"You don't have to tell me anything, that's fine. But that means we are going to have to waterboard you again."

I didn't care. It honestly wasn't that bad.

"Come on," Dempsey said, now sitting in the chair he brought in with him. "I'm tired of doing this. Why don't you give me something valuable?"

"Why would I do that? I'm not getting out of this cell either way. Yes, maybe I'd avoid some torture. Big deal. It isn't even that bad, and I know you aren't going to really hurt me."

Dempsey sighed. "Why don't you at least tell us about the Pakistanis? They are the ones who got you in here. Why are you possibly protecting them?

"Just because it pisses you off."

Dempsey sighed again. "Fine. I hate to do this, but you leave me no choice."

He whistled, and two more Americans came in, both soldiers. Both brainless, crew-cut American soldiers, who say "yes sir" and "no sir" all day and spend all night drinking beer, watching movies about girls they'll never touch and telling their families what it's really like to be around someone truly evil like myself.

"Yes sir," said the tallest one, as he entered my cell. He looked particularly dumb.

"Grab the gurney," Dempsey said, and the tall one went out to fetch it.

"Why are you doing this?" I asked. "You know it isn't going to make me talk. It's just a waste of our time."

"I wish I didn't have to, but it's official protocol," Dempsey said. "If you tell us something, we can stop, and we'll leave you alone with some books. Hell, we'll even let you visit with some of your friends."

"You know I'm not going to do that."

"That's your choice. Unfortunately, though, that choice

means more of the same."

The tall solider came back with the gurney. The other one uncuffed me and then strapped me to it, tightening the straps over my chest, arms and legs, and then wheeled me out of the cell like I was Hannibal Lecter himself.

We passed seven doors on the right: three empty, four occupied, as far as I could tell, which was the exact same as it looked the last time I went down the hallway, about two days ago. On my left was the common area, presumably for dining and recreation, but I don't think anyone was allowed to leave his cell.

Our only regular contact as prisoners was when our meals were served to us men (and I believe there were only men) three times a day through slits in our cell doors that could be opened only from the outside.

There was an advantage being strapped to a board. Gave you some time to observe things, really watch whatever is going around you.

Not that there was too much to see. Just the two soldiers, Dempsey and myself progressing down a concrete empty hallway, my wheels occasionally squeaking as we went.

At the eighth door, Dempsey took a right and walked into a cinder-block room painted a pale white. The two soldiers walked me into the room and, with my arms still bound behind me, put a black bag over my head.

The first time they did this, it really pissed me off, being so helpless. But now I was used to it.

The soldiers slanted the gurney upward at a 30-degree angle or so. My head was at the bottom, my feet a good 2 feet above them.

Dempsey began his questioning.

"Why can't you at least tell me about Pakistan's role?"

"John, I'm not going to get into this. Can you just pour the water over my head already?"

"Akil, why do you make us do this? Just tell us something about the Pakistanis and you can go back to your life. They backstabbed you, they're the reason you're here, why do you insist on protecting them?"

"Come on, John, let's not waste our time. Pour the water on my head."

So he did.

It was the 12th time the Americans had done this to me in the past four months or so, not bad for the alleged "shining city on the hill." The first three or four times, I felt like I was drowning and my heart would race.

I had to give them credit; I never had a sensation quite like that before. That said, I've had far, far worse sensations than it – sensations these Americans could not imagine – but it was unique.

Just not unique enough to get me to talk.

Since, though, the rest went just like this one. As Dempsey poured water on my face, I relaxed and counted off with my fingers. After all, I knew their lily-white lawyers wouldn't let them actually hurt me.

One finger rose, a second, a third, etc. At 10, Dempsey stopped pouring.

"He counted again sir," said one of the soldiers.

"I'm aware," Dempsey said. "Come on, you know the drill, let's do it again."

And so they did. More water on my head, another 10-second count, and then I was vertical again with the bag off my head.

"We are just going to keep doing this, Akil, I hope you know that," Dempsey said. "And I know you don't fear it, but I'm sure you don't like it very much. And it's not going to stop."

He stared at me. What a likable face this man had, his eyes so sympathetic, his jowls slightly drooped, his suit so humble. Looked like a good man, the kind of man who had a daughter who was stressing him out, who would change your tire in the middle of the night, who would forgive you quickly if you lost your temper with him.

Of course, that was the whole point. They wanted to make me feel guilty. Wanted me to feel so bad for poor ol' John who's just trying to do his job.

Truth is, he was probably an even bigger asshole than the rest of them. But he played his part well.

Again, I refused to speak, and he looked down at the ground in disappointment. The walk back to the cell was a silent one.

"Are you sure there's nothing you want to tell me?" John asked, when we reached my door.

I ignored him.

"Okay, your decision," he said, and the men went through the routine of putting me back in my cell.

John's voice was the last one I heard, before they slammed the door shut. "I'll see you in two days," he said.

And he did. Two days later, we did the same thing. And two days after that, we did it again, going through the water-boarding each time.

After that, it went to every day, and soon twice a day. Each time would end the same way – John, looking more dejected than ever, asking me why I wouldn't just say something.

Each time, I looked away, literally biting my tongue to stay silent. As much as I knew what they were doing, I did begin to feel bad for him. One time, his eyes were so sad, his face so morose, I bit my tongue so hard to avoid speaking it actually split open.

It was almost like he was the one being tortured.

A month into it, John came to my cell one day. He looked defeated, per usual.

"Last chance, Akil. Tell me something here. I need something from you."

At this point, his voice would send tremors throughout my head, my brain losing its ability to deal with all this manipulation.

"I don't know what to tell you, John," I said. "I'm not going to say anything. I guess we can just keep doing this if you want, but nothing is going to change."

"You know," John said, "I actually think you're right. I don't think you are going to say anything. So we are going to try something new."

"What is that?"

"You'll soon find out."

With that, he walked out of the room and closed the door. John then opened the slit in the door and I put my hands through it so he could uncuff them, as he always did, and I asked him a question.

"Seriously, what are you going to do?"

"Like I said, you'll find out," John said through the slit in the door. "Although I really wish you didn't have to."

After my hands were freed, the slit slammed shut.

That was the last conversation I would have for six months.

New London, Connecticut
Friday, May 18, 2012; 8:43 p.m.

"I really cannot stand that woman."

For once, Buffalo Bill's was quiet on Friday night. Well, not quiet – the place was mostly packed and filled with all the normal sounds of drunken conversation, forks hitting plates and televisions murmuring.

But at least there wasn't a live band, like there normally was, where it was so loud you couldn't hear the person next to you. I hate when they put the music on so loud you have to shout just to make small talk.

When it is like that, you begin to question why talk at all. You realize then it is like walking through a blizzard – you trek on, because there's blood in your veins and you owe it to yourself to keep living, but that doesn't mean it's particularly fun.

That wasn't a problem tonight, though; there was no music at all. Maybe later, usually later, they'd get some band that was so-so to play all the covers that are expected from such a band. But not for now, so it was quiet tonight, quiet enough for me to deliver one of my patented rants to my reticent friend, Tom.

"I'm just saying, she's a power-hungry manipulator, like all the rest of the motherfuckers. But she's even worse than all of them, because people think she's some sort of groundbreaker or something."

"Yeah, I agree, it's kind of bullshit," Tom said after

swallowing a piece of wing.

"I know. I mean, great, she's a woman. If I were a woman, I'd vote for her, no doubt. I would. Just cause what the fuck, I'm a woman, and I'm going to vote for another woman because it's fucked up there hasn't been a single woman president yet. I get that."

I stopped to take a bite of a Buffalo wing. They were spicy wings, and I was beginning to sweat.

"But she's no freaking groundbreaker, man," I said as I took a sip of my beer. "She's exactly like the rest of them. All she cares about is getting more power for herself and taking it away from someone else."

"I get it, too," I continued. "She sees these asshole white guys getting all the power – heck, she's married to some asshole white guy who got all the power – and she's like, fuck that, why do they get all the power? Why do men naturally get all the power, get to make all the decisions, while I just have to sit back and take it while my husband gets his dick sucked by some new whore each week?"

"But that's what makes her worse, that's what make's her so much fucking worse. See, some rich asshole white guy gets power, that's one thing. He has grown up thinking he is going to be rich and powerful, so when he gets all that power, it isn't anything new. I mean, he is an asshole, but he's always known he was going to be some powerful asshole, so at least he can somewhat control himself."

"Now her, she's a different story. And this isn't true for all women or anything, just her, I can spot it. She is angry – really fucking angry that every white jerk with a well-defined part has moved past her in the pecking order, that she was always pushed aside, always got trampled over. And when she gets power, man, she's going to love it, rub it in every-one's face."

"I don't know," Tom said. "They are all like that."

"Yeah, I don't know, you are probably right."

I finished my wing and slugged a beer. I was talking too much, I thought to myself, and I was driving Tom crazy.

I always talk too much. I have opinions and thoughts about everything and I can't shut them off, even though deep inside I know no one really gives a fuck. And then I see some guy like Tom, or most people, and it seems like they just don't match my intensity.

Maybe I'm insane, I don't know. Maybe they are insane for just sitting, like a dog on a rug, allowing life to happen to them. At least I care about stuff; at least I have opinions on things. Everyone else just acts like things are the way they have to be, and that's just the way it is.

Fuck that.

"Hey lil' brother," my sister Amanda said, laughing.

I rolled my eyes.

My sister, all 5'1" of her, with her dark brown hair and dark brown eyes, was dressed in her black shirt and black pants that everyone at Buffalo Bill's wore. Her shirt was a tight V-neck, with the cut coming down to the beginning of her breasts.

She was just a beer deep, but was acting like it was seven.

"What's going on tonight?" I said.

"Not much," she responded. "Michael is at the bar."

I looked over and there was Michael, wearing a craft beer shirt, and talking with his buddies. He was about 6'1", strong build, tattoos running down both arms.

And he was wearing his Sox hat, backward. He looked like a tool, if you ask me.

"And what are you going to do about it?" I asked.

"Whatever I want to do," my sister responded, laughing.

She laughed a lot more with people around, I noticed. Just about everything she did was exaggerated with more people around.

"So why do you think he's here?" she said, grabbing my arm. "You think he's coming for me?"

"Of course he's coming for you, he didn't just randomly pick this place on a night you always work. Tom, would you go to a bar on a night your ex is working, just because?"

My sister laughed.

"No, I don't think so. Unless my friends or something wanted to go. But no, unless I wanted to see her."

Amanda laughed again.

"What should I do?" she asked, smile on her face. "Should I talk to him? This is so awkward."

"Well, how did you guys end it again? What has it been, like a month?"

Amanda said they stopped seeing each other a month ago, although the last time they slept together was last weekend, when he started texting her around 11 on a Friday, telling her he missed her.

Really, he was just horny. Although, then again, that's probably all it was to Amanda, too.

"I don't know, yeah, a month or so," she said. "Oh my God, it is so weird that he's here. And he's with Alex, that guy is so obnoxious."

"Anyway, are you going to get us some more beer or what?" I said. Tom laughed. Amanda slapped my arm.

"Fine, what do you want?"

"The same thing is fine, Bud heavy."

"I'll have a Blue Moon," Tom said.

"Blue Moon is for pussies," I replied. "'Manda, would you be into a guy who had an orange in his beer?'

"No, I don't think so," Amanda said, and then laughed. "That's kind of lame."

"Sounds like the kind of guy who wouldn't even wrinkle the sheets during you-know-what, right?"

"Exactly," Amanda added. "The kind of guy who orders an espresso at the coffee shop and then spends five minutes blowing on it before he drinks it."

We both laughed.

"Alright, alright, I drink my espresso straight on," Tom said. "Just give me a Bud."

"Be right back," Amanda said.

It took her 20 minutes to come back with our drinks. Oh well, can't complain when they're free.

10:45 p.m.

Tom and I were wrapped up watching the end of the Celtics playoff game. I'm not even into basketball that much, but the playoffs are exciting and it was a close game.

Rondo nailed a shot. "Yes!" I screamed while slapping Tom's hand and downing the rest of my beer, making it about eight or so for me.

Might as well take advantage of free booze.

"Hey lil' brother."

She probably had another beer, at the most, but Amanda was acting drunk.

"I'm watching the game!"

There was 2:32 left, Celtics up by three.

"I need to ask you something quick!"

"Ugh, I'm watching the game!"

While I said that, James picked the pocket of Pierce, dribbled down the court and slammed it home. The Miami crowd went crazy.

"How do you let that happen!"

"Bullshit," Tom said. The game cut to commercial.

"Come on, it's commercial, I need to ask you something quickly."

"Alright, go, what's up."

"You think Mike's into me? He's been checking me out all night."

"Come on, the game's on, I really don't want to talk about this."

"I've gotten you free beer all night! Come on, just tell me, do you think he's into me?"

"Yeah, I don't know, probably. I mean, he came into the bar when he knew you were working and you said he's checking you out. But I thought you broke up with him. Why do you care if he's into you?"

"Forget it, but seriously, you think he's into me?"

The commercial was ending.

"The commercial is ending, I'm going to watch the game."

"Oh well, you're going to want to know something else I have to tell you."

"Oh my God, no, I don't care about Mike anymore."

"It isn't about Mike. I think one of my friends might be into you..."

"What? Who?"

"I thought you were watching the game."

"Can you just please tell me and stop being obnoxious."

"Fine, Julie."

"Julie?" Julie was 5'7", long wavy brown hair, big brown eyes, full lips, athletic build. Overall, a solid 8, if you had to put a number on it (which, apparently, I felt obliged to do).

"Yeah, I don't know, she said you were kind of cute."

"She said I was cute? Come on, hook it up."

"You like her?"

"I don't know, what is this, high school? Come on, just hook it up, give me her number and I'll text her."

"Alright. I'll just text it to you."

"Cool. So wait, what did she say about me?"

"I don't know, not much, just that you were cute. And she liked you were a builder, thought that was manly or whatever."

"Really? Manly, huh?"

"Yeah, I don't know – she's always been into guys with beards, too. But it's going to be weird you dating my friend."

"Do you not want me to? I mean, I don't have to."

"No, it's cool. I want you to be happy. And she's really nice and gorgeous, I'm okay with it."

"She is pretty," as I thought to myself that gorgeous might be a bit of a stretch, but she was attractive, for sure.

"Alright, cool. Well, I'll text you her number."

Amanda wound up going home with Mike that night. Tom and I watched the Celtics blow the game late, and then we went our separate ways, with me walking home tipsy.

I got home about 20 minutes earlier and was checking out Julie's Facebook page on my laptop in bed. She's into reggae and yoga, it looked like. And she likes to post a lot of stupid inspirational Buddha quotes, like, "Three things cannot be long hidden: the sun, the moon and the truth."

Also, she's into traveling and had photos of herself at all these weird places. The Dominican Republic, some place I've never heard of in Eastern Europe, even Japan.

I wondered if she really likes to travel, or just to tell people she likes to travel so she can post pictures of herself in weird places on her Facebook page. Maybe she should just buy a green screen; that would be cheaper.

It looks like she broke up with some guy about nine months ago and has been single since. It was pretty easy to spot the time when she broke up – her Facebook posts increased dramatically, most of them those Buddha quotes.

She was pretty hot, though, and she did have a nice body. And she was cool, I met her a few times, she seemed pretty chill. She'd definitely be a good girlfriend.

I checked out her profile pictures – one rule I learned is that the more a girl changes her profile picture, the crazier she is. Before, she didn't change it that much, but in the past six months or so she changed it like 20 times.

She's getting desperate.

She was 30 now, two-and-a-half years older than me, the age where girls start worrying about kids or whatever. So she's probably all into that, wants to find a guy who will propose within a year so she can post a picture of the engagement ring online.

And then the engagement photos. And then the wedding photos. And then, soon thereafter, the baby photos.

Basically, it seems like half of our life is about getting the right photos at the right time on Facebook. I wonder how a 17-year-old girl with no job, no future and some hit-and-run boyfriend feels when she gets pregnant, knowing she probably won't get the benefit of 100-plus Facebook likes on her baby bump photo.

Then again, maybe she will because she'll be the first of her friends to have a kid. And half of her friends' photos will eventually be them holding her baby, and acting all worldly because they "have a friend" who has a 9-month-old.

I hate that phenomenon – you bring up some personal story about yourself, like your mom died three years earlier. And all some jerk can say is, "I have a friend that happened too, it sucks, man." Like them having a casual acquaintance whose mom also died somehow makes them able to relate with your deepest emotions.

Anyway, I was losing focus. I drank too much beer. Back to Julie. Health nut girl, likes Buddha and yoga and all of that, seems pretty cool. I'd have to take her on some weird date, maybe some coffee shop or poetry reading or someplace where there are tapas and the server has dreadlocks.

I'll figure something out, I'll text her tomorrow. Maybe I'll ask Amanda what to do. As for now, I should probably go to bed.

Saturday, May 19; 6:30 p.m.

"So what do you think I should do with her?"
I was sitting on my red armchair in my light blue liv-

ing room, black iPhone pressed up to my ear. Some action movie was on in the background – *Commando*, I believe – as I was talking to my sister.

She was probably at her apartment in Mystic, half a joint deep. We already talked about Mike – I made sure we got that part out of the way first. And I knew I'd get in only a few sentences about Julie before he'd inevitably come back up again.

"I don't know, she's really into fitness and yoga. You should do yoga with her!"

"Oh my God, I'm not doing yoga with her. I've never done yoga before. And you know how I am, I'd probably fart getting into one of those poses."

Amanda laughed. "That sounds like a good first impression."

"Alright, stop, just tell me what I should do with her."

"I don't know, there's a cool new Lebanese place downtown in Mystic. Why don't you check that out? You can get pitas, a bottle of wine and then take a walk along the water."

"That sounds good, I guess. When do you think I should text her? And you think it's weird asking her to hang out one-on-one before we ever really hung out before?"

"No, it's cool, because you already hung out before. Text her like Tuesday. She knows I gave you her number, by then she'll be wondering why you haven't texted her yet."

"Alright, cool. I'm just nervous, you know? It seems kind of weird."

"No, it's cool. She likes you. Just smoke a bowl before you go, it'll calm you down."

"Alright, maybe that's not a bad idea. Hey, when should I ask her out for, Saturday?"

"I think she works Saturdays. Ask her out for Thursday. Then, even if she has something, you can take her out Friday."

"That isn't too close?"

"Seriously, Dan, it's fine. You're overthinking it."

"Okay, you're right, I'm just nervous."

"Anyway, do you really think Mike likes me? I mean, he..."

At that point, I stopped paying attention.

Tuesday, May 22; 7:30 p.m.

I was sitting in that same red armchair. Another action movie was on. And I was wearing a blue Henley, my chest hair peaking out behind the buttons, and a pair of gray sweats.

It was time for action.

I whipped out the iPhone and pulled up Julie's name. Almost accidentally called her – that would have been embarrassing. But I didn't.

Because I'm a playa tonight. Tonight is the night Dan makes it happen, via text.

>What's up

Whoa. I couldn't believe I just sent that. Without even thinking, and that's what I came up with, "What's up". That's lame. That's lame as hell. What am I doing, just sending a text like that, without even thinking about it.

<Who is this?

I barely stopped myself from writing "the mothering fucking man of your dreams." Instead, I decided to play it cool.

>*It's Dan... Amanda's brother. She gave me your number.*

<*Oooo, hey! (: How are you?*

>*Awesome, thanks. Hard day at work, but I'm cool.*

<*Oh yea, you work for your dad, right?*

Work for my dad? That sounds so freaking lame. But I do work for my dad. And she knows that, I can't lie. And justifying it by saying we are "partners" or something makes me sound like I'm some sort of mental patient who daddy is nice to and lets him come to work with.

I figured I'd just roll with it.

>*Yea, that's right, just building houses across America, no big deal ;)*

<Lol. That's so cool! So you are good at like fixing stuff?

>Not bad.

<*Awesome. Next time I break something, I'll know just who to call (:*

>*Ha, that's what I'm here for.*

It was time to go in for the kill.

>*Hey so speaking of building new stuff, I saw they opened a new Lebanese place in downtown Mystic. Would you want to check it out? I think I have a hankering for a pita.*

<*Lol a hankering? No, seriously my friends and I totally were just talking about that place. I'd love to check it out!*

>*Cool, maybe we could do it Thursday?*

< *(: I work Thursday*

>*Friday? I could push back that other date... (jk)*

<*Lol... okay. I'm supposed to see my grandmother,*

but I should be home at like 6.

>That's fine – want me to pick you up at like 7? Unless you are going to be tired or whatever.

<No 7 sounds great! Sounds fun!

>Cool. See you Friday... looking forward to a pita...

<Me too lol. See you then (:

Dan Berith. Natural born playa.

Guantanamo Bay, Cuba
Date: unknown Time: unknown

I'm slowly going insane.

Three times a day, a meal gets slid through the slit in my cell door. That's the extent of my human interaction.

There are no books in my cell. No TV. No window. Just four cinderblock walls, painted white; a steel door; a cot with a pillow, a sheet and blankets; and a toilet.

That's it. Nothing else.

I do push-ups three or four times a day. Run in place for 30 minutes at a time. Sometimes shadow-box, until I can't punch anymore.

There are no showers, mind you. I haven't had a shower in months. Just day after day of sitting in my own stench, in complete silence, not a single other person to talk with.

I'd do anything for a conversation. Or a book. Even some paper to draw or write on, anything.

But there is nothing. Just me, stuck in this cell, reflecting on how stupid I was to get in here, knowing I'd probably die in this place.

I never had any serious thoughts about killing myself, though.

Figured it was temporary. Figured, eventually, something would change, even though I really didn't have any reason to think so.

I was in a cell in the most heavily guarded jail in the world with not a single person within 8,000 miles advocating for my release. I wondered how my friends were doing in the Hindu Kush, although odds were most were dead.

I suppose the one thing I had to live for was the knowledge that the Americans would never get something from me. Ever. Although, then again, the best way to accomplish that would be to kill myself.

And I didn't really want to do that.

I could just tell John something. Give up the Pakistanis, who cares? At least then I'd get books and interaction with humans, maybe even TV.

I couldn't say anything, though. I'm not even sure why I couldn't, but I couldn't. It just isn't right and, truth be told, holding on to that is the only thing keeping me from going completely insane.

Passing the time is hard. I try to stay positive, try to be active in my 8'x10' cell, but most of the time my thoughts turn negative. Such as what an idiot I am. Or how I should have listened to my father. Or how my cock got me into this whole damn thing. Or about all the people I killed, and how nothing changed. Or about knowing that my oppressors are going to win, and I'm just another ant that's been crushed under their tank tread.

Am I an evil man? Probably. I've done evil things. I suppose I can blame my situation or whatever – it sucked, no doubt about it. But I know, in my heart, it's my fault.

The thing is, I didn't do it to advance my cause or for

70 virgins or whatever. I did it because I was bored. And I figured that doing what I did would be more fun than the other option.

That was true, for a bit. But not anymore. I don't feel very fulfilled spending day after day locked in a tiny room by people I hate, not a soul in the world to talk to, as the Americans watch and laugh.

This is boredom personified. There is no better weapon they can use against me than my own mind, as every shred of anything I had left slowly erodes.

One day – about three months in, I counted the days by counting the meals – John opened the slit in the door. "Ready to say something?" he asked, his voice sounding comforting, empathetic.

My whole body shook when I heard the words, both from shock and because I was so excited to hear another human's voice. "What do you want me to tell you?"

John sighed. "Listen, Akil, you know what I mean. Just tell me, yes or no?"

"No," I said, almost instinctively.

He sighed again. "Alright," and he slammed the slot shut.

Somehow, he made me feel guilty for not telling him anything, as if he were the one locked in a tiny room with no one to talk with. He really was good at his job.

How did I get here? Who I am? How do I relate to this story? Those are the questions you're probably asking yourself. Well, the answer to the third one, you'll find that out soon enough.

The first answer is pretty simple: I was backstabbed. At the time of my "arrest," I was one of the leading generals for the mujahideen, who Americans describe as either freedom fighters or terrorists, depending on where U.S. interests lay at the moment.

As a leading general, I did a lot of work with the Pakistanis. In fact, the mujahideen sect I was part of, I found out later, originated in Pakistan.

Not surprising, really, considering we were based out of the Hindu Kush mountain chain, which acts as a geographic border between the northeastern corner of Afghanistan and the northeastern tip of Pakistan. The mountain chain has a long history of war, beginning with Alexander the Great in 300 B.C. In the past 40 years or so, it's been the site of countless battles between Afghanistan, Pakistan, American and Soviet forces.

One day, I went to meet a former government administrator in Ujnu, a small city in Pakistan. I'd met this man countless times – primarily, he was an arms dealer who would funnel us weapons from the Saudis – and we had to work out the details of the latest shipment. The Americans had grown wise to the roads we used to bring in our weapons, and we had to figure out a new route.

At least, that's what I thought. Within 20 minutes of meeting the man, the four soldiers I brought with me were dead, a bag was placed over my head and I felt a dozen fists beating on my body.

I guess the man made a deal. The bag stayed on my head throughout a flight, and it didn't come off until I was brought here, Guantanamo Bay, Cuba.

I suppose I am lucky. A few years ago, we heard stories that most of our men captured by the Americans would be brought to prisons in some faraway land and tortured for months. Waterboarded, beaten, shackled to the wall, forced to listen to music at high volume for days on end, women interrogators throwing their used tampons at them —everything.

I guess now they just lock you in a room alone and hope you say something before your mind destroys itself. Frankly, it might be more effective.

That's the very short version of how I'm here: backstabbed by a man I obviously should have never trusted. But time to answer the second question: Who am I?

I'm Akil Dhakir, one of the most wanted men by the CIA until a few months ago when I got caught. I'm 28 years old, 5'9", about 188 pounds, stoutly built, strong jaw, darker skin and eyes the color of cappuccino.

Who am I really, though? Where did I come from and why do I do the things that I do?

Take a breath, get a drink and pull up a chair. I'll tell you. I certainly have enough time.

Interlude:
The Making of a Terrorist

*"I don't want to be a product of my environment.
I want my environment to be a product of me."*
– Frank Costello

I grew up wanting to be Batman.

Most days were the same in Zhari, Afghanistan, when I was a kid. We hoed. We deadheaded. Or we picked.

Whatever it took to make the poppy grow.

When I say we, I refer to myself and my father, the great Aaqib Dhakir himself. Even on his wooden leg, my father was a tireless worker, picking and hoeing and trimming until his hands calloused over, never complaining, always energetic for the next task at hand.

Myself, I just kept getting more pissed off. Angry that this was my life. Angry that it was hotter than hell during the day and cold at nights. Angry because I got one day off a week.

But mostly angry that our "product" was used for little more than getting a bunch of European junkies high. That was the worst part, knowing you couldn't take pride in your work.

Well, that's not really true. That's one of those things you say, even though you don't really mean it, because it sounds good. Sure, that pissed me off, but that's not what bothered me the most.

What bothered me the most was there were about six girls in my village, and about 200 guys. And those women were all but promised to whatever man's father could give the most generous offer to one of their parents, which certainly wasn't going to be my dad.

No, my dad was just a laborer with one leg, one son and a wife who Allah took away from him too soon.

So, yeah, basically my life wasn't great. It was either too hot or too cold, there were no ladies around, and all the religious shit did was make me feel guilty about everything. I know, Allah wouldn't appreciate that, but sometimes I think his book was just used to justify whatever the new warlord wanted to justify that day.

But any chance I got – once a week or so – I'd run off to the one mosque in our village, which also was one of the few buildings that had electricity and the only one (or, at least, the only I knew of) that had a TV. There, I'd meet my two best friends – Imran and Zayan – and we'd hang out, tell jokes and talk about all the girls we were gonna get when we finally got out of this place.

And we'd watch Batman.

Keep in mind, it wasn't like we had cable or a satellite disk at this mosque. We had a VCR and a few tapes, most of them religious.

But somehow – to this day, I'm not sure how it got there – mixed in those tapes was one animated Batman movie. It was two hours of Batman running around at night, taking down bad guys and playing with cool gadgets.

I loved it.

Imran and Zayan both made fun of me, because all I wanted to do was watch that video. It got to the point where I recited every word as the characters said it, acting out each fight scene. And yet I kept wanting to watch it over and over again, because I knew it was exactly what I wished I could do.

I wished I could be as fearless as Batman, running around and taking down all the people who wronged me – the warlords, the communists, the Americans, the zealots, and on and on. But I knew I probably wouldn't, at least in the back of my mind. Back then, even though I never said it and never actively thought about it, I probably figured my whole life would be growing that poppy for whatever warlord had the most guns at the moment until Allah decided it was time for me to join him.

So, really, watching that Batman movie was the closest I came as a boy to escaping. It wasn't even hope, because I didn't really have hope, just a fantasy I particularly enjoyed.

Plus, it had this girl in it – Harley Quinn, the Joker's girlfriend. She was hot. I know, she was a cartoon, but she was hot.

Certainly hotter than any girl in my village.

I'm sure, as you are reading this now, you are wondering what role politics played in my life. After all, last I left you, I was sitting in Guantanamo Bay, Cuba, accused of waging jihad against the West. Did I hate the West growing up?

I wish it were that simple. Honestly, most of the time I was thinking about how much my job sucked, or wondering what my mom was like, or what my friends were doing that day, or how I could possibly get laid in this country.

That said, I hated the Americans. They betrayed us. When my father fought with the mujahideen against the Soviets, the Americans supported us, gave us weapons, even helped the warlords sell their opium. At that time, we were skeptical, but we thought they appreciated that we were a group fueled by Allah and they were a country built by men who believed in God as well. We thought that commonality would bind our two countries together, even after the Soviets left.

It didn't.

After the Soviets left, the Americans told us our God was dangerous. Said we were an untrustworthy people.

And, almost overnight, our fighting style went from being described by them as ingenious and resilient to cowardly and unacceptable.

And then they bombed us, just like they bombed all the other countries around us. People told us not to trust them, and they were right.

But it wasn't just the Americans. We really, really hated the Soviets. They were terrible, coming and building a government everyone hated, spreading terror and mistrust throughout our country, and then fleeing in the middle of the night when their godless system (expectedly) failed.

We also hated the warlords who fought over our opium and would put restrictions on us. We didn't trust the Taliban, who were essentially the worst of the worst warlords who put their own version of sharia law on our country and – in one particularly ill-fated move that may or may not have been done to increase the value of their opium stockpiles – burned down most of our poppy fields.

Even the terrorists, who I was later (unfairly) connected with, I hated. Bombing innocent people? Batman didn't do that. Yes, I agreed with some of their points, but you don't fly a fucking plane into a building and kill thousands of people.

That's unforgivable. And, worse yet, it destroyed any argument even rational Afghanis had, as now we were the people who were aligned with the people who were the worst form of evil. And, even worse than that, it meant the Americans now had an excuse to come back in, take over our government, bomb us unmercifully and act like they were doing it in our best interest.

I got their initial reaction – obviously, they had to kill

all the terrorists who killed them (a job they weren't even particularly good at). What annoyed us all, though, was that suddenly it went from killing bad guys to getting their president elected so they could take advantage of our natural resources – all while pretending they were some great peacekeepers.

At least they got smart about the opium. Originally, they tried to talk us out of growing it, telling us to grow things like wheat and pistachios. Pistachios! What a joke that was, although the wheat idea was probably even dumber, considering America itself produces enough wheat to feed the world 17 times over.

Here they were, coming into our country where we make less than a dollar a day in their money, and telling us we should grow something that's even less profitable. We all knew that wasn't going to work.

A few years after they invaded – I believe it was 2005 – they wised up. Even began helping us smuggle out the opium again. Which was good, because it meant steady work for my father and I.

Bottom line, the Americans to us – or, to me at least– were not much different than the Soviets, the Taliban, the warlords and any other group that had any power. They were going to do whatever they could to keep their power and take what they wanted.

The only difference was they were going to put their arm around you and act like your friend as they did it.

Anyway, my life really didn't revolve around geopolitics. Sure, my dad would talk about it with the other men and they'd have their opinions, and some things really pissed us all off. But, at the end of the day, no matter who was in power, we were still doing the same dang thing: taking care of the poppy plants.

So when did it all change? When did I become the evil terrorist I am today? Well, I still remember the day clearly.

It was July 16, 2007.

Just some background: In October 2006, when I was 22 years old, some of the Taliban fighters decided to seek refuge in my village. The Americans didn't exactly appreciate that, so they decided to bomb the fuck out of the place. While we heard the noise, none of the bombs exploded anywhere near the house – or, as you would describe it, the shack – that my father and I lived in.

Astonishingly, there was a pretty limited amount of "collateral damage" from the bombing, particularly considering America's standards. Yet that still meant that along with some Taliban fighters, a woman and her 10-year-old daughter died, and the mother's 6-year-old son got his arm blown off.

Of course, this caused outrage throughout the community, even though we'd been dealing with bombings and senseless murders for years. Many of the men agreed it went too far, the Americans were overreaching their bounds, and something had to be done.

In other words, it was the perfect recipe for a "terrorist" recruiter.

Problem was, those "recruiters" were spread so thin, it took them awhile to get to our place. In fact, it took them almost a year, but they finally came on Monday, July 16, 2007.

I was still 22, and by then a decent laborer in the poppy fields. I had become a foreman, like my father, the leader of a four-man crew. But that day was not a farm day, as the boss had us pour a concrete pad off the side of the main harvest building for a generator he wanted to put there.

For us, it meant me and the guys scratching out a flat 6'x8' rectangle into the ground, building a form from some 2'x6's and then mixing and pouring the concrete. By the time the recruiters arrived, we were done scratching out the rectangle and we were digging narrow trenches for the 2'x6's to fit in.

Around 2 o'clock in the afternoon, with the summer heat up around 40 degrees Celsius (that's more than 100 degrees Fahrenheit, for the Americans out there) and the sweat cascading off our brows, a Jeep with the roof off pulled up. Inside were three soldiers wearing thawbs and long beards and holding AK-47s.

Two of the guys – the driver and the guy in the backseat – looked to be about my age. The third, the one riding shotgun, was the oldest, probably around 30 or so.

"My brothers," he said to our group of four as we put the 2'x6's down and put our weight against our shovels, "how are you today?"

"Fine," I said, speaking for the group.

The man set down his machine gun, jumped out of the Jeep and grabbed a cooler from the vehicle. In it were bottles of water, which he threw to the four of us.

"Drink, drink, relax," he said. "I want to talk with you quickly."

There were four of us in the crew – Taj, Rasool, Mohammad and myself, obviously. Taj and Mohammad were shy 16-year-old twins who did everything I said and spent their free time reading the Quran and obeying their parents.

In a few years, I was convinced they'd become addicted to opium.

Mohammad was 21 and the hero of the group. He had a motorbike, which he drove all over town, and even had a girlfriend. I know, I know – we aren't supposed to have girlfriends, but Mohammad wasn't about to let anyone tell him different.

Me, I was the leader, I guess, although I certainly didn't feel like one. My ideal day was when everyone did what they were told, I could get off in time to hang out with Imran and Zayan for a few hours, and then go home and sleep so I could do it all again the next day.

Taj and Rasool bowed politely after catching the bottle of water. Mohammad, who had his shirt off – he always had his shirt off – drank it in three big gulps. I caught mine reluctantly, staring at this stranger in front of me as I drank.

"So, my friends, how are you today?" our visitor said. "Another fun day tending to the poppy?"

"Actually, pouring a slab today," I said, still staring at the man. "What
do you want?"

"Ha, fair question, my friend," the man said, as his two comrades watched silently from the Jeep. "First off, let me introduce myself. I am Dalir Shafi, and I wanted to invite you four to my party tonight."

"What party?"

"Well, we are hoping all the local men come. It is at your mosque. There shall be food and drink and shooting, if any of you are into that."

Taj and Rasool's eyes nearly jumped out of their heads. Even Mohammad broke a smile.

"Do we get to shoot what you're holding?" Mohammad asked, pointing at Dalir's AK-47.

"Of course," Dalir said. "In fact, we are even having a bit of a competition, and the best shot gets a prize."

"What is this, a fair?" I said. "We know what you are doing. You are part of the mujahideen and you want us to join your ranks."

"Guilty as charged," Dalir said. "I am part of the resistance and I would love for you to join our ranks. I was told to go to this community and bring back as many men as would be willing to come with me, and I hope to get a few, sure."

"That said," he continued, "I can tell already I'll meet my quota, as some men have already told me they'd like to join. So I'm not really desperate for recruits because my boss will be happy with what I have. But I still have enough food, enough drink and enough bullets for all of you, so you might as well come down, have a good meal and have some fun shooting guns."

"Sounds pretty good to me," Mohammad said. "Of course, it'd be better if there were some women there, but I guess one thing at a time."

"Women, you say?" Dalir said. "Then you should join us. The women love the men who join the resistance, even declare 'sexual jihad,' where they promise themselves to any man fighting for the right cause. And you should see the women, particularly the ones from Kabul – they are the most beautiful women in the world."

"Here he goes with the sales pitch," I said.

"No sales pitch, just the truth," Dalir said. "Honestly, I wouldn't want any of you to join for women. I'm sure all of you are capable of getting laid on your own. The women are great, sure, but if that's why you are fighting, you are missing the point."

"Why are you fighting?" I asked.

"Why? Many reasons. With Allah as my witness, I must admit the women don't hurt, despite what I just said. And I was a farmer just like you, and it certainly is a lot more fun than that."

"But that is not really the reason I fight," Dalir said. "I fight because it is bullshit what they do. The Soviets, the Americans, all the warlords. They come in here and push us around because they think it is okay; they think we are slaves who will do whatever they say. And I'm tired of it."

"Especially the Americans. Many years ago they overthrew a government they felt was interfering with their independence. All these years later, they are far more oppressive, yet when we fight back, they declare us terrorists. It's not right."

I could tell Dalir was being sincere, not giving some sleazy sales pitch. Which was great and all, but still I knew in my heart I had no intention of hiding in some cave for six months avoiding bombs and drones, no matter how many women there were in Kabul.

That said, free food and drink sounded good, and shooting an AK-47 sounded pretty fun.

"Okay, I don't want to speak for the group, but I think I can safely say we'll all be there," I said. "Shooting guns sounds fun."

"Yeah, I'll be there," Mohammad said.

Taj and Rasool nodded as well.

Dalir smiled. "Excellent! No pressure, just come and shoot for a bit. Not that any of you guys can, probably. My theory is one of you loses a toe."

Mohammad smirked. "We'll see about that."

"Tonight, then," Dalir said, smiling back. "Oh, and another thing. I'm friends with your boss here, and he said it's okay if you guys take the rest of the afternoon off. So enjoy the sun, see you at around 7."

"See you then," I said, as Taj and Rasool looked at each other and smiled.

At first, I figured I'd spend my afternoon hanging out with some friends for a bit. But I didn't.

Instead, I went to the room in the mosque that had the only TV in the whole town and popped in the Batman movie. Sat there and watched the whole thing.

My favorite part was always the same: when Batman finally got the Joker.

Around 6 that night, with the temperature dropping nearly 25 degrees Celsius off that day's high, I told my father I was going to Imran's.

That was actually true – I did go to Imran's house. I just didn't tell him I was going to a mujahideen recruiting party after.

I got to Imran's house around 6:15 and Zayan was already there. I guess they spent the afternoon playing football (soccer, for you Americans) with some of the other guys in our village. Apparently, they also got off work early, and they waxed poetic about how excited they were for this event.

Well, Imran was excited about the event. Imran was about an inch shorter than me – 5'8", about average height for an Afghani man – and was about my size too, around

175 pounds of mostly muscle. He also was the most religious and defiant of our triad, particularly after the Americans blew up that woman and her daughter.

Since then, he would go on and on about how terrible the Americans were, how Islam is the only true religion, and how he thought even killing innocents was alright in the name of "Arabian independence." Honestly, it got annoying after awhile, so I had no doubt he would sign up tonight.

And I had no doubt he'd do something stupid that he'd think is brave while fighting, and die. So I figured I might as well enjoy my time with Imran while it lasted.

Meanwhile, Zayan was about 6'2", weighed perhaps 150 pounds and, until very recently, had acne all across his face. He seemed excited enough about shooting guns, although I wondered if he was the one who was going to shoot his toe off.

And while he would sometimes agree with Imran and say how terrible the Americans were or whatever, I knew he wouldn't join. Which is probably good, because he wouldn't be much use, anyway.

"Who's ready to shoot some guns?" Imran said as we walked toward the mosque.

"All I know is I'm going to shoot a hell of a lot better than either of you," I said, smiling at him.

"Oh, we will see about that," Imran said.

"Either way, we know we'll both beat Zayan, so we got that going for us," I said as Imran and I both laughed.

"Yeah, okay, we'll see, I'm going to surprise a few people," Zayan said, and then stumbled over a rock.

Imran and I both lost it.

"Maybe you should focus a bit on the walking first

before you try shooting guns," I said.

"Yeah, seriously, best move for the Americans would be to have you join the resistance," Imran said, smiling.

"Whatever," Zayan said.

"You guys going to join, by the way?" Imran asked.

"Well, I know you are going to join," I said.

"Of course. I can't wait. How about you Zayan, you going to sign up and kill some Americans or what?"

"I don't know, we'll see. I mean, seems kind of like a hopeless cause, not sure what I can do."

"Yeah, right, Zayan just doesn't want to share a cave with some other guys, because he knows it'll cut into his jerk-off time," Imran said.

We both laughed.

"So how about you, Akil, you going to join?" Zayan asked me, eager to change the subject.

"Oh, I don't know. I mean, life here does kind of suck, no doubt about that. And it is unfair what the Americans and everyone else do to us, I guess. But I kind of agree with you, Zayan, it's like, what are we really going to change? We'll probably just die in some cave somewhere."

"Come on, man, don't be a pussy," Imran said. "At least you are fighting for something. Better than tilling poppy all day."

"I don't know, I'd rather be tilling poppy and be alive than in some cave dead. Besides, my dad would never let me go anyway."

"Your dad fought in the mujahideen himself!" Imran said.

"That's allegedly why he doesn't want me to do it," I said, now eager myself to change the subject. "I don't know, we'll see. All I know is I'm going to kick your ass shooting guns."

"We'll see about that," Imran said, and we walked on.

I was surprisingly good at the shooting.

Overall, 35 of us wanted to shoot, including my whole work crew, Zayan and Imran. In the first round, they lined up six metal cans on a wooden fence and gave us six bullets each, seeing how many we could knock off.

The top five would advance to the finals. And time was the tiebreaker.

I knocked four cans off in 38 seconds, which I didn't think was going to be good enough. Turns out, only one person got more – one guy got five – and no one else got more than two.

In the second and final round, they pinned a target with George Bush's face on it to a wooden pole, with circles getting smaller to the center, and gave us four bullets each. Depending on what ring you hit, you'd get the corresponding amount of points, with the smaller rings closer to the center obviously worth more.

I was second-to-last to go, and most of the guys hit the target but once or twice, and only in the outer ring. Imran was right before me, and he hit the outer ring of the target twice, for a total of two points, which gave him the lead.

I knew I could do better than that, but the problem was that the guy who hit five cans – Farid, I believe his name was – was going last. Considering how well he shot the first time, I figured I needed a pretty high score to hold him off.

My first shot was beautiful, hitting the second-smallest ring for a total of three points. My next two shots, respectively, hit the outer ring of the target and missed the target completely, for a grand total of one more point.

Realistically, I figured I needed at least a three-point shot to give myself a chance. Well, I did better than that, hitting a perfect bull's-eye on George Bush's nose for a four-pointer.

Eight points total, pretty good.

Next was Farid's turn, and I wish I could say it was dramatic. It wasn't. Turns out the first round must have been a fluke, as he hit the target a grand total of one time, for a score of two.

"Looks like we have our winner," Dalir said after watching Farid's last shot miss left. After a brief fist pump, I shook hands with Imran, Farid and Dalir, and asked about my prize.

"Ah, the prize," Dalir said. "Well, of course, if you join us you get to keep the gun. But we know you don't want to do that."

Dalir winked.

"But we have something for you anyway," he said, and threw me a small black box with a string wrapped around it.

I untied the string and opened the box, which caused a small metal object to fall out. When I reached down to pick it up, I saw it was a retractable steel knife, with a picture of a leopard on the handle.

"Pretty cool," I said, as I showed the knife to the crowd.

"How'd you like to kill an American with it?" Dalir said.

"I don't think I'd like that at all."

He laughed. "Good, you aren't completely insane. Okay, the rest of you, we have some new movies we brought if you guys want to watch them, or you can just hang out in the mosque. Akil, I'd like for you to take a ride with me in my Jeep quick."

Imran, Zayan and just about every other guy there looked at me enviously.

"Uh, okay, I guess," I said, and walked toward Dalir. When I reached him, he put his arm around me and we headed toward the Jeep.

The others went back into the mosque.

The sun had set, ending another day in Zhari, as Dalir drove down the only road we had in my village.

"Where are we going?" I asked, feeling every bump as we drove along.

"Nowhere. I just wanted to talk with you."

"I thought this wasn't going to be a high-pressure recruiting event."

"That's before I saw you shoot."

I smirked a bit, then corrected my lips back to a frown. "Come on, I didn't do that great."

"That was the best shooting display we've seen of any town we ever went to. Frankly, what Farid did in the first round was truly amazing, but we soon realized it must have been luck. But you have a gift for shooting."

"Geez, didn't realize I was that good."

"Most people in this country are terrible at shooting. It's not their fault – they don't exactly have money or access to guns. So I'm not going to proclaim you the greatest shooter in the history of mankind, but you have some natural ability, and I want you to join us."

"Not interested."

"Why are you not interested? Do our politics not align?"

"Not entirely. I agree that all this stuff these other

countries do is bullshit. But I'm not for killing random innocents, either."

"Neither am I."

"You are part of a group that killed thousands of civilians by crashing planes into buildings."

"No, I'm not."

"Uh, you are."

"That's the way they'd frame it, that all of us Arabians
are in one giant group. But nothing could be further from
the truth. The only people I've killed or seen killed are either
American or warlord soldiers."

"Wait, you guys don't commit terrorism?"

"No – in fact, we are completely opposed to it. There
are many different sects within the mujahideen, and we are
part of the largest one, the one based out of Kabul. We all
agree terrorism hurts our cause."

"Of course, no one is going to report on the intrica-
cies of our organization, because most people just see us as
one united, evil group," Dalir continued. "It isn't true. Yes,
we kill foreign soldiers who invade our soil, but we do not
kill innocent people. Our mission is to turn innocents to our
side, not murder them."

"Interesting."

"Let me ask you a question," Dalir said. "You are a
smart enough guy. Do you really want to work the poppy
fields the rest of your life, growing some plant so some piece
of European trash can ruin his life further?"

"Not really."

"Well, that's exactly what's going to happen if you don't
join us. Sure, you might get a wife or whatever, and have sex
with the same ugly woman every day, and till that soil until

your back gives out. You'll spend your last years a burden to society with nothing to show for your life but a career of growing an addictive, life-ruining drug and a few kids who will almost assuredly have the same fate."

"That is, if you live that long. There's also the chance some stray bomb hits or some fight spills over your village, and you'll die a completely senseless death. Is that what you want?"

"I don't think it is as bad as you're making it to be."

"It is. I talk with men my age who didn't join, and they are miserable, and they are only 30. Imagine how they are going to feel when they are 40, their body failing them, with no hope at all? That'll be your life."

"Alright, man, you can just cool it," I said, as the Jeep rumbled on.

"I'm going to turn around now, head back to the mosque," Dalir said. "But let my ask you one last question: Are you worth it?"

"Am I worth what?"

"Are you worth a great life? Where you have women, pride in what you do, excitement every day. Do you think you are worth that?"

"The way you frame things isn't exactly accurate."

"I think it is perfectly accurate."

We drove home in silence.

Early the next day, while my father was still asleep, I snuck out and went to the mosque. There, I jumped in the Jeep with Dalir and headed to Kabul.

I never told my father what I was doing because I was young and stupid and I thought he'd say no. I'm sure he found out soon enough through the village gossip, and I'm sure he was devastated by it.

First his wife, gone while giving birth to me, and now I was gone.

There wasn't a day that went by when I didn't think about him. And on some particularly lonely nights, I would think of what a great man he was and the wisdom he had, and I would cry.

I always thought somehow, someway I'd run into him again. I didn't realize the consequences of my decision when I made it, and how impossible that would be, and the danger I'd put him in if I saw him.

I didn't realize that when I jumped into that Jeep with Dalir, it would be the last day I'd see my father again. Of course, Dalir knew that, but somehow that part was left out of the recruiting pitch.

My first night in Kabul was the wildest night of my life.

Dalir didn't lie – women in Afghanistan apparently do declare "sexual jihad," which basically amounts to they'll have sex with any Arabian carrying an AK-47. By the end of the night, I had two of them – at the same time.

This is coming from a man who never even had a kiss.

I also drank for the first time. In my village, there was plenty of opium. Everyone smoked opium. But I'd never even seen alcohol.

I had two whiskey sours – Jameson whiskey, I'll never forget – and I was completely gone. After the two ladies pleased me, I spent the night in a hotel room Dalir got for us – apparently, the owner was a friend of the resistance – and just thought about how lucky I was.

Lucky I didn't have to till poppy the next day. Lucky I actually would get some adventure. Lucky my life, for once, wouldn't completely suck.

The next morning, I awoke next to the two women I enjoyed. They awoke as well, pleased me again, and then one of them went downstairs to get me a lamb and pepper omelet.

"You are a brave man," the remaining woman said. Well, woman is used loosely; she was probably no more than 16, with dark brown hair, a thin build and stunning blue eyes.

"Oh, I'm not so sure about that. Truth is, I haven't done anything yet."

"No, but you are brave, and Allah will reward you."

"It feels like Allah already has."

The woman laughed. I never did catch her name.

"Seriously," she said. "You are very brave to fight this war. Many other men are too afraid."

"I guess that's true. It certainly beats tending poppy."

The girl smiled and kissed me on the cheek. "Good luck."

The other girl came back – this one not as attractive, a bit thick in the waist with a homely face, but I still certainly enjoyed her company – with the breakfast. I ate mostly in silence, wished them well and met Dalir in the lobby.

"Are you ready, my friend, to do some real work?" he asked as I came down.

"Can't I spend a few more days here?" I asked, smile on my face.

Dalir laughed. "Now you know why I am a recruiter. Hard to beat the benefits."

"Seriously, will I get to come back to Kabul?"

"Yes, of course. But first you must fight. Off to the Hindu Kush we go."

I went willingly, thinking this was all part of some grand adventure. Knowing what I know now, if I had to do it all again, I'd murder Dalir in the lobby right there and spend the rest of my life in that hotel room, with the woman with the stunning blue eyes (and her friend, if she wanted to stick around).

The first six months as a "soldier who follows only one man, the great prophet Mohammad" was awful. I thought tending poppy every day was a bad life.

Nothing was worse than this.

First off, despite the grandiose job description, I had to listen to a lot of people. Basically, I was the lowest grunt in an incredibly hierarchical organization. My job was to do whatever the people above me told me to do, and try not to die.

Still, my day-to-day life included getting into firefights and taking out bad guys, right? Not exactly. It meant carrying messages from one cave to another, and occasionally to a few villages that were relatively close by.

Oh, and while I did it, there was the constant threat of being blown alive by a drone some asshole in Farmland, USA, sitting in air conditioning, remotely piloted from 8 a.m. to 4 p.m., except on weekends and government holidays.

Seriously, our main enemy was just some jerk playing video games. He pressed a button, wiped out a few men on the scene and got a slap on the back by the lieutenant behind him.

For us, that meant another one of our brothers had been killed. And it meant getting a message out to his family that their son/husband/father was dead.

I got that the Americans were trying to win the war and didn't want to put themselves in harm's way. Still, it seemed that murdering people half a world away while sipping coffee took all the humanity out of it.

Not that they cared.

Either way, it didn't really matter. All that mattered was that my job was to hike the mountains in freezing cold weather, often in snow, while trying to stay undercover so some unmanned death machine wouldn't kill me.

Generally, it took me a full day to get to wherever I was supposed to bring the message. Then the people there would give me a menial dinner, I slept in whatever cave or village I made it to, and then I'd walk back the next morning.

And then the process would repeat itself.

Why couldn't we use a cellphone or some other radio device to communicate? Because the Americans would intercept it. Obviously, that'd be bad because they'd hear our message. But worse than that, it would also give away where we were, and we'd quickly be bombed and murdered.

Even the rare day off was awful. We literally lived in a cave, about 30 of us in the "resistance." We ate there, we shit there, and we had no electricity and no way to clean ourselves. So you can imagine how it smelled.

The food was awful – mostly just rice and beans, day after day after day. The guys were mostly older than me – our leader was 48 – and highly, highly religious. There was one imam in our unit, and most of the time people listened to him, read the Quran and chanted prayers.

Meanwhile, our "leader" – the esteemed Naail Saad – was opposed to sex before marriage, modern culture, even music. Any of those topics were forbidden, so I couldn't even tell my comrades how desperately I wanted to see a woman.

All the conversations centered around politics or religion and boring shit like that. Nothing fun. And all the guys allegedly felt strong about the cause, even though deep down I knew they were probably either homicidal maniacs or guys like me, who were tricked into thinking hiding in a cave would be more fun than tending poppy.

Honestly, the more time I spent around the Muslim stuff, the more I thought it was bullshit. It seemed that the whole religion was centered around feeling guilty about everything I wanted to do. And if anyone said that's a stupid fucking idea and they weren't going to live their life fighting their every natural urge, our spiritual leaders would say it's okay to murder them.

Great philosophy.

Of course, I couldn't say that out loud, or Naail himself would murder me. So I just kept my mouth shut, carried my messages back and forth, and tried not to get murdered.

Oh, one last thing. You'd think at least I'd learn a lot about strategy from the messages I carried?

Not quite. Each message was written and put in a steel box. The box was locked, and only a select few leaders had the key.

So, summing it all up, I spent my days risking my life carrying messages I couldn't read for jerks I didn't respect. Even if I were to escape –– which was unlikely, and if I were I'd probably just get caught and be brutally murdered –– where the hell would I go? I was hundreds of miles from my village, I knew no one in the area, and chances were some drone would take me out.

All things considered, my life was a disaster. I should have listened to my dad and just tended poppy.

Somehow, it got worse. Our leader, the great Naail himself, managed to piss off one of the rival tribes. So now we were at war with another sect of the "resistance," meaning that occasionally we sent guys down to some village to shoot at some guys who were allegedly fighting the same guys we were.

My job hadn't really changed, although I didn't have to go to that village anymore to hand over a steel box with some message inside. I was just happy they didn't murder me the last time I went there, when I handed them some message that started the skirmish.

But this latest feud was destroying my morale. Again, I wasn't even totally on board with all the crazy religious shit, but at least we were united against a singular enemy who was being a dick and taking over our country. I could get on board with that. But now that wasn't even true, because we were wasting our resources fighting each other, rather than trying to make a plan that would actually work.

Since I'd been there, we hadn't gotten into a single fight with an American, or killed one. But now we were celebrating when we murdered people who should have been on our side.

I thought our leader was a fucking moron. So far, he'd been lucky because all the firefights had been in the village where the rival sect lived with innocent women and children. So they hadn't been bombed yet by the drones since the Americans didn't want that much bad PR.

But us, we were in a cave, and the Americans would happily murder us. Eventually, our rivals were going to find where we were – probably by following one of the food suppliers who came once every few months or so – and attack. And while we might be able to hold them off, there was a good chance the American satellites would pick up the firefight, know our position and then murder as all from above.

Whatever. My job wasn't to think of the strategy, just to pass stupid metal boxes from one idiot to another, who ranted and raved about Allah but really just cared about having the biggest dick on the block.

Same old bullshit that's gone on forever.

The funniest thing was that Dalir recruited me because I showed some promise shooting. Well, they didn't even give me an AK-47 when I went on my missions, thinking it would take away any chance I had of fitting in and highlighting the chance the Americans might take notice.

It's smart, don't get me wrong. But the idea that I was a great shot and therefore could help the resistance was laughable, considering I didn't hold a gun the whole first year I spent in those fucking mountains.

Finally, some excitement. It only took a year and two months.

Well, that's probably a pretty cynical way to put it. I came back one day from delivering one of my messages and everyone in my unit was dead.

They were bombed and the cave was destroyed. I also saw signs of a gunfight outside the cave and a few dead bodies from the sect we were fighting.

I don't know for sure, but I'm assuming my worry came true. Our rivals likely followed one of our food suppliers – the day before we were expecting a delivery – and found our cave. There, they opened fire and got into a brief firefight that apparently killed four of their men.

If Naail had any brains at all, he would have fled after the firefight. But instead he probably chanted some prayers or something to Allah at the same time some American took a break from watching YouTube to fire a Hellfire missile and blow up our whole dang lair.

You would think I'd be sad knowing the crew I spent the past 14 months with was now all dead. But, truth is, they deserved it. They spent their whole lives hoping to receive some message from the heavens, and finally they got one.

Of course, I still had myself to worry about, and I didn't really love my chances. Here I was, standing in the near zero-degree temperatures of the Hindu Kush, with no way to get food, no weapon and no friends.

Chances are, I'd be dead within a week if I didn't figure something out. Like I said, finally some excitement, right?

I had some things going for me and some things working against me. I did have a backpack with some food in it – probably a couple of days' worth. I had the knife Dalir gave me when I won that shooting competition, whatever good that would do. And I knew the way to most of the villages and secret hideouts in the area, on account of my messenger job.

What was working against me was that our rival sect knew who I was, because I delivered messages to them before. So if they saw me, they'd probably try to kill me. And I didn't really want to just join some other sect and have some shitty job like I had before, although I'm sure I'd resort to that if it became a choice between pride and starving to death.

One option was just to go home. I could walk to a village, try to get a ride somehow to Kabul, and then make my way back to Zhari.

I'd see my dad, who I missed dearly, and my old friends. But it would also mean going back to tending poppy until my back gave out, living an uneventful and ultimately unsatisfying life.

Not that I ruled it out completely. But it wasn't ideal.

Not really knowing what to do, I began walking slowly toward the cave I came from, trying to figure out a plan. But, after about a mile, I realized something: There was a good chance I was on camera.

Chances were, in some room somewhere, some jerk-off American was watching every step I took on a spy satellite. Most likely, the one reason I wasn't dead yet was because they were hoping I'd show them another cave, so they could blow that one up too.

That pissed me off.

That night, it was just me, alone, in the mountains.

Where I was, elevation-wise, there were almost no animals. The Hindu Kush did have ibexes and goats and even some leopards, but they were rare and deathly afraid of humans. Aside from that, there weren't even insects up where I was.

So the normal sounds of nighttime we're all used to — crickets, the croaking of bullfrogs — were gone. It was just complete silence, with no light other than a quarter of a moon, the small fire I made to cook my dinner and the stunning star display up above.

And there was me – and the only people within 200 miles I really knew and could trust were dead and buried in a pile of rocks where a cave used to be. And while I hated my 14 months with them, didn't form a single real connection with any of them, and thought Naail deserved the swift death sent to him, I suddenly became acutely aware of how incredibly lonely I felt.

I also realized why my comrades were so pious. It was because they had no hope. They were fighting just another enemy in a long line of enemies they couldn't beat. All they could hope to do was to endure long enough for our enemy to lose interest or funding and move on to something else.

Even in that situation, there would probably just be some other warlord or some other opportunistic country looking to take what they could from us. It made sense that the "resistance" was so obsessed with the afterlife, considering how awful our real lives were.

So they made up stories. People have been doing that since the beginning of time. When man was ignorant and helpless against some phenomenon – say, electricity suddenly jutting down from the heavens – they made up an elaborate tale about how it must be from an older bearded fellow who overthrew his father and controlled the universe.

In our case, we weren't necessarily ignorant, but we were certainly helpless against the forces that invaded our country and enslaved us. Unable to think of a rational way to overcome it – which I chalked up to a lack of desire, as opposed to a lack of creativity – they simply made up stories about how if they continued rejecting everything they desired, some all-powerful being would reward them in the afterlife.

I was tired of that, though. I didn't want to spend my life making up stories so I didn't have to face the truth. And I didn't want our people to do that anymore either.

That said, what could I do? I was a guy with 14 months of growth on my face, wearing a threadbare thawb, armed with a pocketknife and a backpack filled with rice and beans and little else. The "army" I had was dead, and even if they were still alive, they wouldn't listen to me anyway.

Heck, I'd have to listen to them.

But perhaps therein laid an opportunity. I had nothing, nobody, and yet I was still alive. Somehow, our enemy spared my life, a miracle perhaps, left to live so I could finally lead our country to true independence.

It's just another story, they'd say. But at least it's an optimistic one. One that has something the rest of our stories lack – hope for this life, not the next one.

And, truth be told, I knew I could out-strategize the likes of Naail and others. First off, I would stop fighting our own people. There's time for that later. A simple propaganda campaign could unite us all against one enemy, so at least all of our guns would be pointed in the same direction.

And enough with the caves. We should go to the villages. They couldn't bomb the villages like they bomb the caves. Plus, there we have communities – wives, sons, daughters – we can bring to our side.

We weren't going to win this battle by hiding in a cave and trying to pick off an American convoy once a year. We were going to win this battle by winning the hearts – not the minds, the mind always justifies whatever the heart tells it to justify – of the people in our own land.

Once we did that, there would be no stopping us. Because then each generation would mean another fresh set of troops, ready for battle.

To make that happen, we needed to sell a vision. I'm told the Vietnamese managed to hold off this very enemy we had and created their own nation. We could do the same. We just needed to be unified.

Of course, that was all bullshit unless I could get some attention and respect early. And the only way of doing that, as far as I could see, was winning a few battles and killing a few Americans.

And I thought I could do that. But in the villages, not in the Hindu Kush.

Tomorrow I set off, I thought to myself.

With that, I curled into a ball on the rocky face of a mountain I didn't know the name of, and drifted off to sleep.

And a deep one, at that.

The next day I woke up early to another gray morning in the Hindu Kush. It was cold, so I started a small fire, made some rice and beans for breakfast and then sat. And thought. And thought.

And thought some more.

I knew I had one day of food left, so that meant it would be my last day sitting in the mountains. Which meant I had that day to make a plan. A plan that would establish myself as a leader for the resistance.

And I knew that would mean killing some Americans, without killing any Afghanis. Not an easy task.

Here were the facts. First off, I knew I was probably

still on spy satellite. Which was a bit weird, to be honest, knowing every step I took was being analyzed by some solider in some bunker somewhere.

But I also knew I could use that to my advantage.

Obviously, I couldn't go to a cave. If I did, the Americans would just drop another bomb there, and I'd die along with everyone else. So I had to pick a village, because the Americans wouldn't just blow up a village.

Too much collateral damage.

There were only two villages within a day's walk, although one housed the rival sect that was partially responsible for killing 30 of my comrades. That made the choice easy, then: I was headed to a small village about 17 miles southeast of where I was camped, which was home to some wheat farms and about 200 people.

There was a small resistance sect there of about 10 guys. They were friendly enough with us, as I frequently sent messages to them when Naail was still alive. Their leader was Haroon, a rather thin and clownish man in his 40s who lacked any sense of presence.

That was good. Unlike Naail, who had suspiciously few doubts about his ability to lead, Haroon would question himself. And those questions would be room enough for me to establish myself.

Although the Americans wouldn't bomb the village, I was confident that within a day or two they would send a platoon there to try to make friends and, if that didn't work, blow up some shit.

That was my opportunity. If I could kill that platoon, I could give some hope to the people around me and start the beginning of what I imagined would be a very large movement. The problem was the platoon would likely be composed of highly trained special forces who spent their formative years learning how to murder guys like me.

They also would be backed by air support, ready to fire at any second. And the leader of the platoon would likely be wearing a body camera, which would be sending a live stream to some office thousands of miles away.

If provoked, the air support would likely fire, even if it meant civilian casualties. That would be the worst-case scenario, as even if we killed a few Americans, having innocent people murdered from a seemingly omnipotent force from above would destroy any sense of morale.

Plus, it would mean my death.

And, again, that assumed we'd be able to kill a few of these special-forces soldiers to begin with. These guys were not the 18-year-old brainless dipshits you'd expect in the army. These guys were the most badass motherfuckers of the most badass motherfuckers, who took special joy in murdering people like me.

That was the situation. In my mind, the opportunity (Haroon as a leader, knowing the platoon would be coming) far outweighed the obstacles (heavily armed motherfuckers, trigger-happy bombers circling over our heads, a live stream of our attack). I just had to think of a plan that would work.

So I sat on that mountain and thought. And thought. A few hours in, I took a quick break to eat lunch, took a walk, and then I sat and thought again until dinner.

After dinner, back to sitting and thinking. Finally, just before 9 p.m., it came to me.

That night, it took me awhile to fall sleep. I ran through the plan again and again in my mind, second-guessing every step. Around 2:30 a.m., my brain unable to take anymore, I passed out.

At 8:30 that morning, I woke up, and the plan had hardened overnight in my head like dried cement. I made a quick breakfast of rice and beans – the last bit of food I had – and then began the 17-mile walk to the small farming village that was not unlike the one I grew up in.

The weather that day was perfect, at least for the Hindu Kush. It was still gray, but the air was that crisp fall temperature, which acted like a thousand tiny knives, jabbing you into alertness.

The walk went smoothly enough. The only thing that made it a bit odd was knowing the Americans were likely watching each step on crystal-clear HD.

Six hours later, I reached the village. I found some streams along the way, so I wasn't thirsty. But I was hungry, and the cool air had turned warmer as the elevation got lower, so sweat dribbled down into my eyes and stung them for the last three miles or so.

The first people to see me coming to the village were a pair of 11-year-old boys kicking around a soccer ball in a vacant field. The minute they spotted me, the two quickly scurried off, and I continued to walk toward the one paved road in town.

About 10 minutes later, I saw a small man coming to me over the horizon. A very small man. At first, I chalked it up to perception, but soon I realized his stature was to blame.

"Hello," I said to the man, who couldn't have been more than 4 feet tall.

"Who are you?" he asked in between bites of some sort of homemade cigar he was chewing on. He wore a thawb, a long beard and an AK-47 strapped over his shoulder, which just about touched the ground when he walked.

"Well, I haven't met you before," I said, reaching out my hand. "My name is Akil."

My new friend never extended his tiny hand. "What do you want?"

"I want to talk to Haroon."

The small man's frown deepened. "Haroon doesn't talk to strangers."

"I'm not a stranger. I've sent many messages to him."

"I've never seen you before."

"Well, I've never seen you before either, although there's a good chance I'd miss you."

I could barely contain my smile. "Leave," the small, grumpy man said.

"I was joking, I'm sorry," I said, cracking my most playful smile. "Seriously, though, I have a message for Haroon."

"Where is your lockbox if you have a message?"

"The message is my unit is dead. I figured he should know that."

"How did they die?"

"Their cave was leveled by a Hellfire."

"Then there's a good chance the Americans are watching you now, and will likely come to our village within a few days. Your presence has all but doomed us."

"That's exactly what I'd like to talk to him about."

The small man continued to stare at me with accusatory eyes.

"I'm not exaggerating," he said. "There's a good chance

you coming here will mean our death. If I was smart I'd kill you right now."

"That's exactly what I need to talk to Haroon about. I have a plan."

"A plan to get us out of the situation you put us in?"

"You aren't a particularly friendly man."

The little man kicked me in the leg, hard. I grabbed where he struck me and hollered in pain.

"I'm tired of this!" he shouted. "Do you realize what you've done? You are going to get us all killed!"

I did my best to smile over the pain. "No one is going to die. Take me to Haroon."

"Why should I do that? You already are being followed by the Americans, and they'll follow you exactly to where Haroon is."

"Well," I said, as the pain went away and I stood back up, "they are probably going to follow you now. So unless you never see Haroon again, they are going to find out where he is."

The little man grumbled. "I'll bring you to him. But I don't believe you'll survive it."

I followed the small man into the village, past a string of tiny shacks and farmland. He waddled instead of walked, making for a very long trip to Haroon's home, even though it was only about two miles away.

By the time I reached it the sun had begun to set and my sweat had hardened against my skin. Haroon's home was a shack just like the other 20 I passed, although when I went inside I saw three men kneeling on prayer mats, chanting to Allah, their three AK-47s gently placed in the corner of the room.

When they finished, Haroon – who had a thick mop of black hair atop his head and a wispy white beard across his gaunt face – turned to me.

"Akil," he said. "Do you have a message for me?"

"Hello, sir, my regards," I said as I went to my knee. "I have a message of sorts, although not the formal kind you are used to."

Haroon extended his arm, turned his palm toward his face and flicked his wrist upward, signaling me to stand up. "Yes?"

"The rest of my crew is dead."

Every muscle in Haroon's face dropped. "Including Naail?"

"Yes."

"How?"

"Bomb from a drone. Destroyed the entire cave."

"Where were you?"

"I was delivering a message. When I got back, I saw some dead bodies from Jaul's sect – I believe his men attacked our cave. The Americans must have taken notice and then their drones did the work from there."

Haroon covered his face with his hand and sat down. "I cannot believe Naail is gone. He was so strong."

"I'm sorry, sir. I'm sorry to have to tell you."

Haroon took a deep breath and collected himself. "You know, chances are the Americans followed you here via spy satellite. We are probably next."

"They won't bomb a village with so many innocent people around."

"No, but they will send in their special forces. Frankly, coming here probably means our death."

"No, sir. I have a plan."

"What do you mean you have a plan?"

"I have a plan where we can kill the Americans and unite this village behind us."

"The village already is united behind us."

"Not like this. This plan gives us hope."

"Enough!" Haroon shouted. "You just told me my friend Naail died. I don't feel like hearing about your plan."

"If we do nothing, we will die."

"Enough!" Haroon shouted, and quickly composed himself. "Khaleed will get you some food and water; you can sleep here tonight. I want you on your way in the morning."

"But I have a plan that will..."

"Enough about your plan!" Haroon shouted. "Go!"

And, with that, I left, with the small man – Khaleed, apparently – wobbling closely behind.

"You are a real son of a bitch," Khaleed said. "You have doomed us all."

"Not if you listen to my plan!" I replied.

Khaleed kicked my in the back of the leg and I fell to the ground. "You see that hut over there," he said, pointing to a rundown shack. "There are women there. They'll give you food and water. I expect you gone by tomorrow, just like Haroon said."

With that, the little man turned and went back to Haroon's home. That night, Haroon spent the night praying with his lieutenants, asking Allah what he should do next.

I spent the night sleeping on the dirt floor in a laborer's shack, continuing to work out in my mind the finer details of my plan.

The next morning I was up before the sun rose after sleeping all of two hours or so. As soon as I got up I walked to Haroon's hut, which showed no signs of life.

He was sleeping.

So I waited. Two hours passed – I imagined it went from roughly 5 a.m. to 7 a.m., although I had no watch to really know – until I saw Haroon first come out of his home, his arms over his head, stretching his way into full consciousness.

"Sir," I said, a bit too loudly as I ran up to him.

"You," he said, as he wiped the sleep from his eyes. "What do you want?"

"I seriously do have a plan."

Haroon laughed, an explosion breaking the many thoughts that had been dominating his mind.

"A plan," he said, smiling. "I forget, you are the man with the great plan."

In that moment, I'm certain that if another one of his men had awoke and saw me, Haroon and the other man would have laughed at me and sent me on my way. Or, potentially, they'd realize the harm I'd put them in and sentence me to death.

Luckily, no one did. And with fatigue overcoming the sharp anger Haroon felt toward me yesterday, he relented.

"I'm serious," I said. "Let's face it, you are in a bad situation. The Americans will come today, tomorrow at the absolute latest. It can't hurt to listen."

"I shouldn't listen," Haroon said. "But you obviously have spent quite a bit of time on this. Shoot, I'll give you a minute."

I told him my plan. He laughed again.

"What a clever little plot you have," he said. "You have spent a lot of time playing soldier in your mind, my friend."

"Tell me what's wrong with it," I said, incredulous.

Haroon smiled. "You know nothing of warfare. Or plans. Or anything else. The idea will get us all killed. Really, all we have to do is give you over to the Americans when they come, give them a good dinner and send them on their way, and they'll spare us."

"I thought you were supposed to be soldiers. Fighting the Americans, for Allah. You are going to just feed them dinner and kiss their boots and bless the murder of one of your own countrymen?"

"We are soldiers, but we aren't going to rush into battle because some idiot came here raving about a plan. Seriously, though, if I really wanted to kill you, you would be dead by now and I'd present the Americans with your head. But instead, since I'm sure the satellites are watching us, I'll send you on your way and even give you some food."

"Why would you do that? Why won't you try my plan?"

"Akil," Haroon said, trying – and failing – to disarm me with a smile. "I believe you are a true Muslim and I don't wish you to die. The Americans will probably kill you eventually, truth be told, but we'll see if you are really good at making a plan and killing a few of them. There's your chance to really test your strategies."

I couldn't believe what I was hearing. I became so enraged I punched my leg in fury, which left a massive bruise there the next day.

"I can't believe you! Here you are, a supposed military leader dedicated to Allah to killing your enemy. You have a once-in-a-lifetime opportunity to knock out an entire American unit, but rather than seize it, you laugh at a plan that would bring hope back to our people, and you send one of your own countrymen out to die!"

"My friend, you may leave now, before I change my mind," Haroon said, still smiling. "You have brought death to our front door. Because I am a wise man – wiser than you and good at negotiating – I will save everyone's life here. A ruthless man would just murder you now, but instead I give you an opportunity to save your life and leave you better off than when you started. You should be thanking me for listening to even a second of your babble, and you should already be on your way."

"You're a fucking pussy," I said, jabbing my finger at his face. "That's all you are is a fucking pussy. My one goal in life is to be the exact opposite of you – a man who takes advantage of opportunities when he can has them, a man who kills his enemies when he has the chance. Not some worthless pussy that bows to his enemy and serves them meals and grovels at their feet."

Haroon's face transformed. "Get out of here, now," he said, his face a clenched frown.

With that, I turned and left.

Two days later, nearly starving to death, I stumbled into the village that housed the sect that killed Naail. There, I met the leader – Jaul – who shared my newfound determination to murder Americans. I told Jaul I rejected Naail's leadership, I was glad he died, and kneeled before him, offering my service.

He said I made a wise choice. I'd spend the rest of my military career in his sect, going from village to village killing Americans, having sex with whatever women were around, and watching my closest friends die. Amazingly, I survived and grew strong, eventually leading my own group of 20 men, then 200, then 2,000.

Each murder, each prostitute, each death made the next one easier. Soon, I became a person I barely recognized, strapping bombs to young men's chests and keeping a harem of four teenage women around me at all times.

It was the life given to me, carved out of caves and bombs and poppy fields. I became an evil man, but only because I was surrounded by greater evil, and no more evil than any other general. Was I anything more than a victim of circumstance, where honest, good men were oppressed in a jail of a nation while bad men such as myself were free?

I'm not sure, and I buried all that under the thrill of battle and sex and driving fast and leading men. But what I couldn't shake, even to this day, is the irony of it all.

It wasn't the Americans who made me the man I was, at least not directly. It was my own countrymen in that small farming village just southeast of the Hindu Kush, too scared to fight.

That was not me; that would never be me. I would never till poppy again. I would never do what that white minority demanded of me. I would be free.

And, after awhile, I stopped caring about how I stayed free.

Oh, one more thing. A few months ago, while sitting in my cell in Guantanamo, I analyzed the plan I gave to Haroon, using all the military experience I didn't have when I crafted it.

It was crap.

Back at Guantanamo

Half-a-year since my last conversation

That's how I came to be the evil man sitting in a tiny cell in the most heavily guarded prison in human history. Where I just endured six months of silence, my brain slowly turning into mush.

I was just sitting on the concrete floor that night, my legs straight out in front of me, wondering if I should finally tell John something, figuring he'd probably find out anyway. In the background, I heard the sounds of soldiers running, guns firing and occasional booms from the artillery.

Another drill, I figured; the Americans were always drilling with their blanks. Even the artillery had blanks, although it still made that same ear-splitting noise.

I bowed my head. That's when my entire cell shook. BOOM!!!!!!!

My whole body jolted like I was hit with electricity. My bed came off the ground and rattled back down, somehow managing to stay on all four legs. The water in my toilet splashed up, a few drops landing on the side of my cheek. BOOM!!!!!!!

This time, the jolt was more intense, knocking my bed off to the side, where it came tumbling down onto my toilet and my arm. I pushed it off me, and then the lights flickered, and I soon realized this was not a drill.

Meanwhile, the gunfire intensified, and the screaming became louder.

Bang! Bang! Bang! Something or someone was pounding on my door. What the hell was going on? Was someone coming to kill me?

Bang! Bang! Bang! Bang!

The smashing continued.

BANG!!!

And in came a man, tumbling through my door and onto the floor. Before he could react, I jumped on top of him and smashed him three times in the back of the head, my adrenaline taking over.

I flipped him over and realized he was wearing orange, like myself. I had just knocked out a fellow prisoner, who helped me escape.

So much for a thank-you.

Time for remorse later. BOOM! Another explosion rocked Guantanamo. And the gunfire raged on as screaming filled the air.

With that, I ran out the door and made a deal with myself right there, over the sounds of the firefight: I would not go back to my cell. Either I would escape, or I would die.

Niantic, Connecticut
Friday, May 25, 2012; 2:33 p.m.

It was a perfect day for framing: no clouds in the sky, around 70 degrees. Not too hot, not too cold – you could work the whole day and never break a sweat. The only weather was a slight wind coming off Long Island Sound, which just reminded you that you were outside.

"Give me a number!" my father hollered, all 6'2" of him. My father was a big man, strong in the arms, his light brown hair blowing slightly in the wind.

"Forty-three-and-a-half inches!" I shouted from the roof, hand on the ridge vent. I put my measuring tape back into my belt and finished tacking up the second-to-last piece of plywood with the nail gun.

By the time I finished, my father had already walked up the ladder, a 43-and-a-half inch piece of plywood in his hand. He placed it down on the remaining exposed rafters.

Perfect fit. I nailed it up.

"Looks good," my father said as he surveyed our handiwork. Now that the last of the plywood on the roof was nailed up, the complete outside of the house had been framed in.

"Not bad," I said. "Nice view up here."

I'll be honest, it was two hours from the weekend, and we'd have to start something completely new to keep going. Sure, the view was fine, but really I was just bullshitting to kill time, trying to chop into those last two hours of work.

"Yeah, it's a nice view," which was my father's implicit way of saying, "I know what you're doing, but I'm tired too, and we finished ahead of schedule, so we can bullshit for a few minutes."

"So what do you have going on this weekend?" I asked, legitimately interested. My father should do more on the weekends, aside from whatever chores he could to keep him busy, I thought.

"Actually, I was going to go down to the VFW tonight. Harry wanted me to come. I guess they play cards, so maybe that will be fun."

"Oh, awesome!" I responded, trying not to sound too condescending. "You think this is going to become a regular thing?"

"We'll see. Harry says he plays a couple times a month. Probably just a bunch of old men, sitting around, sipping beer and talking about the Yankees."

"Sounds like you'll fit right in."

"Ha, probably right, although I'll have to bring up the Mets. Probably nobody wants to talk about the Mets, though, they stink."

"No argument there."

"So what are you doing this weekend?" my father asked me. But every time I told him anything – hanging out with Tom, playing football – I felt like he just thought to himself that his son was going to spend another weekend drinking beer and not getting laid.

Sad thing is, whether he felt that way or I just thought he felt that way, he was right. And I knew the fact that I didn't have a girlfriend bothered him a bit.

So I figured I'd give him something to be excited about.

"Believe it or not, I have a date tonight," I said.

"Really?" Now it was my father's turn to try to not act too condescending. "With who?"

"Well, you know Amanda's friend, Julie?"

"Julie, Julie ... I'm not sure I know her."

"You know, the brown-haired one, into yoga and all that stuff."

"Oh yeah, Amanda brought her to the beach last summer, I think. She seems like a nice girl."

"Yeah, definitely, she's pretty too. I don't know, I guess Amanda said she actually wouldn't mind going on a date with me, so I asked her out."

"Where are you taking her?"

"There's a new place in Mystic, The Pita Spot. It has Lebanese food, I don't know. Amanda said she would be into that sort of thing."

"Are you going to pick her up?"

"Yeah, I'm going to pick her up."

"Are you going to get her flowers?"

"Come on now, Dad, nobody gets anybody flowers anymore. She's going to think I'm some sort of creeper if I get her flowers."

"No no no, you have to get her flowers. I'm telling you, if you show up on the date without flowers, she's going to think you're a clown."

"Dad, it's 2012 – nobody brings flowers on dates anymore."

"I'm just saying, girls like it when you bring flowers."

"Honestly, Dad, when is the last time you went on a first date? How do you know what a girl likes?"

"Last first date I went on was 1976, with your mother."

"Did you bring her flowers?"

"Well, no, but you don't want to take after me. You should bring flowers. Seriously, Danny, she would like it if you brought flowers."

"I'm not bringing flowers! Can we just drop it?"

"Alright. I'm just saying, she'll be calling you Dan, Dan the No Flowers Man."

"Seriously, nobody has brought flowers on a date since you were a kid."

"Hey, you do what you want, I'm just saying the custom really is to get her flowers."

"Oh my God, I'm not getting her flowers!"

My father laughed. "Alright, let's go inside, start to lay out all the interior walls."

Ugh. Oh well, two hours until two days of freedom.

Anxiety was starting to build.

>*What should I wear?*

<*What do you have?* My sister texted back.

>*I was thinking of that flannel shirt and jeans.*

<*OMG you are going to look like a lumberjack!*

>*No, it shouldn't be that bad. It's a nice shirt.*

<*You are not wearing a flannel shirt. Period.*

>*Alright fine whatever what should I wear?*

<*Want me to come over? We can drink some wine and talk about it.*

>*Ugh no I don't have time. Just tell me what I should wear.*

<*IDK you should have some cool clothes. You don't have any cool clothes.*

>*This isn't helping! Seriously I am running out of time. What should I wear?*

<*Wear that shirt I got you, show off your muscles.*

>*I look ridiculous in that thing! It's skintight. It looks like Queer Eye for the Straight Guy.*

<*Lol ok. Just wear those dark blue jeans of yours and that button down short-sleeved shirt you have, the pink one.*

>*You think that looks gay?*

<*No it's cute. She'll love it (:*

>*Do you think I should buy her flowers?*

<*OMG You Should Totally Buy Her Flowers!!*

>*Seriously? I feel like it's so lame if I bring flowers.*

<*No honestly she would love that. That's so cute!!*

>*Ugh I feel like I'm a creeper or something going on this date with flowers.*

<*Seriously if you bring her flowers she's going to love you. Guys don't do that kind of stuff anymore.*

>*Probably because they know it doesn't get them laid lol*

<*Don't be gross. Get the flowers.*

>*Fine, I'll buy flowers. They are probably expensive too, plus I have to pay for the dinner.*

<*It's fine. What do you ever spend money on anyway? Good luck! I love you!*

>*Thanks – have a nice night. I'll let you know how it went.*

5:44 p.m.

I was showered, dressed in my pink button-down shirt and dark blue jeans, sitting in my red armchair. The TV wasn't on.

I was anxious.

It was too early to go, or I'd get to her house, like, 45 minutes early. It wouldn't take me that long to get flowers, and I didn't want to just wait in my car for a half-hour.

Unsure of what to do, I walked into the kitchen and grabbed a glass from the cabinet. On top of the fridge was a bottle of tequila, which I used to fill the glass up halfway. Then I grabbed some orange juice from inside the fridge, and filled up the rest of the cup.

"Here goes nothing," I said to nobody in particular.

In three gulps, the glass was empty. I made myself one more.

"You are going to do this, Berith," I said to myself. "You're the man. You can do this."

In three more gulps, the second glass was empty. Burned a bit on the way down.

6:15 p.m.

I was standing in Stop & Shop, in the florist section. There were some really pretty white roses, but they were $19.99. Next to them were some nice white lilies, for $9.99.

I could have bought just one white rose for $3, but that felt kind of cheesy. Something Seal would do, show up with one white rose. I should probably just get the dozen white roses, I thought to myself; they really are prettier than the lilies.

6:17 p.m.

I paid at the counter. She'll like the white lilies fine, I thought to myself.

6:45 p.m.

I was a block from her house, sitting in my car, parked at a local church. I had 15 minutes or so to kill. I shouldn't have left so early.

I downed four Tic Tacs and tried to smell my breath by breathing into my hand and hoping the odor bounced back. It didn't really work. Nervous, I pounded four more Tic Tacs.

I should have brought more tequila, I thought to myself. I wondered if I had time to run over to the package store and grab a beer real quick, although I wasn't even sure if they sold single beers.

Ah, I'll just wait, I figured. By the time I did that, I'd be late.

7:01 p.m.

"Hey!"

I had begun to walk to her apartment building's front door, but she was already walking out.

"I live on the first floor, so I saw you coming," Julie said, smiling.

What a pretty girl she was. Her hair, long and brown, came down over her shoulders. Her skin was tan and clear, her eyes big and brown, and those lips. She had great lips – a great smile, really – and, lucky for me, that smile was in full gear.

"Ah, well that made it easier," I said, smiling, as she walked toward me. Suddenly, I was very excited to be exactly where I was.

Julie was wearing a green tank top below a thin blue sweater, left unbuttoned. Her blue jeans were tight and intentionally faded, and she looked both comfortable and beautiful at the same time.

"You look so nice," I said, still smiling.

"Oh, thank you!" she said as she reached me. Then, we awkwardly hugged.

A beautiful girl who Amanda assured was into me. This was going to be a good night.

"I have something for you in the car," I said as I walked toward my crappy green Mazda. Somehow, now, as I walked toward it, the high fuel mileage and low cost of ownership didn't seem as appealing as it did when I bought it.

I should have taken my work truck, I thought to myself. I'm a construction worker after all, with a beard. I should have a manly car. Not some douche-bag Mazda.

"A gift?" she asked, excitedly.

"Something like that," I answered.

I walked to the passenger door side and opened it for her, and she thanked me as she went in. I grabbed the white lilies from the trunk and gave them to her as I came around the driver's side door.

"I got these for you."

When she saw them, her eyes – already prominent – doubled in size. In that moment, she looked so beautiful.

"Oh my God, they are so beautiful," she said. "I can't believe you got me flowers!"

"Really? Okay. I thought you were going to think it was lame."

She laughed. "It's not lame at all," she said, smiling. "It's very sweet. Very adorable of you."

She lunged toward me and gave me a kiss on the cheek.

"Thank you, they are very nice," she said.

I guess the old man knew what he was talking about after all, I thought to myself as I drove to the restaurant.

7:16 p.m.

We pulled up to the restaurant, easily finding a spot. A little too easily, frankly, as it seemed nobody else was there.

"Looks like we have the whole place to ourselves," Julie said, smiling.

"Guess so," I said.

We walked into the restaurant – a yellow, single-story building with big windows lining the front and "The Pita Spot" written in white on the glass. When we walked inside, there was an interesting aroma in the air – something exotic, I couldn't put my finger on it exactly.

A Lebanese girl – probably a bit younger than me, with dark skin, dark eyes and perfect curves – was there to greet us. She was gorgeous.

"For two?" she asked.

"Yes, please." As I walked in, I realized the tequila was beginning to kick in a bit. Either that, or I was just excited to be in this exotic-smelling restaurant, on a date with a beautiful girl, being seated by another dark, beautiful woman.

The inside of the place was a dark yellow, with Lebanese idols and drawings lining the walls. The table was simple – square, with a deep red tablecloth on top, and two place settings.

"This place is cute," Julie said after we were both seated.

"I just hope the food is good," I said. Julie smiled. We both grabbed our menus and began our search.

"So, Amanda tells me you are into yoga," I said after we made our choices – I got the filet mignon pita, and Julie ordered the chicken shawarma one.

"Yeah, totally, I just find it so freeing," she said. "Do you do it?"

"Me?" I said. "Ha, no, I don't do yoga. I don't know, I'm not sure if it is for guys like me."

"So many guys take our class!" Julie said. "You should

try it, it's so hard."

"Ha, I don't know, seems kind of more for girls," I said.

"It's not at all! Seriously, it's really good for you."

"No, yeah, you're right, it sounds cool. I'm sure it is good for you. I'll have to try it sometime."

And then, a brief moment of silence. Not a long one – maybe 20 seconds or so – but it was a bit awkward.

"So, uh, what do you do again?" I said. "Still doing the waitressing thing at AJ's?"

"Yeah, unfortunately," Julie answered. "I mean, the money's pretty good and the people are great, but I don't think I want to do it the rest of my life."

"Oh? What would you like to do instead?"

"Well, I know this sounds stupid, but I'm really into photography. I always thought I could do something with that."

"Oh, really? That's cool. Maybe work for a newspaper or something?"

"No, not a newspaper or anything, the media is so negative. I don't know, I would love to just go to Africa for like a month, and just take pictures. It is just so beautiful there, I really would like to go."

"Oh yeah, that would be a cool job," I said, thinking that it doesn't really sound like a job at all.

"Yeah, I have this idea, actually, for a photo book. It's called 'What Does Love Mean To You,' and what it would be is just talking to people throughout Africa and asking them what love means to them. And then I could package it into a book, I think it would be really cool."

"Huh," I said. "Interesting question."

"So what does love mean to you, Dan?"

"Ha-ha, that's a good question."

The first thing that came into my mind was my dead mother, and having her back. The question made me miss her – bad. I probably should have just said that. I would have gotten some sympathy points.

But I didn't.

"I don't know, really. I can't really even answer that question, I guess. What does love mean to you?"

"Love, to me, means to be completely free. To be completely one with nature. I just feel like nature is so peaceful, so relaxing, and when you are in it, you don't have to worry about a thing. You know what I mean?"

"Nature is peaceful? Don't animals, like, kill each other for crossing their pee lines or whatever? I don't know if that's so peaceful."

"No, you know what I mean. I just feel like being outside, there's something spiritual about it."

"Yeah, I guess. I always preferred working outside to inside, I can tell you that much. Although I'm not sure I get the whole spiritual effect, with the air compressor running and the smell of nail-gun oil on my hands, ha-ha."

"So that's what you want to do with your life, to build houses?"

"Uh, yeah, I guess, I don't know. I mean, it's what I've done my whole life."

"I just think it is so cool that you get to create every day."

"Ha-ha, yeah, I don't know – I guess create is one way to put it. We follow the plan, I guess, but yeah, it feels good to be able to see what you built each day. I like it."

"Cool."

Another 20 or 30 seconds of silence, finally broken up by our waiter, Charles, with our dishes.

"It looks delicious," Julie said.

"Don't you think they could have gotten a Lebanese guy to be the waiter," I said, half-joking. "Might have helped with the whole credibility thing."

Julie gave out a snort of fake laughter.

Two bites in, disaster struck. Thanks to the force of my jaw, the tahini sauce shot out the back of my pita and got all over my pink shirt.

Julie laughed, for real this time.

"Oh my God, that probably wasn't too smooth," I said, turning red. "Well, so much for being cool on the first date."

Julie laughed again. I did my best to clean it up, but it left a pretty good stain on my shirt.

Once I finished my cleaning, we ate, mostly in silence.

"That was delicious," Julie said, once we were done. I ate all of mine, and after Julie ate only half of hers, I ate the rest off her plate.

"Indeed," I said, slapping my belly. "I'm full, though. So, hey, I was thinking, though, after I grab the check we could grab a drink at The Steam House down the street."

"I love The Steam House. My friend works there, so we go all the time."

"Oh, awesome. Well, yeah, let's do that, give us some time to talk without having to worry about spitting out food or anything like that," I said, smiling.

"Sounds good," Julie said, smiling.

The tequila had kicked into full gear as we sat at a table in The Steam House. The table was a real oak top, and there was a massive old drill press behind the bar.

To me, it was a place that was trying entirely too hard. Julie loved it.

"Can I get you guys a drink?" the waiter asked.

"Do you have any IPAs?" Julie asked.

"Yeah, we have two new ones, actually. One from a brewery out of Old Lyme, it's called Pirate Larry's – it is very hoppy, so a bit of a fuller flavor. And there's another from Silver Cap Brewery in Cranston, called The Hobbit. That one isn't as hoppy, and a bit lighter of an IPA."

"Oooh, they both sound so good, it's tough to choose," Julie said.

"Would you like to try them both?" the waiter asked.

"That would be fantastic," she answered.

The waiter went back to the bar and got a sample of each beer. He came back, and Julie downed them both.

"Oh, wow, that Pirate Larry's really is hoppy, but I sort of like it," she said. "I'll do that one."

"Awesome, good choice," the waiter said. "And for you, sir?"

"Oh, I'm not too picky, I'll just get a Bud."

"We actually don't have that. We do have two lagers on tap, though – one from..."

"Sure, no problem, yeah – whatever one you think, you know better than me. Surprise me," I said, smiling.

"You got it," the waiter answered, and then went to the bar.

"They have Pirate freaking Larry's but they don't have Bud," I said. "I guess I only have one thing to say – *arrrrrre* you kidding me."

Julie forced out another snort of fake laughter.

She did look pretty, though – man, she really did. I don't know about this Africa shit or this freaking "what does love mean to you" crap, but she was pretty hot.

And she was into me, right? I mean, she was the one who asked Amanda to ask me out. She had to be into me, man, for real.

The bartender came back with the lager; I forgot the name the minute he told me. "Thanks man," I said, and he went off.

"Salud," Julie said, lifting her Pirate Larry's beer into the air.

"Salud," I responded, and we touched glasses, and I took a sip. "You know, this actually isn't bad."

"Probably better than Bud, I bet," Julie said.

"Ha, probably right."

We stared at each other for a minute. The lighting in the bar mimicked candlelight, and for the first time all night, there seemed to be some genuine chemistry between the two of us.

"So why did you ask Amanda to tell me to ask you out?" I asked, smiling.

"I did no such thing!"

"Seriously?"

"Well, I might have told her I thought you were kind of cute," Julie said, smiling seductively. "So I guess I wasn't too disappointed when you did."

"Ha, well, good," I said, looking back at her. "I'm not

sure what you'd want with a boring old construction worker like me, but I'll take it."

"Oh, you're not boring. Tell me, Dan, what do you want in life? Surely there's more to you than building houses."

"What do I want? Oh, I don't know. I guess it's time in my life I get a girlfriend or whatever, I don't know. I mean, I've only really ever had one girlfriend, I guess, and she was kind of insane. So, I don't know, I guess that's probably what I would like."

"You've only been in one relationship?"

"Well, yeah, I don't know, I guess I'm not good at the whole dating thing. And, you know, I mean I work with my dad and some other guys, so it isn't exactly like I'm meeting a lot of girls or anything. So I guess that's why I was excited, you know, when Amanda said that you, you know, whatever."

"Oh, well, that's nice," Julie said. "Well, what do you want besides that? Do you hope to travel? What do you want your life to be remembered by?"

"Ha, geez, tough questions here. Um, yeah, I like to travel, although honestly I haven't done it much really since I was a kid or whatever and we used to go with my mom and dad. I don't know, just kind of work or whatever, but yeah, I would like to do something."

"I feel like," I continued, "I don't know, I sort of work, go home, work, repeat, you know? I mean I work hard and work's cool and all of that, you know, but I'm bad at the other parts of life, I feel like sometimes. I mean, I love hanging with my boys and all of that, I guess, although most of them are moving away and stuff."

"That sucks," Julie said. "I know how that is."

"I don't know," I said, stuck on my previous idea, "everyone thinks there is some amazing, great life set out for them. But you want to know something? Most people die and there is no great, amazing life. They had a family, they did their job, they spent their last few years sitting in some chair watching the news, and then they die."

"I mean, that's sad to say, but maybe that's all that's cut out for me. You know, I'll work, maybe I'll get married, I guess have a kid or whatever, save up just enough money to have a miserable retirement, and then spend my last few years yelling at Dan Rather or whoever is reading the news at that time."

Julie was just looking at me.

"I don't know, maybe there is no great adventure awaiting me. Maybe I'm just destined to be boring, destined to get 3 inches of an obit written about me in the local newspaper when I die that my whoever bought, and then forgotten about. Maybe that's all I am and will be, 3 inches in some newspaper, and then I'll cease to be remembered."

Julie held her glare. She was engrossed, but engrossed in the way you are engrossed watching a fly trying to get out when they get stuck between the screen and the glass window. You watch for a bit, to see if they can find the hole in the screen they flew into, and then finally you open the window and save them.

"Well, maybe I'm just being optimistic, but I think there's some adventure in all of our lives," she said, gently opening that proverbial window.

"Yeah, I suppose so. Maybe, maybe I just haven't found it yet."

After that riveting speech, the romance of the moment,

so tangible a few minutes before, was gone. We finished our drinks. I paid $16 for them, after tip – $16 for two drinks! Fucking Pirate Larry's – and we walked out.

10:11 p.m.

I drove her home pretty much in silence. I got to her place, stopped the car, and it was time for the most awkward part of the night.

"Well, I had a really good time tonight," Julie said.

"Yeah, definitely, we'll have to do it again," I answered.

"Yeah, just text me or whatever."

Then, I reached over, unsure if I was going to go for the kiss or the hug. Julie was proactive – she went for the hug, ensuring I couldn't go for the kiss.

"Well, have a nice night," she said.

"Yeah, totally, sleep well," I answered.

She opened her door and got out. "Bye!" she said, as she slammed the door shut.

Why the fuck did I go on that speech, I thought to myself.

It was a quiet drive home.

Guantanamo Bay, Cuba
Date: unknown; Time: unknown

BOOM!!!!

The prison shook and the lights flickered as I fell to the ground exiting my cell. Must have been a mortar.

BOOM!!!

Another, shaking the prison. This time, I grabbed the doorjamb while still on my knees so I wouldn't fall.

Bang, bang! Bang, bang! Bang, bang! Bang, bang! Over and over, on the door of every cell, were men just like me banging to be released. They sensed freedom and their instincts were taking over.

I looked around. Astonishingly, despite the desperate noises coming from the inside of the cells, the cellblock itself was empty.

I thought about saving the other prisoners for about a second, figuring I could capitalize on the confusion, even though must of us would probably die. But I had no key for the doors and no real idea how to free them, so I decided to worry about myself.

That meant getting out of the jail, quick. It sounded like both mortar explosions came from the front of the jail, so I ran to the back.

And began to think.

I was wearing an orange jumpsuit. The minute an American saw me, he was going to shoot me, and that would be the end of Akil Dhakir. Which is better than going back to that cell, but not precisely ideal.

I figured if I could change my clothes, I'd be able to blend in among the confusion and potentially escape. Although how was I possibly going to get a new pair of clothes in the middle of a firefight?

I could kill an American, but even if I did, I'd have to find a place to undress him and steal his clothes. That would probably take me at least three minutes, and I doubted I'd find an American so alone I'd have three minutes to do all that.

Speaking of which, it was strange that my cellblock was so empty. Why? Is the threat so big? And what is the threat, anyway?

The thoughts continued, along with my legs. I reached a door marked "EXIT" at the back of the block, but instinct stopped me from opening it.

There was a chance, if I opened that door, an American would see me in the corridor and shoot me on the spot, I thought to myself. Dead. I could just wait in my shockingly empty cellblock, but that would probably just delay my capture. The goal was to avoid it.

Ratatatatatatatatat! I heard machine-gun fire in the distance, along with the screams of Americans shouting orders. But mostly, I heard the prisoners banging on their cells.

I stood staring at that steel exit door, wondering what to do, frozen in the moment. My heart was racing. My nose smelled freedom, but something was telling me if I opened that door I'd be greeted with a bullet to my head.

Suddenly, the door opened. In a flash, I hid behind the opening door.

"Check it out," one American said to another. "If you see any cell open, call it in immediately and shoot any prisoner."

There were two of them, both wearing helmets and

fatigues and carrying M16s. I made my move.

Surprising them from behind, I hit one – the shorter one – directly in the back of the neck as hard as I could with a closed fist. I heard a crack – I broke his spine, instantly.

The second turned around, swinging his gun at my face. I managed to get my arms up just in time, but pain radiated immediately through both forearms as they smashed against the steel barrel.

The gun ricocheted high into the air, with the soldier firing bullets into the concrete wall and ceiling of the jail. Sensing an opportunity, I kicked him in the nuts – hard – which caused him to drop the gun, fall to the ground and yelp in pain.

"You motherfucker!" he screamed.

I jumped on top of him and began punching his face, over and over. A few shots hit his helmet, but most caught him in the nose, the right eye and the jaw – or what was left of it.

By the end, bits of teeth were scattered across his chest, my hands were covered in blood, and his head was an amorphous blob of liquidated skin and bone.

The American next to him was in deep shock, paralyzed from my punch. I grabbed an M16 and shot him in the head, and then began to undress.

The soldier I just shot in the head was taller than me by a few inches, so the jacket sleeves ran to the base of my thumb. But it was fine, and with the helmet on, I looked like just another American soldier, eager to kill some Arabs.

It was time to open the steel door and exit. It opened to an empty, white-block corridor that went straight for about 20 feet and then took a 90-degree angle right. I ran through the corner, reaching yet another steel door with a small, square glass window eye-level on it, and opened it up to the warm night.

I had my machine gun pointed in front of me, where I saw five American soldiers huddled around a man who must have been their leader.

"Did you see anyone in that cellblock, Martinez, and what happened to Marquis?" the man shouted at me as I walked through the door.

I looked at him, and for an instant we locked eyes and he realized I wasn't Martinez. Before he could say anything, I opened fire on the unsuspecting group and killed all six of them.

And then I ran, as fast as I could, until I hit a chain link fence that surrounded the facility. It was 20 feet tall, barbed wire all around the top, but there was a door about 30 feet or so to my right.

I ran alongside to the door and saw it had some sort of electronic locking system. I pointed my machine gun at it and shot the thing to hell, which set off an alarm that nobody was going to pay attention to.

The bullets tore the locking device right off the thin wires of the fence and I began kicking down the door. After a strong thrust with my right leg that nearly put my foot through the chain link, the door relented, and I was outside the prison walls.

Or so I thought. There were 200 feet of well-lit grass until the start of the jungle. Although I knew the Americans were busy dealing with whatever threat they were dealing with, never before had I run so fast as I sprinted toward those trees.

I literally dove into the jungle when I finally reached it, rolling down a hill I didn't see. At the bottom, despite bleeding from my hands and with a whole new collection of bumps and bruises gained from the tumble, I laid there for a second and began to laugh hysterically.

I was free.

After a minute of euphoria – after all, I just got out of America's most infamous prison – the pain began to flair. My left forearm, where I blocked the one soldier's gun barrel, was killing me. My entire body was sore from the tumble I took. And I still had no idea what the hell was going on.

Who launched the assault? There was no way it was from Afghanistan, half a world a way. There was no way the Americans' surveillance would miss any sort of convoy coming over here, particularly one that was heading toward their best-guarded prison.

I figured I'd better find out before I went any farther. So I climbed back up the hill – my arm shooting in pain with each movement – and peered through the Cuban night. I still heard the sounds of machine guns and Americans yelling orders, although it was clear the fighting had died down.

I saw that the attackers came from the north, as that's where all the action was happening. They probably surprised the Americans – hard to believe, considering the surveillance – with a few mortars and took out a few guards before the highly trained American forces mowed them down.

I was at the southeast end of the prison, way too far away to clearly see whoever was responsible for the ambush. But I briefly saw two men before oncoming American soldiers took them out, and I could make out they were wearing a uniform of some kind.

Interesting. Terrorists didn't wear uniforms. Was an actual country behind the attack? What country? Again, what country could possibly make it all the way to Guantanamo without being detected?

It didn't make much sense to me, so I figured that question would just have to remain unanswered for now. Besides, by then a bigger one started to crawl into my mind – what the hell was I going to do now?

Well, I knew one thing for sure: It certainly didn't involve me waiting around at the edge of the jungle for the Americans to spot me again. With that, I headed back into the jungle, my M16 over my right shoulder, my left arm hanging limply by my side.

After a couple of minutes I could no longer hear the gunfire. Which, ironically enough, was my only comfort.

There's nothing quite like walking through the Cuban jungle in the middle of the night, with no idea where to go. Sure, I've spent plenty of time walking around at night in the Hindu Kush, but there weren't really any animals there and I always had a decent idea of where I was.

In Cuba, it seemed like everything moved and a thousand eyes were watching me. I couldn't go more than three steps without tripping over something and falling hard on my right side so I wouldn't put any weight on my left arm.

For the five years before my imprisonment, I did everything I could to get away from the Hindu Kush. At that moment, trying to navigate through a jungle that scared the shit out of me, with the Americans trying to catch me, I would have done anything to go back.

It was the snakes that really got to me. Tell you the truth, I don't know a damn thing about which snakes live in the Cuban jungle and which ones don't. But all I kept imagining was one of those suckers slithering up my pants, sinking its teeth into one of my balls, and clamping on like a second dick.

Fuck it, I told myself, fuck all of it. I'm the first man in history to escape from that prison. I'm not going to let some fear about some stupid fucking legless reptile stop me from getting away.

The next step, my right foot came down on what I first thought was a root. But I looked down and saw it was a big snake – I couldn't really make out the colors in the night – that wasn't too happy I just stepped on his back. He picked his head up, hissed at me, and then slithered away faster than I could blink.

That's all I needed. I began to run in fear, tripping over a small bush four steps in and falling onto my broken arm. The pain was no problem, though, because when I hit the ground I felt something touch my skin – probably just a leaf or another bush – and I swore to Allah it was another snake, ready to make a meal out of my nuts.

I got up again, running as fast as I could, screaming like a banshee as the helmet I stole from the American flew off my head.

That's when I felt the bullet hit my shoulder.

New London, Connecticut
Saturday, May 26, 2012; 8:33 p.m.

Three beers deep. Sitting on my red couch in my living room staring at my flat-screen TV. Alone.

Thinking what an idiot I was the night before.

Julie was hot. She wanted to go on a date with me. How did I blow it?

Then again, sure, she was nice enough, but she was kind of a weirdo. What was that "what does love mean to you" crap?

That's what made it so frustrating: I was better than her. I didn't need Julie. She's some freaking waitress; I'm a partner in a construction company who makes $67,000 – most of it tax-free – per year.

Can she build a fucking house? Does she have any real marketable skills at all besides a flat stomach and the ability to laugh at some jerk's jokes? Could the next dude who fucks her handle even one day framing with our crew?

Probably not. It'll probably be some fucking nancy who thinks he knows something but doesn't really know anything.

Then again, he's going to be the one fucking Julie, while I'm sitting here, grabbing my crotch and thinking about how I fucked it all up. Why did I go on the speech? What the fuck was the point of that speech? Sorry for all the swearing. I was three beers deep, after all.

Oh well. Truth is, it isn't like I'm some great entrepreneur. I'd been working with my dad since I was 12 years old, just sweeping up the job sites back then.

I hated it back then, thought it was just some crappy job my parents made me do for punishment or something. They probably just realized, looking back, that I'd never listen to teachers, never make it in school very far, never really be able to get any other job but swinging a hammer.

Either that, or my dad just needed some help on the job.

Here's my real theory on my dad and why he wanted me to work for him: Sure, he's nice to everyone, but at the end of the day he thinks to himself most people are sacks of shit who stare at computers and jerk off all day.

If something breaks, they don't know what to do. If society collapsed, what good would some Excel spreadsheet be then? Meanwhile, his work was real, meaningful work.

As he raised me, he probably heard the same thing every day. Dan needs his diaper changed. Dan needs new clothes. Dan doesn't like tomato sauce on his spaghetti; he just likes the noodles in butter and cheese.

Granted, my dad was always a great dad with that smile on his face, but deep inside his mind he's probably thinking who the fuck does this Dan think he is anyway. He's another sack of shit like the rest of them who spends his days reading comic books and waiting for the next episode of whatever show to come on.

So the minute I could be of any use on the job site – and trust me, I wasn't much use at age 12, but I could sweep sawdust – he was going to put me out there. He was going to make a man out of me, not like those other amorphous blobs who sit in front of their computer every day doing just enough not to get fired.

He was going to make me a man, just like he was, who would have a use no matter what happened to the society around us.

After all, we don't have any control over all that, and my father was not a man who trusted the ability of others too much.

The ironic part is he made me more dependent on him than ever. My house, my work truck, my job, all from him. I had all the skills to do it on my own, but I never had, really. I'd gotten jobs on my own, even ran the crew alone for six months one time while he was out after surgery, but he was always there.

I called him just about every night during those six months, and sometimes even on the job, to mull over nearly everything that came up. Could I have done it myself?

Yes, I know I could have. But I didn't.

What the hell was I thinking about? I was supposed to be thinking about how I messed it all up with Julie.

But maybe I just laid out exactly why I screwed it up. See, that next guy who fucks her, he probably won't have some dad hanging around, talking him through every little obstacle he encounters.

No, he'll probably have some asshole dad who said, "Go out, son, do it on your own." And you know what? He did.

While I'm left here, pounding a Bud heavy, with no girl to speak of. Watching some basketball game on TV I don't even care about.

I finished my beer and forced my buzzed ass back to the refrigerator. I opened the door and saw there were three cold ones left, but I was getting tired of drinking alone.

I figured I should just go to the club, get as drunk as I want and take a cab back. I know, I thought to myself, I shouldn't go, it's expensive and all that and probably bad for my soul, and it makes me a super fucking creeper.

But fuck all that. I just fucked something up, bad, with a hot girl who was just there on a platter.

This was an exception. I need some female attention.

I'd been there for over an hour, sitting on a stool at the bar by myself, and not a single girl had talked to me. It sucked.

Oh well, at least the whiskey was good.

I was working on my second glass of Jameson's, no ice. Meanwhile, every time someone walked into the place, I checked them out while simultaneously hiding my face.

After all, the last place you want to run into someone you know is at the local strip joint.

I don't go there all the time, I really don't. And god-damn do I feel guilty about it, okay? Truth is, I went there about once every other month or so.

Well, that's kind of bullshit. Maybe once a month, and then I spend the next two weeks regretting it because either I spent too much money or I felt like some creeper.

But what the hell: I was a single guy, I wasn't going to drive home and, sure, it sucked that these girls had to strip for a living. But you know what would be even worse?

Working as a stripper and not making any goddamn money. At least I gave them some cash to blow on whatever strippers blow their cash on. Heck, I was making their lives better and boosting their confidence.

And they were going to dance for some fuckhead or dance for a nice guy like me. That's an improvement, right?

After all, I wasn't going to stalk them or try to kill them or anything insane like that. So fuck that guilt shit.

"Another Jameson?" a chubby bartender – wearing black panties, a black corset and nothing else – asked, noticing my newly empty drink.

"Hell, why not," I said, probably not nearly as smooth as I thought I did.

Fuck that guilt shit indeed. I wasn't going to think about any of that tonight, I was just going to allow myself to fully let loose.

Now I just needed a girl to talk to me...

10:24 p.m.

The DJ was pounding some pop song so hard the walls in the club were shaking. There were about a dozen guys at the bar, in various groups.

There was one set of three, plus two sets of two and four solos. The set of three and two of the solo guys were talking with girls, and one guy occasionally straggled off to the back room, holding hands with a stripper.

The rest of us just sat staring ahead, nursing our drinks, pretending that we couldn't care less if some girl talked to us or not. Even though, in all of our minds, we were the most appealing ones in the room.

Behind us was a stage where a thin, homely, brown-haired girl with small breasts and a Cesarean scar on her stomach was doing a three-song bit. A few guys were sitting around her in big, plush red chairs, blankly staring ahead.

She'd earned about six dollars so far, spread haphazardly across the stage. Seemed like the market for small-breasted brown-haired homely girls with C-section scars wasn't too strong.

Behind the stage were circles of plush red seats surrounding tiny tables. Those were filled with groups of guys, half of them making small talk poking fun at the homely, small-breasted girl on stage while nursing their drinks.

The other half were having awkward conversations with strippers, with the guys sitting farthest away from the girl telling the guys sitting closest to the girl to "get a dance already, you pussy," or something along those lines. Occasionally, the guy closest to the girl listened, leaving the guys sitting farther from the girl to make awkward small talk and secretly hope the stripper would sit closer to them next time.

Meanwhile, not a single girl had talked to me yet. Although a Latino girl with frizzy hair, no ass and tattoos running down both of her arms was about to change all of that.

"Hey baby," she said as she walked up next to me and put her hand on my back. "What's your name?"

Her breath smelled of cigarettes.

"Dan."

"That's a hot name."

"You really think Dan is a hot name? I mean, come on, we all like to believe our own hype, that's probably why we come here, but you got to give me more than 'Dan's a hot name.'"

She laughed. "It works on most of the guys."

I flashed her a smile. "I bet it does."

"So what are you doing tonight, Dan, besides cracking jokes about how hot your name isn't?"

"Just drinking."

"Mind if I sit down?" she asked seductively.

"Sure," I responded, which prompted her to pull a chair next to me and stretch her legs across mine.

"My name is Sasha," she said.

Sasha had covered herself in some sort of perfume, but it was no match for her cigarette breath. And her voice was so throaty – mannish, almost – that the idea of spending money on her, or even continuing the conversation, didn't exactly appeal to me, even three beers and three whiskeys deep.

"What do you do, Dan?"

"I build houses."

"That's hot," she said, smiling and looking directly into my eyes, her legs still stretched across mine. "I love a man who can fix things."

"Oh?"

"Yeah, I like a manly man. You look like that with your beard and all that, you know. You're pretty cute, you know that Dan?"

It was my turn to smile. She was a pretty good saleswoman.

"You aren't so bad yourself," I lied.

"Want to have some real fun?" she asked, and then winked at me.

"Well, I hate to do this to you, but there's another girl I've sort of been looking at."

Normally, I wouldn't ask one stripper to be my courier to another, but I was six drinks deep and didn't really want to spend more time talking to a girl with cigarette breath and two arms full of tattoos. That thought made me feel bad for her, but not bad enough to not continue with my demand.

"That girl, the one with the, uh, white lingerie" – I stopped myself from saying overflowing tits – "she kinda pumps me up. Think you could hook it up?"

"You're going to use me as your pimp?" Sasha asked,

still with a smile on her face, as she pushed me away with her hand. "You got to buy me a drink then."

"Okay, tell you what, you get her over here, then I'll buy you and her whatever you want to drink."

"You got a deal, Dan. Her name's Nikki, by the way."

"Sure it is."

Sasha laughed and walked over to Nikki, who was talking to two guys sitting in those red plush chairs surrounding a table, but it was clear it wasn't going anywhere. My messenger whispered a few sentences into Nikki's ear, and she began walking right at me, smiling, breasts jiggling as she stepped.

"I'm Nikki," she said, when she finally reached me.

Nikki was hot, at least to my Cro-Magnon brain. She had long, brown hair, big brown eyes, full lips, tight stomach and a big, firm ass. Oh, and as I already mentioned, just a perfect, juicy pair of tits.

And goddamn do I love tits. Especially while drinking whiskey.

"Hey," I said, smiling. Nikki put her hand on my back and my entire body tingled. "You are fucking hot."

The words came out half-slurred, but Nikki didn't care, and neither did I. She laughed – the strangest, most contagious laugh I ever heard.

"Nice laugh too," I said. I'm sure at this point, Nikki saw me as little other than a pile of money just waiting to be deposited in her bank account. But, truth is, that's exactly what I wanted to do.

"So I told Sasha if she brought you over here I'd buy her a shot. How about I buy you a shot as well and then take you for a dance?"

"Sounds good to me," Nikki said. Sasha was standing right behind her, but, honestly, I hadn't even noticed until right then.

"So what do you two want?"

"Fireballs!" Sasha said.

"Fireballs it is."

Three shots and $23.50 later, post-tip, I was ready to go. "So about that I dance," I said, looking at Nikki.

She smiled and grabbed my hand. "Let's go."

10:43 p.m.

A man can get depressed about a lot of different things. But there's one thing that can always make him feel better about it, at least for a minute or two: the attention of a beautiful woman.

Even if you have to pay for it.

That was my experience, sitting in a bar stool at The Pink Lady Gentleman's Club that Saturday night, just coming back from a dance with Nikki. She was smiling, flushed even, laughing at my every joke, and couldn't take her hands off me.

Why couldn't she? Because she was getting paid. But a part of my brain convinced the rest of me a part of her was actually enjoying herself, and that was good enough.

Man, she was hot. Not hot in the traditional way, as any girl who has two tattoos on either side of her lower back could probably never be considered classically beautiful.

But hot in the way you want a girl to be hot when you're drunk on a Saturday night at a strip club and you plan on taking a cab home.

"So you build houses?"

"Yeah, pretty much build everything."

"So if something broke, you could fix it?"

"Absolutely. Why, you have something broken?" Nikki laughed.

"No, I just think that's really hot."

"It's empowering. It's a skill that will hold up no matter what happens, no matter how the economy changes. There is always going to be a need for someone to build stuff, and I'll always be able to build stuff."

"That's really cool," she said, smiling at me and rubbing her hand on my thigh. "You're pretty cute, you know?"

"You're pretty cute too," I said, smiling at her.

"Why don't we go to the back and have some real fun?"

"Sounds amazing. Let me get one more drink and we'll go. You want a shot?"

"Why not?" she said. Her breath didn't smell like cigarettes, and whatever perfume she had on – heavy as it was– smelled good to me.

And then, suddenly, my plans of wasting a sizable chunk of my bank account went awry.

"Get the fuck away from me," some man yelled from across the bar.

Nikki and I both turned and looked. There was some guy – a white guy, about 6 feet tall, wearing a baseball hat backward and a blue-and-white striped oversized collar shirt – shouting at Sasha.

She began to cry. Apparently, he enjoyed her cigarette breath about as much as I did. But at least I had the common courtesy not to scream at her about it.

"I don't want no fucking crack-smoking spic getting

near me," the man said, now rising from his chair. "Keep your fucking hands away from me."

Before any bouncer could react at the club – there were three in the place – I ran toward the man. When I reached him, he turned toward me and I punched him in the face.

Crack! I could hear his nose shatter.

The jerk took a few steps back, shouting in pain, blood running down his face. He put his hands to his nose, saw the blood and immediately lost his mind.

He threw a punch. I ducked. He threw another. I blocked it well enough. He threw a third, I ducked again and uppercut him in the stomach, hard.

He doubled over, going to his knees.

Before I could do much more, two of the bouncers finally arrived and grabbed both of my arms. Once they did, I broke out of a trance and realized the music had stopped and everyone at the club was staring at me, including the DJ behind the mike.

For a second, there was silence. The bouncers both looked at each other, confused about what to do, my arms still cradled in their grasp.

The man behind the mike interrupted the quiet.

"Give it up for this guy," he said to the bar, and pointed at me. The place exploded in applause, the loudest coming from the strippers around me.

"Get this man a drink! Champagne room is on us!" The place broke out in a cheer again.

In that moment, the DJ could just as easily have said what an asshole I was. Or said nothing and the bouncers would have thrown me out.

But he didn't. He pumped me up. Those three sentences, looking back, were a defining part of my life.

After hearing the words and the applause that went with it, the bouncers, now smiling, let go of my arms and patted me on the back. "Way to take care of that piece of shit," one of them said.

I walked to the bar where the chubby bartender was looking at me, grin on her face. "What do you want?"

"A fireball, for myself, Sasha and my friend Nikki over there," I responded, grinning myself.

The bouncers, meanwhile, grabbed the man in the backward hat by the arms and began carrying him out of the bar.

"I'm going to fucking kill you!" the man screamed at me, but one of the bouncers just twisted the guy's arm, and he yelled in pain.

"They'll tell him he has two choices," said the chubby bartender in the slutty outfit that no one wanted to see her in, as she made the three shots. "They'll tell him either he can file a report and risk arrest himself, or he can just go home and forget it ever happened. Just about 100 percent of the guys choose the latter."

"Sounds good to me," I said.

Sasha then came up to me and kissed me on the cheek. She had been crying and I suppose it was a nice moment, but the overwhelming smell of cigarettes on her breath ruined any chance of butterflies.

"Thank you so much," she said as she hugged me.

"No problem. Let's drink our troubles away."

I felt an arm on my back and turned toward Nikki. She was grinning as well.

"That was really hot."

"Oh, just another day's work," I said, barely containing the pride inside me.

She laughed. By then, the chubby bartender had passed us our three shots, and we drank up.

After recovering from the face you make after drinking whatever alcohol is in a fireball, I felt another arm on my back. This time it was the DJ.

"That was awesome, man," he said, as he put out his hand.

"Oh, honestly, no problem," I said as I shook it, a little embarrassed by the attention.

"I was serious, bro," the DJ said. "Champagne room on us."

"Well, I guess I'll have to take you up on that," I said as I placed my arm around Nikki.

"Sounds good to me," she said.

I shook the DJ's hand again. "I suppose violence has its rewards sometimes," I said.

Nikki and the DJ both laughed. "Indeed," he said.

Nikki grabbed my hand and led me to the champagne room.

11:18 p.m.

During the third song of our five-song dance, Nikki put her massive breasts on my manhood, unbuckled my belt and unzipped my pants halfway.

She crawled up my body, putting her right hand between my legs, underneath two layers of cloth. "This is for being so brave tonight," she whispered in my ear.

She began rubbing my cock. "And for being so cute,"

she said, and laughed. A song later, I went, wetting my pants and Nikki's hand.

"Sorry," I said.

Nikki laughed again. "Why are you apologizing? That's the point, right?"

I laughed back. "I suppose you're right."

"Okay, I'm going to clean off my hand," Nikki said. "Did you enjoy yourself?"

"I certainly did."

Nikki laughed again. "Good. You should come see me again soon."

"I think I might just do that."

Another laugh from Nikki.

11:48 p.m.

I took a taxi ride home that night, my pants wet, the fare overpriced. But I didn't mind.

Guantanamo Bay, Cuba
Time: Unknown; Date: Unknown

When the bullet struck me in the shoulder, I screamed in pain, falling to the jungle ground squarely on my back. Perfect: my left arm broken, my right shoulder with a bullet through it.

I screamed in pain again, as the blood began running down my stomach and puddling around me. The blood felt warm as it ran against my body; maybe it would even have tickled a bit, if my shoulder didn't feel like the devil himself was sticking his finger through it.

"Who fucking shot me?" I screamed. "Who shot me?"

I heard the pattering of four feet and the breaking of vines and branches. Apparently, whatever pair pulled the trigger was now coming to finish the job.

The pain subsided slightly, but I continued to scream. Half in pain, half because I knew my life was about to end a mile outside of Gitmo.

When the two men arrived, I had already made my peace. I was a bad man. I'd done bad things. Maybe this was best.

"Akil," screamed a younger man with patchy growth where a beard should have been, wearing a thawb and carrying an AK-47. "Ahmad, it's Akil Dhakir!"

I heard the footsteps of another man intensify, and then abruptly stop as he reached me and leaned over my mutilated body. He was an older man with a thick salt-and-pepper beard, dark brown eyes, white hair narrowly showing at the bottom of his headdress and a creased brow.

"I can't believe it," he said softly as we locked eyes. "It is you."

Immediately, he turned to the younger man behind him. "We need to stop the blood and get him to the sub as quickly as we can." With that, he took off his headdress and wrapped it around my wound, hard.

I screamed in pain when he tightened it, but once it was knotted, I could feel that the blood stopped running. That helped to subside what was left of the pain, although I began to grow weak.

Very weak.

"We thought you were an American," the old man said, putting his hand flat against my army jacket. "It makes sense now – it was the best way to avoid being seen."

I nodded, a light display starting to take over my vision.

"Can you walk?" he asked me.

I smiled, feeling the energy flow out of my body through the hole in my arm. "Like a rooster," I said, and laughed.

And out I went.

I'm not sure if I actually woke up before getting to the boat or I imagined it later on. But I have a clear vision of being outside myself – like a spider monkey sitting in a tree – watching my body get carried out of the jungle by that young man who couldn't fully grow a beard, no matter how hard he tried.

I remember him being scared and the old man just ahead of him looking intense, chopping down branches and stomping over weeds to clear the path.

And I remember seeing myself, my face without a single line of worry, and the most peaceful smile I'd ever seen plastered across the front of it.

The next thing I knew, a splash of water hit my face, and my eyes were overtaken by a flurry of blinks.

I looked around and saw I was at the front of an inflatable life raft, the waves bouncing me slowly back and forth, like a mother gently rocking her baby to sleep. My shirt was off, my shoulder heavily bandaged, my left forearm wrapped with a thick layer of tape.

The old man was looking over me, with the young man behind him, steering the raft's tiny engine.

"Drink," he said, and poured cold water out of a plastic bottle down my throat. It felt like gasoline getting poured into a tank that had been empty for so long, the inside was covered in a thick layer of red flaking rust.

All told, he poured about half the bottle into my mouth, until I coughed and spit a gulp back up. "More?" he asked, sitting over me.

"Yes," I said, weakly. He poured more, and I could feel it spread throughout my body, restoring every muscle it touched.

"Where am I?" I said after we were done.

"About 10 miles off the south coast of Cuba," the old man said, still sitting over me, although his eyes grew less concerned.

"Why?" I said.

"We are meeting up with some newfound friends," he said.

"And who are you?"

The old man put a finger to his lips. "Rest," he said. "They'll tell you everything once you get underwater."

"Underwater?" I said softly. "What the hell am I going to do underwater?"

Just then, the waves changed abruptly, from the sway of a comforting mother to the shake of a hungover father. The young man cut off the engine, and I began to hear mechanical noises that seemed frightfully out of place in the isolation of the Atlantic.

"What is that?" I asked, weakly.

"Your ride," the old man said. "Coming up for a breath. We are going to get you in that thing."

"How?" I said.

"You are going to be brave," the old man said. If probably anyone else at any other time in my life told me that, I would have strangled him on the spot for being so patronizing. But, lying there on the inflatable bottom of the raft, teetering on the edge of consciousness, it gave me comfort.

The machine noises got louder and louder, the waves got rougher and rougher, and I began to worry that we were going to tip over. I heard something break the seal of the ocean, touching the warm air, the water rushing off its sides.

"Here it is," the young man said again, excitedly. "I can't believe we actually did it, here it is!"

The old man grunted. "He isn't in there yet."

Using what felt like all my energy, I picked my head up and looked over the side of our tiny raft. Sure enough, there was the very top of the black hull of a submarine, emerging from the depths.

"I'm going in that?" I asked, my head collapsing back onto the pillowy raft bottom.

"It's the only way you'll get out of here alive. I know you're hurt, but if you want to live, you are going to work with us to get you in that ship."

"Alright," I said.

The engine of the sub reverberated through the night, but the dominant noise was the gallons upon gallons of water rushing off the steel the ocean once possessed. The water coming off the top of the vessel helped kill the waves, though, like calming hands over hot clay, and soon the air was still again.

The submarine had risen.

After a few silent minutes, a hatch popped open and a dozen lifejacket-wearing sailors came out. Then, a long pole – it had to be 40 feet, at least – was passed through the hatch, the sailors turning it perpendicular to the boat.

As this was happening, the old man was busy putting a

lifejacket on me – he was careful not to move my shoulder too much, although it still hurt like a bitch – and put his own on. "Okay, they are going to pass that pole to us. Hassam will grab it and pull us tight to the sub."

I nodded.

"Now, normally they throw a rope to us and you'd climb up. But obviously you don't have the strength to do that. So I'm just going to tie your lifejacket to that rope and they can pull you up."

I nodded again.

It all unfolded exactly as the old man said.

I'll tell you, I've had plenty of regrettable moments in my life, a few great ones, and a few where I almost lost my mind (most of those involve me sitting in solitary confinement in Gitmo). But never did I have a moment where I felt as helpless as I did being slowly dragged up the side of a submarine, as if a fisherman was pulling one of his lobster pots out of the water.

At least it didn't hurt. The old man tied it right so it wouldn't.

When they pulled me up they saw my injury, and one of the men speaking a language I couldn't identify picked me up and put me over his shoulder. It hurt like hell when my left forearm – the broken one – smashed against his muscular back.

A few more grunts, and down the hatch I went, down under the water where even the Americans couldn't find me. Once the hatch closed, it was official: I had become the first man to successfully escape from Guantanamo Bay.

New London, Connecticut
Sunday, May 27; 4:45 p.m.

"Yo," I shouted as I walked through the front door of my father's condo, carrying French bread and an eight-pack of Guinness. "Brought the bread and the libations."

Sunday dinner at my father's house. A tradition.

When Amanda and I were kids, my mother did it every Sunday. Always the best meal of the week – often pork roast or ribs or occasionally prime rib. She'd cook all day, dessert and all, and we'd sit around and eat and talk about whatever.

Mostly sports, my father and even my mother loved sports. The Mets, the Giants, UConn, whatever. Amanda would try to bring the conversation around to something she wanted to talk about, i.e., herself, but mostly it drifted back to sports.

Up till when my mother died three years ago, we were still doing it just about every Sunday, even though Amanda and I had moved out. It was our once-a-week get-together where we would talk about whatever was happening in our lives, sports, Amanda and our new favorite topic: politics. We loved arguing politics.

"Just throw the beer in the fridge," my father shouted from his balcony as he tended over his grill. We were having ribs tonight, one of my father's specialties.

"Oooh, Guinness?" Amanda said while chopping up cucumbers for a salad. "I'll have one."

"You got it," I answered. "Hey Dad, you want one?"

"I guess I wouldn't be opposed."

"Well, that's an awfully complicated way to say yes, but you got it."

After my mother died, we stopped having our Sunday meals. My father, he wasn't too well off during that time. He didn't say much, certainly never complained, but you could tell, it was tough.

Real tough. On all of us.

He had just finished my mom's dream house for her about 200 feet from the beach in New London. They hadn't even been there six months when the doctors found the spot on her lung. Three months later, she was dead.

For a year, my dad still lived in that dream house. He never left except for work or for necessary stuff like shopping, just would stay home all day and clean and make that house perfect. His nights, he didn't tell us what he did at night.

One time, I went over there unexpectedly to drop off a tool I borrowed from his shed. As I walked by his living room window, I peeked in and saw him sitting on the couch, crying.

I put the tool away and went back to my car and blasted the radio real loud on my three-mile ride home. I tried to forget it, but that image would pop into my mind sometimes right before I would go to bed, and I knew I wasn't going to sleep whenever that happened.

One day, about a year after she left us, my dad put the house on the market. He said he thought the market was right, it was too much for him to take care of, all that. I just don't think he could take it anymore, but I figured I wouldn't pry too much.

The house sold quickly – my dad actually made a profit off it – and he moved into a condo right in downtown New London. He made some friends there, would walk to restaurants and the VFW downtown, anything he could do to stay busy.

And he started having Sunday dinners again.

The first few were quiet, somber affairs. One time, after my dad burned a pork roast, I made up some excuse and left early. That night, I just laid in my bed, staring at my ceiling, trying not to think of anything at all.

But the dinners improved. Slowly, they improved. By now, they were mostly happy affairs where we again talked about sports, Amanda and, of course, politics. We still loved to argue politics.

"So did you see what happened at Guantanamo?" I said as I started the process of pouring three Guinnesses into three mugs.

I was still hung over from the night before, despite sleeping for most of the day. Still, I took three Advil before I came over and pounded three glasses of water, so I was feeling about as good as I could, considering the circumstances.

And despite the headache, I was energized from the night before at the strip club, even eager to re-create it. It was a long time since I'd felt that alive.

"I know, I can't believe it," Amanda said. "That was messed up."

"Did you see what happened in Cuba?" I said as I walked outside, offering my father a glass of beer. "Crazy."

"It was crazy," my father replied as he grabbed the beer from my outstretched hand. "I guess they killed 12 Americans."

"Yeah, and about 1,000 Cubans and prisoners. What were they thinking? Why would they even try it?"

"He thought he could catch us surprised. That Castro,

he's hated America forever. He figured this was his chance, I guess."

"Why do they hate us? I mean why just randomly hate us for all that time, and you are going to risk your country's life on it? Sounds insane to me."

"They hate us for the same reason we hated the Cowboys all those years. People hate whoever is at the top."

"First off, the Cowboys have sucked for years and I still hate them. Second, that seems like a stupid reason to throw up some attack you know is only going to get swatted down."

"They are just evil people, some of these dictators. They would kill you any chance they got, that's how they got the power in the first place. They just want to kill Americans."

"I guess. I don't know, sounds extreme to me. They couldn't have thought it would possibly work."

Amanda walked to the back deck.

"What are you guys talking about?" she asked.

"Oh, just the Cuban thing, it was crazy," I answered.

"I know, what was with that?" Amanda said. "You think the Arabians were in on it too?"

"Well, I watched the news today and they said they weren't," my father said. "Good thing none of them escaped."

"Yeah, I guess they killed Akil Dhakir in the fight," I said. "Although who knows – you really think the Arabians didn't know anything about it? Sounds suspicious as hell – and even if someone did escape, you think they would tell anyone?"

"People there are just so crazy," Amanda said. "Did they really think they were going to do anything to us?"

"I know," my father said. "They just can't help themselves – like I was telling Dan, they are just evil people. That's how they got into power in the first place: In those countries, if you aren't the most evil person, someone is going to kill you."

"Yeah, I'm just happy no Arabians escaped," I said. "They are nuts."

"That's pretty racist," Amanda said.

"It's true!" I said. "I mean, all these other people get along fine in America, and you got these Cubans and these Arabians – especially the Arabians – and all they do is just run around and kill each other and try to kill us. I mean, what the hell is wrong with them?"

"You can't just say everyone from the Middle East is some maniac," Amanda said. "It is just an evil few. We have the same amount of evil people here in the United States. Look at that guy who blew up the Oklahoma City building, he was just some regular white dude."

"Yeah, I guess there are evil people everywhere," I said. "It just seems like an inordinate amount in the Middle East, and I guess Cuba too. I mean, maybe it is that Muslim stuff, I don't know – they teach jihad against nonbelievers. And you see how they treat women."

"How do they treat women?" Amanda asked.

"You haven't seen that?" I asked. "They stone them to death for cheating on their husbands and they, like, aren't allowed to talk outside the home to any other guy. Hell, they barely ever even get to leave their home. They are just second-class citizens."

"They are really bad to them," my father chipped in.

"Oh, I didn't know that," Amanda said. "That's pretty messed up."

"Oh well, what are you going to do," my father said. "Anyway, ribs are done. Set the table."

"I set the table already," Amanda said. "Salad is ready too."

"Alright, well, sit down, let's eat," my father answered.

6:05 p.m.

The meal was done and the dishes were washed. That left the three of us sitting around the television in the living room of my father's condo, watching the Celtics on TV. Another playoff game, likely the last one the team would play this year.

"So what have you guys been up to?" my father asked while sitting on the sectional sofa he was sharing with my sister.

"Oh yeah, little brother, how did the big date go?" Amanda said.

"Oh, you know, alright I guess," I replied from the comfortable confines of my father's brown recliner.

"Come on, is there going to be a second date?" Amanda said.

"I mean, I really don't want to get into it," I said as my face turned red and I instinctively looked down. "It went fine, I guess."

"Come on, lil' bro, I set the whole thing up, you got to give me some deets."

"Deets?"

"Yeah, details. Stop stalling and give me some deets."

"Um, alright, there isn't much to tell. We went to that new Pita place in Mystic, it was alright. I don't know, she was a little weird, I think. I mean, you know she's going to Africa to ask people what love means to them?"

"Oh yeah, she's been talking about that alleged trip for years. Wake me up when she finally goes."

"Wait, what?" said my father, who had remained silent on the couch. "What is she doing?"

"I don't know," I answered, "I guess she wants to go to Africa to ask people what love means to them. She thinks it is an inspiring question, I guess."

My father shook his head and laughed. "I just don't get it."

"Anyway, I don't know, I don't think there was a love connection," I said. "She's pretty and all that, but she's a bit artsy or whatever – not right for me."

"Another ship coming," Amanda said with a smile on her face.

"Toot-toot," I replied, mimicking the sound a boat makes when it pulls out of harbor.

My sister rolled her eyes and my dad laughed.

"So what does love mean to you?" I asked.

"Who you asking?" Amanda said. "Me?"

"You? We all know what love means to you. A compliment every five minutes and bottomless pockets."

All three of us laughed. "Shut up," Amanda said in between giggles.

"No, Dad, seriously, what does love mean to you?" I said.

"Love? You know, that's a good question. What does love mean to me? You know, love really means to me doing what you want to do, not worrying about anything else. I think things happen to you and you kind of realize what is actually important and what isn't."

"What happened to you?" Amanda asked.

"Oh, you know, the tough times," my father said. "Obviously, when your mom died, but also even going through the military and all that. And you kind of realize you might die any day and it puts things in perspective."

"What kind of perspective?" I said.

"Just that you realize what matters and what doesn't. Like you stop caring about material stuff. And you realize the things that matter are things like you guys, the family, obviously mom at the time. But also, while I'm living I want to do what I want to do, not what anyone else thinks I should do."

"Building houses?" I asked with a snicker.

"You laugh, but seriously, that's what I want to do. I could sit in an office and draw plans or whatever, but I would rather be in the field, working, building houses. That's actually fun for me. And when I'm home, I want to enjoy time with you guys and hang out with a few of my friends, and I'm not going to worry about anything else."

"So I guess," he continued, "that's what love means to me."

"That's pretty good," I said, and then was quiet for a bit.

Somewhere off the coast of Cuba
Sunday, May 27, 2012; 9:57 p.m.

The past week or so had been a haze.

First off, apparently I was underwater, in some cramped submarine bed with a morphine drip in my arm.

Luckily, there was a surgeon aboard who took my bullet out, set my broken left arm in a cast and pumped me with so many painkillers I could barely remember a thing.

In my rare moments of clarity, I asked whoever was around how I got there, whose sub it was, where I was going. Largely, I was ignored.

Finally, I got the pain under control. The left arm didn't hurt at all, while the right shoulder – where I got shot – itched and was uncomfortable but wasn't particularly painful. I walked around for the first time earlier today, and sitting up in my little bed, I figured it was time to get some answers.

"Where am I?" I asked a male nurse who walked in. He couldn't have been more than 22 years old, wearing a blue Navy uniform with darker skin and thin, almost Asian eyes.

He looked at me confused.

"Where am I?" He muttered something in a language I assumed was Russian.

"I suppose you don't speak any language but Russian? How about English? Arabic? Spanish?"

"No," he said through his thick accent.

"How about the captain? I'm sure the captain speaks English at least, we can use that."

He looked at me and shrugged his shoulders and then said something in Russian I didn't understand.

"The captain," I said, instinctively putting my arms out to act like I was driving a ship. "The leader."

Again, he said something in Russian I didn't understand and then asked with his hands if I needed to use the bathroom. When I said no, he walked out of the room.

Great.

10:11 p.m.

Apparently, my nurse understood more than I gave him credit for. Either that, or he just alerted the doctor that I was up and talking.

Regardless, the nurse came back about 15 minutes later, the doctor with him.

"Hello," I said, smiling. When you haven't talked to anyone in a week, and before that spent months talking to people who were only trying to manipulate you, you get very excited over the opportunity for an honest conversation.

"Hello," the doctor answered in a heavy Russian accent of his own. It appeared this man knew just slightly more English than his nurse, who didn't know it at all.

The doctor was about 40 or so, a handsome, healthy-looking man with clear pale skin, blond hair and light blue eyes. It was amazing to me to see how different he looked from the nurse, who looked almost Oriental, and yet still they fought under the same flag.

"How am I doing, doctor?" I asked.

"Good, good," he answered. I figured that was probably one of about 15 English words he knew.

"Will I survive?" I asked, not really meaning it, but asking anyway.

"Friend," the man said with such heavy Russian overtones that it took all my concentration to understand what he was saying. "I get captain. He'll talk."

11:00 a.m.

It took a long time to get the captain.

"So I finally get to meet the man who has been using up all my medical supplies," said a wiry, tall, mustached Russian man with a heavy accent in a deep blue Navy uniform and a brimless blue hat that covered most of his thinning brown hair, as he walked into my cramped room. "My name is Captain Pavel Emin."

"Thank you," I replied. "Awfully nice of you to give me a ride, Captain."

The Russian smiled. "Wasn't exactly my decision," he said in his thick Russian accent, although it was clear enough and he was fluent in English.

"So I'm assuming I'm on a Russian sub. I guess my question is, why is one of the world's most wanted men on a Russian sub."

"We teamed with the Cubans."

"The Cubans? What does that have to do with anything?"

The Russian laughed. "You really don't know much, do you?"

"There hasn't exactly been a television on where I've been."

"Okay, okay, let me take you to the beginning."

"Four months ago, Fidel Castro announced he had Stage 4 liver cancer and probably had six months to live or so. And he said his biggest regret in his life was that the Americans had built a base where they torture in his own country, and the Cubans did nothing about it."

"Okay, so did Cuba declare war on the Americans?"

"Quite the opposite, actually. Castro's own brother said he was delusional from all the treatment he was getting and said basically that while he didn't condone what happens in Guantanamo, it was American property and Cuba wasn't going to get involved. And that was the end of it, at least from an official Cuban government perspective."

"Okay, but somehow I feel like that isn't the whole story."

"Strong deduction, my friend, considering you are underwater in a Russian submarine. The fact is Fidel sent a heavily coded cable to us directly, saying he would like some help. Of course, he knew we weren't going to take on the Americans directly, but something a bit more clandestine."

"Such as a submarine?"

"More or less. See, Castro is still very popular in Cuba and still has a strong following. He knew he could get a decent enough gang of rebels to attack the base on his behalf. But he knew any attack would obviously be crushed by the Americans and likely do no lasting damage."

"So then why attack? It would only strengthen their resolve."

"Well, that's where the submarine came in. He wanted to embarrass the Americans. So, yes, he was going to attack the base, even though he knew he couldn't overthrow it. Of course, he didn't tell the rebels that – he told them they could shit fire and punch through walls – but the real intention was freeing some of the prisoners."

"To what end?"

"He figured it would be seen as a national embarrassment to the Americans. That they couldn't even stop a gang of revolutionaries from invading what is advertised as the most heavily guarded prison in the history of mankind. He figured he would die with that as part of his resume, the man who broke into the unbreakable prison."

"I guess he succeeded."

"Well, not precisely. The revolutionaries attacked last week, as you saw. All told, there were 3,000 of them, against about 10,000 Navy soldiers. In the end, about 1,000 of the revolutionaries were killed; the remaining 2,000 were captured. On the American side, around 12 men died."

"That few?"

"Most of the deaths came from some initial mortar shots that hit the prison, the ones that probably got you free. The Americans were very well-prepared for the attack and easily took out the revolutionaries."

"They do train constantly."

"It paid off. We had two Arabians we were going to send off to collect fugitives, but with the attack going so poorly we decided not to send them in."

"I'm assuming that's the two who shot me in the arm?"

"In fairness to them, you were wearing an American Navy jacket. But yes. You were incredibly fortunate to find them."

"So I am the only one who escaped?"

"Yes."

"So the mission was a failure?"

"Not quite. Although, according to the American media, nobody escaped."

"It sounds like a failure to me, then. What's the good of me escaping if no one knows about it?"

"Well, we are going to inform the world."

"What do you mean? Are you going to announce that I'm free? That would indict you guys, which I'm sure Russia wouldn't be happy about. It would start World War III."

"You don't understand. Frankly, we figured only one or two of you would escape. We called our two Arabian friends off because we didn't even think that was going to happen, but our whole plan really was based on just a fugitive or two."

"So tell me the plan."

"Well, it's pretty simple. We are going to drop you off somewhere in the United States. And you are going to make your presence felt."

"What do you mean, make my presence felt?"

Pavel smiled. "You are going to do what terrorists do. You are going to raise terror."

"You mean kill as many Americans as possible?"

"Precisely."

"You know I've never killed an American before who wasn't a soldier. In fact, I've never killed an American before who wasn't a solider and wasn't invading my country. I'm not just going to be dumped somewhere and kill a bunch of innocent people."

"You are one of the most wanted terrorists in the world."

"Because I was good at killing American soldiers. Not for killing random innocents. Frankly, I'm not sure the description terrorist is even accurate."

"Listen, my friend. I'm going to drop you off on the shores of the United States. That's my orders. What you do from there is your choice. But I don't understand why you would show mercy now, considering what they did to you."

"Well, even if I wanted to do that, how am I going to make that happen alone?"

"I told you, we planned for only having one or two men escape. So we decided to give you some help."

"How much help?"

"Five of your best men."

I had begun wondering who my best men could possibly be.

"Listen," the Russian said. "It'll be a few months before we drop you off in the United States. In that time you can make up your own plan on what you want to do."

"If you think I'm just going to go on a murderous rampage, you're insane."

"Your men don't seem to have a problem with it. In fact, they seem very excited about the idea."

"I'd really like to know who these men are."

"Well, that's the next surprise. I heard you can walk, and frankly we need this bed free if one of my own men gets hurt. So I'm kicking you out. There's a change of clothes in the bathroom over there" – he pointed to the bathroom I'd been using all week – "so you can change. When you're ready, Seaman Romanov will take you to your men."

"Okay," I said. With so much information dropped on me, I was too numb to muster a question.

"Good. I have to get back to piloting this ship. I'm sure we'll talk soon."

And with that, he left.

1:37 a.m.

Five of my best men. Right.

Romanov led me to a small room, presumably once an office, converted into rough barracks for five of my warriors. If you could even call them that.

There was Ahmad Essa, the fat gunman. Claimed to be an artillery expert, but was most famous for shooting his own toe off with a pistol. Since then, he walked with a limp, his belly swelling from inactivity.

There were Caleb and Hassan Masih, the infantrymen brothers who couldn't stop fighting. They constantly bickered about everything from food to girls to guns to the point that we put them in different units. The only thing they could agree on was that whenever there was gunfire, they'd both find the biggest rock to hide behind and take the time to practice their prayers to Allah.

Next was Raja Kouri, the scout who claimed to be 23 but looked no older than 17. His alleged beard was little more than patches of whiskers that abruptly ended where his cheeks met his jaw, only to start again on his upper lip. Despite being nearly 2 meters tall (more than six feet), he might have weighed 70 kilograms (154 pounds American), earning an Arabic nickname that loosely translated to "The Needle."

And then there was Omar Baba, who had all the makings of a great solider. He was well-built and handsome, his almond skin and chiseled features giving him the appearance of an Arabic action star. His voice was deep, his bravery was unquestioned, his effort unmatched.

There was only one problem with Omar: He was dumb. Incredibly, outrageously dumb. And not dumb in the way you want your men to be dumb: Give him a gun and tell him where to shoot. No, dumb in a dangerous way, dumb both innately and because of his lack of knowing how dumb he was.

Every command, every order we gave to Omar in the Hindu Kush, he'd have his own suggestion. And it was invariably both idiotic and dangerous, yet despite our pinpoint explanations of why it was so dumb, Omar would not be deterred. We tried everything against him – force, screaming, cajoling – but nothing would stop Omar from thinking of his own idiotic ideas and then stubbornly sticking to them, no matter what the cost.

Ahmad would be lazy, would tell me he did things even though he didn't, but I could deal with that. He truly was a good shot, and he did know his weapons.

The Masih brothers would be fearful and run, but they could be intimidated to do what I wanted for short stretches – so long as they were kept apart. Raja was thin, weak, unimposing and immature, but he was also eager to make a name for himself and would follow my words blindly.

Those four I could deal with.

Omar, though, he would be tough. There was no way to corral Omar. No matter what I said, no matter what I did, he would argue with me, fight me, tell me how I'm wrong and present his own idiotic idea.

I had no plan to deal with Omar. So I improvised quickly.

"Hello," I said to the men after Boris led me into the room. "Thank you so much for joining me."

"Akil!" Raja said excitedly. He ran up to me and shook my hand, telling me what an honor it would be to serve under my command.

The Masih brothers followed suit, shaking my hand and speaking over themselves about how they wound up in a Russian submarine 30 miles off the coast of Cuba. From what I gathered, the Russians sent an envoy – a man on my team eager to get a sizable paycheck – to recruit for the mission.

Most likely, after the recruitment was done, the envoy

was given a bullet instead of a paycheck. The Russians would not risk being connected to my escape.

I saw Ahmad sitting on his bed, his massive belly pouring out of his white V-neck undershirt and over his brown denim pants. He nodded politely, unwilling to get up to greet me.

Omar, meanwhile, ignored me. He knew his brief power over the other four men was now conflicted, and he was refusing to show me any sign of submission.

Quickly, I ran through each man's motivation for coming. The Masih brothers likely took the deal because it meant being far away from the caves they were living in and the bullets that went with them, to the relative safety of the Atlantic Ocean. The same reasoning was likely utilized by Ahmad as well, although he was perhaps more motivated to get away from the work that came with fighting on the front lines, as opposed to the danger.

Raja took the ride for the same reason many young men do anything: He figured it would be an adventure, something he could tell his family, his friends and – most importantly of all – potential mates. Plus, it was a chance to work for me, a man he clearly idolized.

Omar, though, did it for one reason and one reason only: power. In the Hindu Kush, he had no power, for no man with any brains would ever give an egomaniac moron like Omar any authority, and he was certainly unable to command it for himself.

But this mission would pit him with the weakest of his colleagues, a golden chance to have what he so sorely wanted: the ability to tell others what to do.

I dashed that chance, which made Omar very angry,

and therefore very dangerous. Which is exactly why I was forced to deal with him.

"I can't believe you escaped," Omar said to me, unsmiling.

"Some say I have a gift for doing the unexpected," I replied. "But I'm glad to see you've kept these men under control and organized while I was gone."

Omar appreciated my acknowledgement of his alleged leadership. Fact is, I would bet that all four men would be happy to put a bullet in his head if they had the chance.

"It wasn't easy," he said as an unsettling smile spread across his face.

I pointed to the holster on his hip, which held a pistol. "A Makarov?" I asked.

"Yes. The Russians gave it to us."

"Can I see it? I've never actually held one."

"Sure," Omar answered, and he handed me the gun.

I held it out in front of me with both hands, analyzing it. "Where's the safety on this thing?" I asked.

"Right there, just above the trigger."

Omar always liked to be asked questions he knew the answer to. His jealousy of me slowly began to fade as he started to think he could ultimately command me as well.

"Ah," I said, feeling it with my thumb. "So simple, so eloquent – beautifully designed."

"You talk about that gun the way you should talk about a woman," Omar said, laughing. Omar was always eager to take jabs at anyone around him, and I was more than eager to give him the bait.

I smiled. "Ha, you are a funny man, Omar. It's critical for a leader to be funny."

The other four men were taken aback by this praise, but to Omar, they were words he had spent his life thirsting to hear. When I said them, his cheeks turned red in full blush, his head lifting, his guard abruptly dropped.

It was what I expected him to do.

In a second, I flicked off the safety and pointed the Makarov at Omar. One blast later, and his forehead was splattered over his bed. From there, I turned around and looked at the other four men in the cabin.

"I am your leader. Omar didn't understand that, and he paid the price."

The other four men stared at me, aghast.

"Do any of you have a problem with that?"

The men said nothing.

"Good. Truth is, we have no friends on this ship, aside from whoever is in this room. The Russians might like us now, but that loyalty is as thin as a leaf. One gust of wind the other direction, and we're all dead."

"The only way we will get out of this alive," I said, "is if you listen to exactly what I have to say and trust each other completely. If those tenets are broken, we will die. Any questions?"

There were no questions.

"Okay. Clean this up. I need to go to bed."

Raja and the Masih brothers took care of the mess, the Masih brothers carrying the body to the ship's repository. When the Russians saw, they reacted in the same manner they'd react when they saw the menu for the next day's breakfast, and continued on with their work.

The Masih brothers now feared me, even more than they'd fear the bullets in a firefight. They knew if they tried to hide during battle, I'd kill them, so they would now fight for me.

Young Raja needed no convincing, but Omar was becoming a plague to him. Raja had begun to think that he too knew things he didn't really know, that he too could question what he was told.

The shot with the Makarov took care of that.

Ahmad, he was Ahmad. He wasn't going to overthrow me either way, although I had the distinct feeling he found Omar irritating. So he was grateful to me, at the very least.

Now I had a crew, a crew that would fight for me. It wasn't a talented crew or a particularly skilled crew, but it was a workable one, and that could be good enough.

That's good, because I was going to need it. Now all I had to do was figure out a plan.

New London, Connecticut
Tuesday, May 29, 2012; 8:43 p.m.

I was sitting in my red reclining chair, red blanket on my lap, wearing sweatpants, an Incredible Hulk T-shirt underneath a UConn long-sleeve thermal, beer in my right hand, staring at the TV. The Mets were losing 7-2 in the bottom of the seventh inning.

My house was silent, aside from the commentary by Gary Cohen and Ron Darling.

I went home that night directly after work, heated up a box of spaghetti and a jar of sauce for dinner, and spent the rest of the night sitting in that chair, getting up only to go to the bathroom and grab a beer.

David Wright grounded out to third with a guy on second base to end the inning, and likely any real chance for the Mets to win. I turned off the TV and stared blankly at the black screen.

Silence.

Wednesday, May 30; 9:48 p.m.

Same as Tuesday.

Saturday, June 2; 9:23 p.m.

Tom and I were sitting at Buffalo Bill's, between a pile of Buffalo wing bones and a pitcher half-full of beer. Tom sat in a dark wood chair, myself in a booth, with a photo of Muhammad Ali taunting over the lifeless body of Sonny Liston just above my head.

The bar was painted a dull red, the walls decorated with crooked photos of strong men in tight-fitting clothes putting balls in baskets, swinging bats or smashing into each other; the wood floors were sticky. Our waitress was a petite, brown-haired girl with bright blue eyes and a heavily padded bra, but Tom and I were none the wiser.

"Goddamn dentists," I said as I took a swig of my beer. "They are so fucking full of themselves."

"Where is this coming from," Tom said, chuckling.

"I go to the dentist this morning and they want to charge me nearly $6,000 for some root canals or some shit. It's, like, three hours of labor for them total and they want 6-freaking-grand."

"Geez, that's crazy," Tom said. "It's a broken system."

"It's just they think they are so freaking important. Big

deal, they know how to look at an X-ray and figure out the most expensive thing a person needs to get their teeth fixed. I mean, they act so holier than thou because they can fix a freaking broken tooth."

"You going to do it?"

"I don't know, I mean the price is so exorbitant I don't want to just on principle. Plus, I don't really have six grand just laying around."

"Can you get a second opinion?"

"Yeah, I guess so, it just pisses me off. I'm so sick of their fancy language and whatever, they just piss me off. And then the guy spends the whole time talking about his stupid 3-year-old kid. Why do I care about your 3-year-old kid? I never ever care about your lame story about what your 3-year-old did, ever. It might be interesting to you, but trust me, it is never, ever interesting to anyone else."

Tom laughed. "I know, we have this guy at work. You get stuck with him and he just goes on and on about his kids."

"I know! It's like, I get it, if you have little kids, your life pretty much sucks and you just have to spend 1,000 percent of your time with them, so you have to justify it somehow by making fun of them or enjoying the 16 weird things they do. But don't bum us out too by making it clear how lame your life is that the only thing you have to talk about is your kid's karate class or some shit."

Tom laughed. "Yeah, not like our lives."

It was my turn to chuckle. "Seriously. Now you and I, we have the exciting stuff, spending Saturdays at Buffalo Bill's eating our weight in Buffalo wings. Those are the stories people want to hear."

We finished off our beers and I poured out the rest of the pitcher, refilling both of our glasses three-quarters of the way. "So what do you think of the waitress?" I asked.

"She's pretty hot, I think," Tom said.

"Yeah, definitely. Oh well, I probably won't really say anything."

Tom laughed slightly. "That's the spirit."

"Least I can do is get drunk, right? I feel like getting drunk tonight – we should do something fun."

"Oh yeah, what's that?"

"I don't know, maybe bowling? At least we get out and do something, not just sitting at this table trying to talk over the crappy music and watching some random game."

"Alright, I'm in."

"Cool, let's finish these beers and we'll head over to Groton to bowl. We'll grab another pitcher there, I think they have a bar there."

"Sounds good."

We both drank up.

10:44 p.m.

Madonna was blaring over the crappy bowling alley sound system. The beers were poured, sitting perilously on the slightly angled scoring table, the rest of the pitcher on the dirty, cracked linoleum floor. The walls had two sets of blue-and-white horizontal stripes running down them, interrupted by graphics of bowling balls smashing into pins.

And I was down 14 pins. On my last frame. Basically, I had to get a strike or a spare to win, anything else I'd lose.

The bar tab on the line.

I walked up to the alley calmly, or at least as calmly as could be expected, considering the situation. As I reached for the ball – a 12-pound green one, the only one I tried that had holes big enough for my python fingers – I stumbled slightly, a side effect of the alcohol.

Tom sat on the third of three gray plastic chairs, nursing his beer, not saying a word. "It's like a dream to me," garbled out of the speakers, and I couldn't help but sing along.

But now it was time to bowl.

I stared down the pins, visualizing my ball hitting the crease between the front two, sending them all flying in a brilliant display of satisfying destruction. While the image was blurry, the noise, that sublime noise, filled my ears.

I was ready.

I took my three steps forward, my arm cocking back slowly and then violently straight ahead. When the ball came off my hand, my fingers were singed, the urethane orb flying 3 feet into the air before crashing down on the oiled wood and beginning its spinning assault toward the helpless 10 pins.

There was only one problem – the path was off, just ever so slightly. The ball missed the front pin completely, smashing head-on to its astern brother, which sent it violently into the air.

The ensuing chain reaction was loud and impressive but ultimately disappointing. Eight white soldiers had fallen, but two – the front one and his comrade to his immediate back left – stood unshaken.

Knock down those two, and the victory would almost assuredly be mine. Leave them standing, and I'd be stuck with both the loss and the bill. "Feels like *flyingggggg*," boomed out over the speakers, breaking my concentration and doubling my heart rate. I looked over at Tom, and he was still sipping his beer, stone-faced.

I grabbed the ball again from the claw crane, took two steps toward my target and held it just below my chin, eyeing things up. I pictured the two survivors falling, the complete annihilation of my red-ringed enemies. The sound I heard in my mind was a softer one, but not the least bit less satisfying.

Again, I took my three steps forward, and again I cocked my arm back. This time, though, my arm's thrust was much slower, my hand releasing the ball when it was contacting the ground, my fingers escaping unscathed.

The throw was straight and perfect. The ball went forward triumphantly toward the front pin, exactly as I pictured, on course for certain victory.

The ball struck the front pin, sending the victim directly upward. Down it crashed, past the remaining pin, and harmlessly rolled to the back of the lane.

I kicked the claw crane.

My opponent laughed.

"What made that so fucking frustrating was that the throw went exactly as I pictured it to go," I said. "And I still didn't get the spare."

Tom just smiled. "Want to play again or get out of here?"

"Come on, how long have you known me? Double or nothing."

"Ha-ha, what's double?"

"I don't know, I got the beer next time."

"Alright, I'll play one more."

"Cool. Man, I'm still pissed that ball didn't go in."

"Just can't handle the pressure," Tom said, smiling.

"I guess not, choker. Atlanta Brave they'll call me."

At least I got to make fun of the Braves. I sat back down and filled up my beer as Tom set up the next game.

As I waited for the computer to reset and Tom to bowl his first frame, I noticed a fat man two lanes over, scarfing down his plate of nachos in between gulps of beer at the scorer's table. He was watching his 8-year-old daughter, who was bowling.

The fat man was white with short, straight, light brown hair and a thick beard. He was wearing a blue button-down denim collared shirt tucked into his dark brown Dickey's, and black work boots. His daughter, who also had brown hair, but much longer, was wearing a threadbare "Little Mermaid" shirt and blue jeans.

The little girl rolled a strike and broke into a dance. "Did you see that daddy!" she shouted, as her father continued munching down his nachos.

"Not bad," he deadpanned, a frown on his face and bits of tortilla shooting out of his mouth as he talked. "Now you have to do that every time instead of just some of the time."

"I thought it was a great shot," I said loudly from three lanes over, so the girl and her fat fuck of a father could hear.

The fat man looked over at me, his neck now a mound of flabby, crinkled skin.

"Pay attention to your own game," he said, angrily.

"I'll pay attention to whatever game I want to pay attention to," I said, even louder this time. "And if I see a great shot, I'm going to compliment it. Unlike someone else."

"She's been fooling around all night. I'm not going to compliment every single success like those parents you see on Dr. Phil."

"Maybe she's fooling around because her fat dad keeps her at the bowling alley past 10:30 at night while he stuffs his face with nachos."

The fat man smashed his hand against the table. "You leave us alone or I'll make you leave us alone."

"Oh yeah!" I said back, now standing up and my face beet-red. "I'd like..."

By now, a bowling alley employee had walked over and grabbed my shoulder.

"We don't want any trouble," the acne-faced, pencil-thin, shaggy-haired employee said.

"Sorry," I said, quickly calming myself down. "I'm not sure what got into me. Come on, Tom, let's go."

I chugged my beer and we went off to the bar to pay our tab. We'd already paid for the first game of bowling, and since we never started the second one, no bill was outstanding for that.

"What was that?" Tom said as we waited for the bartender to cash us out.

"Nothing, he was just a fat fuck, that guy. Who brings their 8-year-old daughter to a bowling alley at 11 at night and spends the whole time eating fucking nachos and drinking beer?"

"I guess so. But still, I mean, why are you getting involved?"

The bartender came over and I handed him my debit card. "I don't know, man, sorry about that. Glad that attendant stepped in."

After we paid, we walked out of the bowling alley. In the parking lot, we saw a group of bikers surrounding one man, arguing with him. Suddenly, one of the bikers threw a punch at the man and knocked him to the ground.

"Next time keep your hands to yourself," the biker said as his friends did their best to be intimidating. The bikers – there were seven of them – were all wearing leather vests, with four of them wearing no shirt underneath.

The man on the ground was wearing tight black jeans, a button-down oiled-up blue mechanic shirt, and a dirty red hat. He had long, curly hair and a grizzly (and rather disgusting) beard.

"What are you guys doing?" I shouted from across the parking lot. The seven bikers all turned around and looked at me.

"Go start the car and drive over here, ASAP," I told Tom, my stare giving him no room for argument. He walked off to the car.

The bikers slowly approached. It appeared the man who punched the other guy was the leader of the group, his large arms covered in blue tattoos.

"What the fuck do you care," the leader said halfway across the parking lot, their victim still on the ground. The head biker had long brown hair that cascaded past his shoulders, a tightly groomed beard, light blue eyes and a bandana tied around his head.

"I just don't understand why it takes seven of you pussies to take out one," I said as I watched Tom get into his car and pull it out of the spot. If they took a few more steps forward, Tom would actually pull behind the bikers, forcing me to run through them to escape.

"You're going to see how much of a pussy we really are in a few seconds when we beat your fucking face in," the leader said as the septet moved closer.

"Hey, by the way, are these your bikes?" I asked, pointing to a row of seven motorcycles that obviously belonged to the group. Meanwhile, I spotted Tom pull just behind my approaching enemies.

The men didn't answer, but I needed no confirmation. With a stiff kick, I knocked the bike closest to me over, causing a domino effect that left all seven lying on the ground in a pile of smashed mirrors, broken chrome and leaking gasoline.

"You motherfucker!" the leader screamed as the group ran over a second too late to stop their motorcycles from smashing to the ground. In a flash, I darted to my right, and jumped and kicked the biker at the end of the line in the chest. He went down, immediately, leaving some of his comrades to stop and check on their fallen friend and the rest chasing after me.

Tom pulled forward to meet me and pushed open the side door, allowing me to jump in. One of the bikers reached Tom's trunk and smashed it with his fist, causing a massive dent that did nothing to stop the accelerating Honda from leaping onto Route 1.

"Woo-hoo, what a rush!" I screamed inside the car. "That was one fucking ride!"

"What the fuck was that, you maniac? That guy fucked up my car!" Tom said in the most animated tones I've ever heard from him.

"Come on, you can't tell me that wasn't fucking worth it!" I said, my heart pounding.

"Bro, I can't believe you did that – you are out of control tonight," Tom said.

"Whatever, dude, that was a thrill," I said, my high coming down.

"Also, you are going to pay to fix whatever he did."

"Come on, dude, the car sucks anyway. I'll just buy you beers and wings next time."

"Alright, fine."

"Relax, dude, we have something to tell our grandkids. Plus, I'm sure that fucked-up guy was happy for the interruption. Did you notice he ran away during the chaos?"

"Actually, I didn't see that. That's good."

"Yeah, totally. Hey man, honestly, we saved that dude, he was getting absolutely fucked up."

"Alright, I guess."

The rest of the ride was relatively silent. Tom dropped me off at my house, said little more than "see you again soon," and took off.

My night was far from over, though. I went inside my house, put on a nicer shirt, and then left to drive to the strip club.

Two hours, $268 and a hand job later, I was sitting in the VIP lounge with Nikki, my pants ruined and our songs over.

"See me again sometime," she said, smiling.

"I think I'll have to take you up on that," I replied, smiling back.

She laughed, put her shorts back on, waved goodbye and walked back to her job. I got up, got into my car and started the ride home.

It was another good night.

Part III: America's Pastimes

"The American pastime is juiced."
– Jose Canseco

New London, Connecticut
Monday, July 9, 2012; 10:34 a.m.

Marcus Stuberd walked into the counseling services building on the corner of Jay and Hempstead Street wearing a dark blue button-down shirt, tucked into his black jeans, and a black Boston Celtics cap, brim unbent.

He came through the entrance of the wraparound porch, opened a Victorian door with chipped white paint, and entered a lobby that was dominated by a grand staircase leading up to the second floor.

There, an overweight blond woman in her mid-20s sitting behind a corner desk greeted him.

"Hello," she said, smiling, looking Marcus up and down. For a second, she imagined what his 6'1" body looked like underneath his button-down shirt.

"Yo," Marcus answered, looking in every direction but at the chubby blonde. She gently brushed her blond hair back, but that did little to grab his attention.

"So, can I help you?" the chubby blonde said, smile on her face.

"Yeah," Marcus said, and he reached into the front pocket of his black jeans and pulled out a crinkled piece of paper. "I'm here to see O'Reilly. Heather O'Reilly."

"I'll call her right now," the blonde said, still smiling. She pulled up the receiver of her desk phone to her ear, her chubby finger hitting a few buttons. "Yes, Heather, I have someone to see you."

She was silent for a moment while Heather answered back, then nodded and put down the phone.

"She's ready to see you. Walk right up those stairs, make

a right, last office on the left."

"Thanks," Marcus said, still unsmiling, still looking in each direction but the chubby blonde's.

"No problem," she said, smiling, and Marcus walked up the stairs.

The building was constructed in 1907, which meant it had tiny rooms instead of big ones, thick oak slates for flooring and intricate white trim around each window and along the perimeter of the walls. The steps of the stained staircase creaked each time they met contact with Marcus's size 12 feet.

When he reached the top, he turned right, as the chubby blonde had explained, his hand still on the guardrail that now served as a safety barrier separating the wide corridor from the first floor it overlooked. On the walls were a few framed news articles detailing fundraisers the counseling center ran and new programs it launched.

After a few steps, the barrier ended and he was surrounded by offices on both sides – two on the left, two on the right. The last one on the left had a black sign on the oak door with white letters that read "Heather O'Reilly, Counselor".

Marcus turned the gold-brushed knob and pushed open the door, and a pencil-thin, 30-year-old woman sitting behind a desk, typing on her computer, greeted him.

"Hello, I'm Heather," the woman said when she noticed Marcus, and gestured for him to sit in the padded chair located just beyond the front of her desk. Heather was a short, white woman, about 5'1", with short brown hair, fair skin, striking steel blue eyes and a body completely devoid of fat.

"Nice to meet you, I'm Marcus," the tall athletic black man said as he sat in the chair, his eyes scanning the office.

The office had a thin, faded green carpet that looked like it was installed in the 1970s and never got updated. The walls were a darker green and mostly bare aside from Heather's framed counseling license from the State of Connecticut and her framed master's degree from Eastern Connecticut State University.

"You're late by five minutes," O'Reilly said. "And I don't allow hats in my office."

Marcus took his hat off, rolled his eyes some, his frown tattooed across his face. "Won't happen again."

Heather opened the bottom drawer of her desk and pulled out a manila envelope. She opened it up, scanned the contents quickly and looked at Marcus again.

"So it looks like you're here via court order," she said. "We have 10 appointments scheduled as part of your parole. You have the right to switch counselors in the middle of our treatment if you'd like, but I find it is much more effective if you see one person for all 10 appointments."

"Alright," Marcus said, his eyes still scanning the office.

"That means I like to figure right away if I'm going to work well with a patient or not. Because, like I said, switching in the middle generally leads to no real progress, as does spending 10 sessions with someone who I'm not a match for."

"How do you do that?" Marcus said, his vision now firmly affixed toward the right corner of the room, 45 degrees away from Heather.

"Well, the first question I always ask is do you really want to change, or are you here because the court said you have to go?"

"What does that mean, change? Why should I change? Are you saying there's something wrong with who I am?"

"I'm not talking about the person you are, Marcus. I'm talking about the choices you've made. Namely, selling drugs."

"How do you know I sell drugs?"

"That's what you were arrested for and ultimately pled guilty to."

"Cops don't know shit. Just trying to keep me down."

"Are you saying you don't sell drugs?"

"I do what I have to do to make a living. You talk to people who don't want to talk to you to make your cash. I make people feel happy to make mine."

"You think drugs make people feel happy?"

"It makes them forget how much this place sucks for a few hours, at least. That's as close to happiness as most of my customers are going to get."

"When you say this place, do you mean New London?"

"I mean fucking Uncle Sam and his good ol' boy country. This country wasn't made for some African like me, this country was made for one person and one person only: the white man. And what does the white man like to do? Fuck the rest of us in the ass. So if I can make a few people who are smart enough to understand that happy, then I'm going to do it."

"Sounds like you think selling drugs is a noble profession?"

"It's as noble as any other profession, aside from professions like yours that are paid for by taking money out of our pockets, against our will."

"I have a feeling very little of the money you make is taxed, Marcus."

"Why should it? Very little of the money a lot of companies make isn't taxed. I just don't have the money to hire some CPAs to get away with it, so I get busted."

"I see."

"No, you don't see. That's a perfect example of how this whole country is built to fuck people like me. Rich white guys don't pay taxes and they make the cover of Fortune. I don't pay taxes, I get arrested."

"You aren't here because you didn't pay taxes."

"If I did pay all the people who get paid by taxes – police, judges, lawyers – I wouldn't be here. So it's the same crime."

"It sounds like you have a lot of resentment."

"Oh wow, I can see they taught you a lot at that fancy university you went to. Of course I have resentment, and now I'm forced to talk about that resentment to some stuck-up white bitch who doesn't have the slightest idea where I came from or why I do what I do."

"So then why don't you tell me, Marcus. Where did you come from?"

"I came from these streets, but not the streets you walk down getting a coffee or drinking cosmos with your ladies. The back streets where you die if you talk shit and the only way anyone feels free is when they do the product I was arrested for selling. That's pretty fucked up, making life so miserable on us that only drugs make us happy, and then making those drugs illegal."

"Did your mother raise you, Marcus?"

"The TV raised me. The streets raised me. My mother

and my grandmother lived with me, but all they did was smoke and drink while my mother acted like a whore."

"Are you telling me your mother was a prostitute?"

"I am telling you what I just told you, I said it simple enough. My grandmother was disabled, we lived off that, but I told myself when I was young I wasn't going to live off of some white man's guilt no more."

"So you started selling drugs?"

"I did what I had to do to stop taking your pity. Isn't that the point of all this assistance, anyway, to get off of it? I'm the American ideal; I worked hard so I don't have to accept some white man's guilt by doing something that makes people happy. And now the police told me I'm wrong."

"There are other jobs, Marcus, aside from selling drugs."

"What are the other jobs for people like me? A guy raised by a drug-addicted grandmother and a drug-addicted mother who didn't even graduate from some shitty high school, lives in the hood and, worst of all, has skin the wrong color? What job is there for me, working at fucking McDonald's wearing some fucking costume the white man thinks I look funny in so he can drop his nuts on me, and I just have to take it for $8 an hour? Fuck that, I'm not working for some cock-sucking white man who thinks he can tell me what to do for motherfucking $8 an hour."

"Marcus, why do you hate white people so much?"

"You know the thing about it, I don't even hate white people. It isn't a racial thing. I actually met a few crackers I could tolerate. It just is what they represent."

"What do they represent?"

"Listen, all they represent is that they are the baddest

dicks on the motherfucking planet. And they built this place and they stole us from the fucking jungles of Africa to live here just so they can tell us what to do. That's what they are, that's what they represent, they think they are the baddest dudes on the block and they'll do anything to prove it."

"And you don't think you'd do that if you were in charge, Marcus?"

"You know, maybe I would. I guess there isn't any point to having power unless you can make people suffer – Orwell said that, you know, bet you surprised I've read him – and I guess that's true. White people just represent everything wrong with human nature."

"So that means there's a white person in you, Marcus. Metaphorically, of course."

"There was one white man who tried to be in me before, one of my mother's 'friends.' I pushed that motherfucker away and kicked his dick with my boot and he never bothered me again. But yeah, I see what you're saying and it's true, I'd probably act just like those white motherfuckers act if I was in charge."

"How can you hate white people then? Are you just jealous?"

During the course of their conversation, Marcus's body language had changed remarkably. At first, he was slumped back in his chair, his body and eyes turned toward the corner of the room. But now, his body and eyes met Heather squarely, his shoulders leaning toward the counselor. And after her question, he paused his diatribe for the first time and thought.

"You know, I don't really hate white people, I told you that," he said, his voice softer and more controlled now. "I love white women, I can tell you that," he said, and smiled for the first time. An ugly, discomforting smile, but Heather's facial expression never changed.

"Are you dating one now?" she asked.

"I don't know about dating. But fucking one, yeah, for sure I'm fucking one. But I can't help myself, pardon my honesty, but I hate fucking just one chick."

"Well, tell me about the girl you are having relations with now."

"She's one of these white chicks who likes to fuck black guys. I don't know if they do it because they are saying fuck you to their asshole dad or they just know we bring it over some lame-ass white guy, but she can't get enough of my black dick."

Marcus said that in part to get a reaction from Heather, but her tone, her eyes and her face remained unchanged.

"What does she do?"

"She's a stripper. At that club in Groton."

"How did you meet her?"

"I went down to the club one night and I saw this brown-haired girl with the most perfect tits I'd ever seen dancing there. And I told my boys I was going to fuck her, and by the next night I did. And we've been fucking ever since."

"How did you pull that off?"

"I went up to the girl and told her she was fine as hell but I wasn't going to drop my money like the rest of the cracker fools just for her to rub her ass against my jeans. So I told her I'd take her out the next night instead, took her to one of those fancy places white girls like. And two hours into our date, she had my cock in her mouth."

"Sounds like you are pretty good at this."

"Whatever Marcus wants, Marcus gets."

"I doubt you wanted to get arrested, and yet you did."

"You have a quick answer for everything, don't you. But I'm back on the streets, aren't I? And all I have to do is talk with you nine more times."

"What I want for you to realize is you can hustle without having to sell drugs, that's all."

"Did I just hear a white girl use a black man's word, hustle? Normally something like that would piss me off but I'll let it slide, because it's accurate. Truth is, I am a hustler, and like I said, I get what I want, and that includes any white woman I damn well please. Including that fat blond bitch that sits at the desk downstairs."

"If you ever say something like that again about one of my colleagues, I'll kick you out of this program and you can serve the rest of your parole in jail."

"Alright, sorry, sorry," Marcus said, the first time he'd apologized to anybody in a long time. Maybe ever.

"Now, you mentioned this girl. I know you're acting all big and bad, but you wouldn't have mentioned this girl specifically unless you actually liked her."

"I don't know if I like her or whatever, but she's cool."

"What's her name?"

"Jen. Jen Thompson."

"Have you had sex with any other girls since you started talking with Jen?"

"No, actually, I haven't. It's been like two months, too."

"Doesn't that say something to you?"

"Yeah, I guess it does. Here's the thing, though, she's been pissing me off lately. She's mentioned this white guy who came into the club a few times, and I know when people bring up other people, most of the time it's because they're crushing on them."

"You're right about that. What does she say about him?"

"Nothing dramatic. She just relayed some stories she told about him, bullshit like that."

"You going to do something about it?"

"I was thinking about it. I was thinking about finding out who this bitch ass was and fucking him up."

"If you do that, you'll go to jail."

"No one has to know about it."

"I'll know. And I'll let the right people know."

"You know, most little white girls are afraid of some black guy like me."

"I deal with guys a lot scarier than you, Marcus. You're not scary. You're just angry. Over these 10 sessions, I'm going to make you realize you don't have to be so angry all the time."

"You know what would make me less angry? Fucking up this bitch ass white fool who thinks he can make head-way with my girl."

"You think that will solve any of your problems?"

"It would solve one of my problems."

"Just like the drugs you sell solve problems. But have you ever seen any of the people you sell drugs to get their problems solved – like, actually, really solved – from taking those drugs? Or does it just add one more problem to their list?"

"They'd have problems either way, they're addicts."

"But you're not. You don't have to act like this, Marcus. You don't have to beat this guy's ass and you don't have to sell drugs to make money. Believe it or not, there's a lot of programs for guys just like you so you don't have to sell drugs, and you'd be able to do what you wanted to do without worrying about being arrested."

"Whatever, maybe. This white guy still pisses me off."

"You're jealous. The question is, are you jealous because you actually like Jen? Or are you jealous just because this guy is potentially getting what you've deemed yours?"

"Truthfully, probably the latter. I wouldn't have even mentioned Jen's name unless I knew about this white guy she was all about. Because I'm so pissed off about it, I want her more."

"Sounds like you want what you can't have?"

"Isn't that what this country's based on? Isn't that what we were raised to know?"

"Oh boy, another political statement."

"What's wrong with making a political statement? White people make political statements all the time and they get praised for it. God forbid a confident black man actually make a political statement."

"The reason I'm annoyed when you mention these political statements is you speak in generalities. But life isn't about generalities or what's happening in the world, it's what you can control. I'd listen to your political statements if you had any way of enacting any of those changes, but until you stop selling drugs and realize you don't have to beat up everyone who threatens you, no one is ever going to listen or care about your political statements."

"That's pretty strong words coming from some privileged white girl."

"It's strong words because it's the truth. The problem is you haven't heard the truth in a long time, Marcus. You're attractive and you have power in your neighborhood, so girls want to be with you. And when a girl is desperate for a guy, they don't ever tell them what they really think about their lazy views. And the guys you hang out with, they either are dependent on you for drugs or work for you. They don't tell you the truth either. So you have these conversations and people agree, but you might as well be having them with yourself."

"You are a pretty tough counselor, Ms. O'Reilly."

"Well, guess what, our session is almost over. Like I said, I'm normally pretty good at deciding if I can work with a client or not. I think I can work with you for nine more sessions and maybe even get some results. Do you want to work with me?"

"Yeah, I actually do."

"Then prove it. Don't mess around with that guy you were talking about. If you do, I'll find out about it, I promise, and that will be the end of our sessions."

"Alright, fine. He's just some chump white boy anyway, thinks my girl's name is Nikki."

"Why does he think her name's Nikki?"

"Because that's her stripper name," Marcus said, laughing.

They spent the last 10 minutes of the session talking about Marcus's childhood, all the guys his mother introduced him to when he was a kid, and his drug operation – mainly, he sold coke and pot, but he occasionally dabbled with some of the "hippie shit" too, LSD and shrooms. At the end, he agreed to meet with Heather next Monday at 10:30, and promised to be on time.

Marcus thought about getting the chubby blonde's

number when he walked out. Not that he'd tell his friends, but he liked tubby white girls, and he could tell this one would be all about it.

Instead, he just politely said goodbye to her and walked back onto Jay Street.

New London, Connecticut
Saturday, July 14, 2012; 10:37 p.m.

At O'Malley's on State Street. Eight beers deep. A Narragansett in front of me, half-gone. And the bar was beginning to spin.

"Fuck you."

That's what I wanted to say to the 5'9" piece of shit standing next to me. He was wearing a pink-collar shirt, collar popped, with plaid cargo shorts and sandals. He gelled his brown hair to mimic a wave and was talking entirely too loudly to a blonde and a brunette who looked like they crawled out of an H&M photo shoot.

"You are so ridiculous," the target of my rage said in his nasally, high-pitched voice, big stupid smile across his face.

"OMG, I'm not being ridiculous!" the blonde said, her hair perfectly manicured. Yes, she actually said the letters O-M-G. "You should go for it!"

"You don't just go up to some girl you've been friends with for years and just ask her out," he answered. "I mean, that's so freaking awkward."

"She is totally into it," said the brunette, who was wearing a green tank top and skintight jeans that she bought with rips in them. "You should seriously ask her."

The conversation was pissing me off. This nancy with

the over-styled hair drinking the vodka and diet seltzer should just ask the fucking girl out. This idea that he was talking it over with two girls made me think he was just some sissy who politely asked his lady each time he wanted to get laid.

Then again, who was I. I was sitting in some preppy bar by myself, dressed in a Batman shirt, not a single girl talking to me. In fact, no one was talking to me, except the bartender once every 20 minutes to bring me another Narragansett.

Hell, even if a girl were to talk to me, I'd probably only fuck it up anyway.

That idea just pissed me off more. Why the fuck was I there anyway?

I was there because I woke up at 9 this morning, went to the gym and then just sat on my red couch. Sat there for hours on end, first watching a movie and then reading this horror book, and back to watching some crappy movie at 4.

At 6, when the movie mercifully ended, I grabbed a steak-and-cheese grinder and ate it while I watched the Mets. Sitting on my red couch, steak juice running into my beard, watching the Mets get shut out by the Braves.

And the whole time, not saying a word, not getting a single text, not a single phone call. Aside from paying for the steak and cheese, I hadn't talked to a single human all day, just cooped up in my jail cell of a house, watching the goddamn Mets lose another game to those Southern fuckers.

Around 8, I began drinking the four beers in my fridge, which ended around 9:35. Hungry for more, I drove to this overrated Irish bar in New London, sat at the bar and started ordering beers, pretending to care about some Red

Sox game I don't give two shits about.

I figured I should go out, meet some people, broaden my horizons. Instead, I was just sitting at the bar, getting so sloshy the room had begun to spin, and every person in the place was pissing me off.

I should have just gone to the club and paid my $150 bucks for Nikki to get me off. But that's disgusting, that's not what a man should do, paying for some whore to dingle with his manhood.

No, I needed to go out with normal people, have an actual conversation that didn't cost more than a few Narragansetts, and maybe actually meet a nice, normal girl who doesn't wear a thong to go to work.

It didn't work. I didn't belong with these people who pretended not to see what I see. Wasting their money on ridiculous outfits for what exactly? To give their "significant other" a hard-on? Or some random guy/girl across the bar? Just because they enjoy looking like some fucking idiots with nothing better to do but doll themselves up with fancy clothes and hair gel?

What was I even talking about? I was drunk and not making sense. The only thing I know for sure was the pink shirt-wearing pansy needed to ask that girl out or I was going to rip off his fucking head.

"So did you guys hear about John and Amanda?" my friend in the pink shirt said.

"Of course, it's all over Facebook," the blonde said.

"So ridiculous. I can't believe they are fighting online. I mean, it's one thing to argue, but why are they doing it on social?"

That word, social, took me to the next level. At that

point, while I was drinking my Narragansett, I couldn't stop daydreaming about the many ways I would take this guy out.

My favorite was one where he attacks me from behind and beats me senseless. He talks to the blonde and the brunette afterward, bragging about it, how's he going to post about it on "social." They laugh, with me on the floor of the bar, seemingly unconscious.

But I'm not. I get up, face covered in blood, and tap my pink-shirted friend on the shoulder. His face – the look of horror – is an image I cherish in my mind.

Then come the punches. Three to the face – right jab, left cross, big right hook – take him down. A few kicks in the stomach to finish him off.

He's fine, no broken bones, not even any lasting scars. Just a memory, that's all.

Meanwhile, the brunette and the blonde leave with me, back to my place.

It was a nice daydream. His nasally voice broke me out of it.

"Seriously, they are such a f-ed up couple. I heard she cheated on him, too."

"Will you please shut the fuck up?"

The man in the pink shirt turned around and saw it was me who had just interrupted his conversation, head down over my beer, the beard hair around my mouth coated in a thin layer of Narragansett.

"Excuse me?" he said, his own face a mixture of anger and fear.

"I said, will you please shut the fuck up? I'm trying to get drunk here and your annoying, nasally, communist voice is seriously harshing my mellow."

"Uh, excuse me, we are at a bar. At a bar, people talk. Get used to it."

"You're right, people talk, just like I'm talking now. And I'm telling you to shut the hell up before I rip off your goddamn head."

"Listen, buddy, I don't know what your problem is – I'm just trying to have some fun with my friends. I don't want to start anything."

"Are you fucking those two?"

"What?"

"I said, are you fucking those two?"

"No, we are friends. Unlike you, I actually can be friends with women."

"You're right about that. The only girls I hang around with, I fuck."

"Then I doubt you hang out with many girls."

The blonde and brunette snickered. In response, I picked up my can of Narragansett and smashed it onto the hard wood floor, watching it shoot beer in 37 different directions.

By the time the bartender turned around, I already had that pussy lifted up by the front of his shirt, both of my eyebrows making 45-degree angles toward the top of my nose, his face pure white.

"I will fucking kill you right now, you pathetic waste of space," I said as the bouncer ran over, shouting at me to put him down. Before it got any more serious, I did as the bouncer suggested and straightened out the front of the nancy's pink button-down.

"Now have a nice night," I said, a maniacal smile snapping onto my face, a look of horror remaining on his. By the time the bouncer actually grabbed me, I had already turned to the exit.

"Get the fuck out of here and never come back," the bouncer said as I passed him.

"You have a good night too, bro," I said, smile still plastered on my face.

Once I crossed the threshold and hit the heat of the summer night, the anger, which had briefly subsided into my gut, rose again. I screamed an animalistic roar and forcefully brought down both of my fists into the front of my thighs, which left two plum-sized bruises there the next morning.

There was a demon inside me.

I began walking down State Street, fury in my heart and destruction in my mind. Not destruction of a person, per se, but destruction of the lifeless things that controlled us, the objects we saw every night on TV that enticed us to own them. In that moment, I declared war on American consumerism, and I was committed to winning.

Two blocks from the bar, I reached my car and popped the trunk. Inside was a baseball bat I always kept in there – I suppose so if a spontaneous home run derby broke out, I'd be prepared.

Or perhaps I kept it there for this exact moment, although that gives far too much weight to divine providence and not nearly enough weight to the credo I subscribed to, random chance.

Either way, it was a good bat, 33 inches of black metal with the replicated signature of some long-dead baseball player near the handle. It would be my weapon tonight in my battle against the machines.

I closed the trunk and continued my path down State Street, and headed to the parking garage for some high-end condos on Bank Street. The people who lived in the condos and parked in that garage were the worst breed of Caucasian: affluent, unsatisfied and relentlessly condescending.

After I walked on some back roads I didn't know the names of, I reached a parking lot with a mechanical arm intended to keep mere worker bees like myself out. Just beyond the arm was my target: four concrete floors of BMWs, Audis and every other car made significantly more expensive by the metal decal on the front.

I ducked under the mechanical arm and grabbed the bat with both hands. It was time to swing.

I started with those decals, smashing each one with the force of a man who hadn't been laid in over a year. On the third car, an alarm sounded, and I knew my time was limited.

So, realizing my new goal had to be to create as big a mess in as short a period of time as possible, the glass came next. There, I did not discriminate – windows, windshields, side-view mirrors – it all felt good to me.

As I smashed, shards of my lifeless enemy would strike back at me, cutting my arms and shoulders. The pain was like cold water during a long hike, refueling my body and refocusing my mind on the opponents that lay before me.

Seven or eight cars in, I realized the police would soon arrive, and I had no intention of spending my night in a 6'-by-8' cell. No, I had another place in mind, and no blue shirt was going to keep me from it.

So I ran, taking my bat with me and throwing it into a dumpster hidden in the shadows about three blocks down.

I ran two more blocks and then took a turn down a side road, my pace then slowing to a walk, calming myself to the sounds of police sirens.

It took me about another 10 minutes to get to my car, feeling every heartbeat as I went. But externally, I was calm and composed, and that control saved me from a night in jail.

When I reached my car, opened the door and sat in my driver's throne, I finally allowed myself to relax. Truly relax.

I had escaped, I had won my battle, and now it was time to celebrate.

Off to Nikki I went.

1:07 a.m.

I was sitting in a red plush chair in a sleazy strip club, too cheap to do anything other than nurse a domestic beer and run my hands over the cuts the rebounding glass caused, watching tattooed women with asses looking like mounds of mashed potatoes try to seduce Navy sailors and clubbed-out guys, when the obvious question hit me: What the fuck was I doing with my life?

I came here to pay $150 to some girl so she would tug my member. That's the only way I could get laid, with a receipt. And not even really laid, just a hand job that made me hungrier, meaner, angrier in the morning.

What the fuck was wrong with me? I wasn't a terrible-looking guy (right?) and perhaps not even a bad guy. That said, I rarely even talked to women, and when I did, I fucked it all up, like with Julie.

My father was a good man, my mother a great woman

when she was alive, my sister normal enough. Why was I so fucked up? Why couldn't I just meet some normal, nice girl, instead of relying on a stripper with plastic tits and money on her mind for an ultimately unsatisfying sexual release?

Worst part, the one I wanted – Nikki – was off with some freaking communist right now, some squib wearing a blue button-down and a silver chain around his neck. She'll come back, I know that, but still, the delay forced me to think about how fucking pathetic I'd become.

And then there was the whole case about smashing up a parking garage filled with expensive cars. Why oh why oh why would I do that?

How were we going to get work? Who would hire a contractor who'd gone to war against a fleet of parked cars?

Would I get arrested? How could I ever pay for the damage? Was there video of me doing this – would this outburst make me just another YouTube fool?

Luckily for me, there was no video – although part of me wanted to see it, to be honest – but I didn't know that at the time. I didn't know anything, other than I probably shouldn't waste another $150 bucks on a hand job from Nikki, considering the legal expenses that were likely to come.

Finally, I couldn't take it anymore, the rational side of my brain finally winning out. A few hours too late, but it won out, and I walked out of the strip club and began what I thought would be a lonely car drive home.

Three minutes after I left that hole-in-the-wall club, Marcus Stuberd walked in.

Groton, Connecticut
Sunday, July 15, 2012; 1:10 a.m.

Marcus walked in, alone. It had been a long day – he dropped his phone on the ground and the screen broke, one of his old girlfriends started texting him again, and one dealer didn't have the full amount.

But that wasn't the worst part of it all. It was his mom, his motherfucking mom who thought she could hide something from him.

No one can hide shit from Marcus, and she didn't even try particularly hard.

A few weeks ago one of his boys said he had a new source of heroin. Marcus hated dealing with heroin, preferring weed. Rich white kids would spend their dads' money or whatever they earned working at Banana Republic on weed.

Clean, easy sales where everyone was cool.

Heroin was a different story. You dealt with strung out motherfuckers who stole TVs from their parents and busted car windows to steal a GPS for another high. It was messy, dirty work that Marcus hated doing.

But his boy, he had a big source of heroin. Endless amount, almost. Didn't even know where it came from – word was it was some South American shit – and Marcus didn't really want to know anyway.

The less he knew about the supply, the less anyone would bother him. Sure, some local yokel cornbread cop might bust him for carrying some, like what happened to him a few months before, but it wasn't no sting operation bullshit.

No one was going to put any real time and energy busting some local drug dealer who was just making enough to pay his bills and buy some clothes and maybe get a steak every once in awhile, especially if he didn't know anything. His ignorance was the key to his business.

Still, heroin made him nervous. But the truth was, if you had a source of heroin, you might as well have the Federal motherfucking Reserve. You were printing money faster than you could spend it, and the cops were so overwhelmed by bigger fish they wouldn't do anything about it.

Greed getting the best of him, he started selling that shit about a week ago. One of his first customers, according to one of his boys?

His motherfucking mom. And that good-for-nothing motherfucking cocksucker Rick.

Rick spent six years in jail for armed robbery and had another dozen arrests for domestics. And now Marcus's mom was hanging out with him again, doing drugs, getting high as hell, and then Rick would probably beat the hell out of her.

He knew why that motherfucker was around and why she was injecting that shit in her arm again. It was the cash Marcus was giving her.

Marcus's mom had lived in the same house off Coleman Street forever and worked at the high school as a receptionist at the front desk. But since his business had taken off in the past year or so, Marcus started giving her $500 a week each Sunday in exchange for home-cooked fried chicken.

He knew it was a mistake, but he loved his mom and he didn't like that she was just scratching by. Marcus was making $3,000 to $4,000 a week, tax-free. Surely he could give his mom some of that so she could actually go out to eat every once in awhile and maybe drive something better than her 1998 Ford Taurus.

All that money did, though, was act as manure and attract that fucking insect Rick to her. She probably quit her job at the school, Marcus figured, too embarrassed to show up one day with holes in her arm and bruises on her face. Now she was probably spending her days doing drugs with that cocksucker, watching old TV shows and talking about how the government doesn't give a fuck about people like her, he figured.

They were probably stealing again, Marcus figured – no dopehead can go long before having to steal. For what? So she could give money back to Marcus via one of his soldiers for a couple of hours of feeling alright.

He'd spent the night drinking Cognac and coke with his two boys, Jamal and Snake, while watching some movie on Netflix. His two boys spent the night talking like they always do about how they gonna do this and they gonna do that and how LeBron ain't no Jordan or even no Kobe. After three hours of the same conversation they'd been having since they were 10, Marcus wanted to see his bitch.

Alone.

He knew he was going to go into the strip club, see her grinding on some white dude, and he was going to get fucking pissed. But he wanted to get pissed, he wanted someone to act as the outlet for his anger in that moment.

Just another ungrateful white bitch taking her tits out to get what she thinks she wants, Marcus thought to himself. She needed a fucking slap to reality on what it's really like to hustle without having to put a dick in your mouth.

She needed to feel some pain.

He walked into the club and sat at the bar. A waitress whose pillowy breasts were barely confined in a tight black corset and whose grenade-launcher thighs and Southern grits ass were spilling out of a pair of black panties asked him what he wanted to drink.

"Cognac and coke," Marcus said. He was wearing a Red Sox hat, brim unbent and turned slightly sideways, along with faded, loose-fitting blue jeans and an Aeropostale shirt.

The waitress did as she was told.

Marcus took a sip of his drink, looked around and didn't see Jennifer anywhere. Probably putting her tits in some guys face, he thought.

Why is my motherfucking mom with that guy, he thought to himself? Why does she want to be with some wife-beating bitch who can't hold a job and only cares about her money? Why is she on those drugs again when he'd spent all that money on her rehab?

He stopped looking around the room for Jennifer, pretending to watch some baseball game on TV and sipping his Cognac. He knew she'd come up to him when she saw him, be all excited as if he was thinking about her or some shit.

He was thinking about her, alright. Thinking she's about to get what the bitch deserves.

Ledyard, Connecticut
1:15 a.m.

I was supposed to take a right when I left the club, back to I-95 to New London. To my shitty home where I would have to listen to the tenants scream at each other or their kids in the middle of the night.

But I took a left. And now I was in the middle of east bumfuck, Ledyard, not knowing where the hell I was or what the hell I was doing and beginning to realize I just fucked myself.

Why would I smash all those cars with that bat? What was wrong with me? All those rich people wouldn't just forget about something like that, they were going to put real money into finding me.

And then what? I was going to get arrested for smashing up 13 cars for no particular reason? Who's going to want to hire me or my father then?

Oh yeah, I know you, you're the insane person who caused $500,000 in property damage for no damn reason. Yeah, I'd love to have you build my house, that sounds like a great idea.

I was fucked. F-U-C-K-E-D fucked. Fucked fucked fuck fucked fucked fuck. What was I going to do? What was possibly going to be my excuse? Where the hell was I driving?

I'll just tell them I had a psychotic break. Yeah, that's a good idea, I'll be the guy who works with power tools who is prone to violent outbursts. The court will love that.

Maybe I'll tell them some sap story, that some girl broke up with me or something. And then I'll be the guy who all the girls want to date, the kind of guy who if you ever break up with me, I'll just get angry with a bat.

Girls love that guy, right?

Another left turn, another road I didn't recognize. I didn't really know where I was, and I definitely didn't know how I was going to get out of this situation.

Maybe I'll just confess my sins. Tell them exactly what

was going through my mind, whatever that was. I'll do community service, even more than what's assigned to me. Have the newspaper do a story about how I reformed, about what a mistake it was. If any client asks me about it, I'll tell them it was the dramatic moment that changed my life around.

I'll start going to church, stop drinking alcohol, start working harder than I ever worked before. This could serve as a turning point, one that catapults my life back into a normal direction. I'll even stop hanging out in strip clubs, get a real girlfriend, maybe even have a kid some day.

Crazy as it sounds, this might be the best thing that ever happened to me, I thought to myself. My wake-up call. I'll confess tomorrow, tell my dad everything. He'll be disappointed, sure, but I'll make it work.

Hell, the insurance will take care of all the damages. Sure, my rates will go up ridiculously, but that'll serve as my penance. My reminder. If I stop going to strip clubs because of it and stop blowing $150 on backroom hand jobs, it'll save me money.

Yes, that's exactly what I'll do – it makes the most sense, I thought to myself. Tomorrow, I'll be a new man, a reformed man, a man who does the right things. Who is a net positive to society. Who doesn't swear, doesn't think so negatively about everything.

Tomorrow, my life really starts, I thought to myself.

But that was tomorrow. I should have one last celebration of the life I used to lead, I figured. Throw some money around – I deserved it, before my slow march back to respectability.

And that meant going back to the club for one last dance with Nikki.

Groton, Connecticut
1:23 a.m.

"Oh my God, what are you doing here?"

Jen, aka Nikki, was exalted to see her boyfriend at her place of business. She hated working weekends, leaving him to his buddies and all the girls who texted him. He said they were dealers or friends or whatever, but she knew what he was really up to, and she knew the nights she worked were his play nights.

Why she was with a guy who cheated on her, she didn't know. Then again, he was handsome, confident, made lots of cash. He also had that beautiful, big dick. She loved his penis; licking it, swallowing it, feeling it inside her.

So strong. So powerful. So masculine.

"Where were you at?" Marcus said, unsmiling.

Jen, whose hands were on her man's shoulder, remained smiling. "Oh, just with some guy, making some money."

"By grinding your ass against his dick?"

She remained smiling. "Well, I mean basically, yeah," she said while laughing her one-of-a-kind laugh.

"You think you can come up here and touch me smelling like some guy's cock you just rubbed all over yourself?"

The smile broke.

"First off, I didn't rub his cock on me. I gave him a lap dance and he paid me good money for it. He was a complete gentleman about it, too, which is much more than I can say about you right now."

"Oh, now you like this cracker? I assume he was a cracker?"

"He was white, yes."

"What did this cracker do, he say?"

"He said he was in the Navy but now does engineering at Electric Boat."

"You let some cracker squib put his hands all over you and you rubbed your tits and ass all over his dick and you just come up to me all excited and expect me to be excited to see you?"

"Marcus, you really are starting to act like a jerk. You know what I do. It's not like I ever hid it from you. Heck, we met here."

"Yeah, and how do I know you aren't going to find some other dude here? That makes me feel really good."

"I don't want any other guy! Although now I'm starting to question that! You didn't have any issue at all when I was working here – I remember asking you that night and you said only a bitch would tell his woman what to do. And now you come here and you want to tell me what to do and it's really starting to piss me off."

"You're pissed off? I'm the one who has to deal with the fact my girl is a professional slut. You know what they call a professional slut?"

"What's that?"

"They call her a fucking whore. A fucking cornbread whore who sucks some squib's dick for some money to buy some worthless purse or some shit she don't need."

Slap! Jen slapped Marcus across the face and walked out of the back of the strip club, crying.

Two security guards came up to Marcus.

"Just some woman issues," he said to the two men, both bigger than him. "You know how that is."

"You just got to get out of here, man," said the larger of the two guards, a man with darker skin and indiscriminate ethnicity. "We just don't want any problems."

"I was just out the door anyway," Marcus said, and he exited the club.

He too went through the back door, past a few people leaning against the outer wall who were smoking cigarettes. Soon, he saw Jen, crying against her car, wearing a light jacket over her lingerie.

"You're such a fucking asshole," she said as he walked to her. "You know what I do, I've never tried to hide it. You know I need the money. And all you can do is be a complete asshole about it."

In that moment, Marcus knew exactly what she wanted him to say, exactly what he should have said. And when he was a few years younger and hornier, he probably would have said it and they'd be having outrageous make-up sex an hour later.

But he was tired of manipulative white bitches who think they can cry and make some guy grovel for forgiveness. He was tired of them using the threat of their emotions to bend men to their will.

He was tired of women, period, particularly those who spent the money he gave them on drugs, alcohol and some bitch-ass wife beater named Rick.

"You are a fucking whore," he said to Jen. "A dirty, cheap whore who does whatever a man wants for a pocket full of singles. That's all you are and all you ever will be – a cheap, dirty whore who doesn't deserve the G-string she's wearing."

"You fucking asshole!" Jen screamed. She ran into him

and began punching him in the chest as hard as she could. Three shots in, he grabbed her arms.

"Don't hide from the truth, you fucking whore," he said. "That's all you are is a dirty fucking whore."

Jennifer struggled and broke her arms free. She ran two steps away from him, grabbed the 3-inch heel off her foot and charged after him with it. Again, he grabbed her arms, rendering her attack useless, and resumed his hate-filled monologue.

"Look at you, nothing but a helpless whore," he said. "You are as powerless to me as you are to the guys who give you $20 to suck their little white dicks."

With that, she wriggled an arm free and slapped him across the face, hard. Without thinking, he struck her back in the face, sending her to the ground in a heap.

In that moment, Dan Berith pulled into the back parking lot, $150 already spent in his mind on 30 minutes with Nikki.

Groton, Connecticut
1:29 a.m.

Park in the back. Someone might see your car if you park in the front, I thought to myself.

No one is going to see my vehicle. It is the middle of the night and my car's dark green. No one is going to be driving on 184 and then all of a sudden be like, "Hey, that's Berith's car."

Just park in the back, will you? What's the big deal.

Fine. I'll park in the back, I told myself. The conservative voice in my brain won out.

If only it could have won out in the next battle.

As I pulled around, I saw a white woman wearing a thin red hoodie slap a tallish black man across the face. Shocked, my eyes were glued on them as I pulled into a spot.

The next move really surprised me. In the blink of an eye, the black man threw a right hook at the woman, his fist connecting with her left cheek, sending her down as if she'd been shot.

"What the fuck," I shouted to myself.

My car now parked, I ran over to the two, quickly noticing that it was Nikki on the ground. The black man was standing over her, showing no emotion and making no attempt to help her up.

"What the fuck is wrong with you, man?" I shouted at him.

"Yo, stay out of this, it doesn't concern you," he said.

"I see a guy punch a girl, I'm going to get concerned," I replied. "Can you at least help her up?"

"I said, back out of this, bitch, it don't concern you. It's between my woman and I. You ain't never had a fight with your woman?"

"It never ended with me punching her in the face."

"Keep your opinions to yourself, you little cracker. Get the fuck out of here."

"Why don't you get the fuck out of here, you piece-of-shit woman beater?" I said as I walked up to him.

He pushed me. "What did you just say?"

"I said you're a piece- of-shit woman beater who doesn't deserve this girl anyway."

"Who the fuck are you to tell me what I do and don't deserve, you fucking cracker?"

With that, he pushed me again, and my last fiber of restraint broke. I charged toward the black man, who was taller but thinner than me, and tackled him to the pavement.

"You piece of fucking shit, I should fucking kill you right now," I shouted as I mounted him. As I got on top of him and cocked back my right arm to rain punches on his head, he threw the perfect right jab that hit me directly in the nose, splitting it open upon impact and jolting me off him.

Now he had the advantage, as he jumped on top of me and began throwing punches. Nikki, meanwhile, had gotten back up and was pleading for peace, but no one was listening.

I covered my face with both of my arms but he was getting strong shots on my forearms and on the side of my head. I knew if I stayed there any longer, he would knock me unconscious and he could do to me as he pleased. Blood, meanwhile, poured out of my nose, down my beard and onto my chest.

The black man cocked his arm back to hit me with a shot that almost assuredly would have broken my arm or smashed my head into the ground and knocked me unconscious, but Nikki grabbed it. He turned for just a second to look at her – the exact second I needed.

In my haze I noticed an object next to me. I grabbed it; felt it was hard and figured it was exactly what I needed to get this dirtbag off me, even if my mind never fully processed what it was. I swung the object as hard as I could with my right arm and connected with his left ear and temple. He was knocked unconscious immediately, falling harmlessly to the pavement.

"Are you alright?" Nikki asked me, and then her face changed to one of surprised recognition when she saw who I was. "Dan!"

"Nikki, are you alright?" I asked again, half-expecting a hug.

"You killed my fucking boyfriend!" she screamed, and then went over to the black man, trying to feel for a pulse. "You killed Marcus!"

Before I could tell her he wasn't dead, just unconscious, I heard a police officer scream from behind me, "Get your hands in the air, now!"

Without thinking, I did as the policeman said and turned around to see two Groton cops approaching me. I would find out later the police were called when Marcus and Nikki were fighting outside, and arrived by the time I had nearly killed him.

The cop grabbed me from behind and pushed me into his car. The next thing I remembered, I was sitting in jail.

Groton, Connecticut
3:34 a.m.

I was sitting in a cell in the Groton Town Police department, my shirt still covered in blood. Marcus was in the interrogation room, being interviewed by police.

The cops had already taken my statement. Luckily for me, they didn't ask many questions about where I was earlier in the night, when I thought it would be a good time to go all Babe Ruth on a stable of parked cars. I gave my account of the fight as honestly and as completely as I could, with the officers showing no emotion to any of my responses.

I assumed they were going to ask my, Nikki's and Marcus's accounts of the events and then come out with some version of the truth. What helped me was that Nikki had a massive black eye, so there was no denying Marcus had punched her.

Otherwise, I don't believe either of them would have told the cops that part.

No matter what, though, I knew I was screwed. I knocked out a man and probably would have killed him if I'd swung just a bit harder. The right thing to do would have been to call the police on Marcus, instead of trying my hand at frontier justice.

But even if I wasn't charged, I'd be screwed. It would be in the papers, I was sure, and I'd have to tell everyone I knew why I was in a strip club parking lot at 1:30 in the morning by myself.

My sister would find out. Any girl I'd ever want to date would Google me and find out.

And my father would find out. That was the worst part, knowing my father would find out.

Would this cripple the business? It almost certainly would if I was arrested, no matter how the court case turned out. Every potential client would Google my name and see I was arrested for assault at a strip club, and there would go any chance of getting the job.

And what if they found out about the parking lot incident? I'd be going to jail for probably a few years, where I'd become some nice black man's girlfriend.

There's nothing I can do about it, I told myself. They aren't going to find out about the cars, there were no cameras. They aren't going to arrest me for the assault; it was

Marcus's fault. I was acting in self-defense.

Somehow, that justification must have worked. Because after I told myself that, I laid down on the metal cot in my cell and fell into a deep, dreamless sleep.

Somewhere 800 feet below the surface of the Atlantic Ocean
Sunday, July 15, 2012; 2:10 a.m.

The past few weeks had been one sustained headache.

I'd spent it with four other men in a cramped room, underwater, surrounded by dozens of sailors wearing stupid uniforms who didn't speak our language.

The sub made all kinds of irritating noises – from the constant hum of the engine to the random, high-pitched squeals across the sonar. And the sailors were either yelling at each other in harsh tones or laughing uproariously in bawdy ones.

Oh, and the food was terrible. Half the time, I wasn't entirely sure what I was even eating, just some combination of sodium-infused protein and sodium-infused vegetables.

My crew wasn't exactly the most fun crowd to hang out with, either. Caleb and Hassan did not stop bickering the entire time. Who knew what first. Whose idea it was to come on the boat. Who killed whom in some battle that they probably made up anyway.

Even who gets the top bunk. They were like schoolchildren.

Conversely, I was convinced Ahmad and Raja were psychopaths. I tried to confide in Ahmad my concerns about killing a random collection of innocent people. He shrugged and said it had to be done, as if it were like getting a tetanus shot or something.

Raja was even worse. His obedience extended far beyond me – he was hopelessly committed to "Allah," or at least the Allah his previous commanders laid out for him. He honestly believed that when he died, he'd be awarded 70-some-odd virgins for his part in the jihad.

What a fucking idiot.

Still, they saw me as the leader and were looking to me for a plan. And I still didn't have one yet.

One thing I had was plenty of excuses for not making one. The ship was too loud. The four other guys were getting on my nerves. The food was bad. I couldn't stand the Russians anymore.

The real problem: I was scared. The best I could hope for when the Russians dropped us off – oh, and by the way, they had yet to tell us where and when they planned to do that – was to be captured, tortured and sent back to Guantanamo.

That was the best-case scenario. Much more likely, I'd be killed, giving me probably a few more weeks or so to live.

I was only 27 years old, and yet I was facing almost certain death.

I'd spent the last five years living mostly in caves, in a jail cell or underneath the ocean. At least I got laid a lot in those caves.

Damn, I really wished we had women on the sub. I had masturbated a few times, when I (thought) the other men were asleep. I'm sure they did the same. Hell, I was sure if I asked for it, Raja would do it for me.

But, for the most part, I'd never been so sexually frustrated. Who knew that facing my death would make me so horny?

Back to making a plan. If I were to murder a bunch of innocent people, how would that help our cause? The Americans would just see me as yet another in a long line of insane Muslim terrorists who hated people in the Western world because they have Kraft macaroni and cheese and we don't.

But I didn't really know what else to do. It wasn't like I could just show up and demand to debate the president or something. The Americans would just arrest me or murder me and never tell anyone I escaped to begin with.

What I really needed were hostages, to demand coverage. We'd have to strike quickly once we got into America, before we were found out. But I also knew I couldn't trust Ahmad or Raja because both of them would likely kill indiscriminately.

Especially Raja. Ahmad had no qualms about killing whomever, but he was also pragmatic. Raja thought the more Americans he killed, the better.

I was seriously considering sending him to cause a distraction, while we got ourselves some hostages. My hope was he'd be shot quickly by some alert police officer and I wouldn't have to deal with it anymore.

So that would leave the four of us to get some hostages and demand a camera to make our point. Here was the thing, though – we needed fear on our side. The only way some idiot local news station was going to put us on TV would be if we put so much fear into them they'd crap their pants too much not to.

And that would mean killing some innocent people.

There was no way around it. Maybe I could get Ahmad to do it...

From the New London Day on Sunday, July 15, 2012:

Police: Two Men Arrested For Fight Outside Gentleman's Club

Groton — Two New London men were arrested early this morning for their alleged involvement in a fight outside of The Pink Lady Gentleman's Club, according to Groton Town Police.

Police arrested Dan Berith, 27, of 30 Montauk Avenue, New London, and Marcus Stuberd, 26, of 37 Coleman Street, New London, on assault charges early this morning. Berith was charged with aggravated assault with a weapon and Stuberd was charged with two counts of aggravated assault and disorderly conduct.

Police allege that Stuberd struck a woman outside of The Pink Lady at approximately 1:33 a.m. Berith saw the assault and the two men then assaulted each other, with Berith later striking Stuberd with a woman's shoe.

Berith refused medical treatment at the scene. Stuberd was taken to Lawrence + Memorial Hospital for precautionary measures and was later released. A female victim was also taken to L+M Hospital for precautionary measures.

Stuberd is also facing previous unrelated charges for possession of marijuana with intent to sell. Berith was released with a promise to appear and Stuberd was released on a $500 bond.

The short blurb didn't even make it into the Sunday paper because it came in too late. The author, Jim Franco, a copy editor at the paper, saw the press release come in through the fax and figured he'd throw something up on the web quick.

Franco did little more than rewrite the press release, adding the part about Marcus's other arrest only because he remembered editing a story about that a few weeks before.

If that was the only story about the fight, both Berith's and Stuberd's lives would have gone on mostly the same. Sure, some embarrassment for both, but it would have blown over soon enough.

Except it didn't.

A Hartford Courant reporter, Andrew Harris, saw the press release when he came in at 9 a.m. for his eight-hour Sunday shift. Harris, 22, had been working at the Courant for less than a month after graduating with high honors in journalism from Emerson.

Ninety-nine out of 100 reporters would have just rewritten the press release as Franco did and moved on, since the story wasn't all that much different than the 20 or so other assaults the police summarized each week. Sure, a bit strange with the shoe, but just two more drunk idiots fighting at a strip club, most reporters would say.

But Harris was not most reporters. He was 22, underpaid and hungry to prove to the world what a great journalist he was. And he mostly covered town politics – mill rates, school budgets, that sort of thing – so he hadn't grown the cynical shell about police coverage indigenous to most crime reporters.

So he made a call – Berith's phone number was mis-

takenly listed in the police report – that initially went unanswered. Harris left a message and wrote a story similar to
Franco's, and that could have easily been that.

But Berith did call back about three hours later, angry
over the arrest and the fact that his name was already in
the newspaper. His interview, and the updated story that
included it, would change his life.

From the Hartford Courant on Sunday, July 15, 2012:

'Modern-Day Lancelot' Arrested For Beating Man With Stripper's Shoe

*Groton – A self-proclaimed "modern-day Lancelot"
was arrested this morning for allegedly assaulting another
man with a stripper's 3-inch high-heel shoe outside of a
local gentlemen's club.*

*Dan Berith, 27, of New London, was charged with
assault after he allegedly struck 26-year-old Marcus Stuberd with a stripper's high-heel shoe outside of Groton's
The Pink Lady Gentleman's Club at approximately 1:33
this morning. However, when interviewed this morning,
Berith said he only struck Stuberd after seeing him assaulting his girlfriend, a stripper at the club.*

*"In the old days, people would be praised for doing
something like that, standing up for a petite woman
being assaulted by a 6-foot tall man," Berith told the Courant. "The way I see it, I'm a modern-day Lancelot, not a
criminal."*

*Berith said he was in the parking lot when he saw Stu-
berd punch his girlfriend. Police confirmed Berith's story,*

charging Stuberd with domestic assault.

"I get it, you don't want people taking the law into their own hands," Berith said. "But I broke up this fight while it was still going on. That's a big difference than coming in later and beating up some guy."

Berith said he struck Stuberd with a shoe because "it was the closest thing to me." He has never been arrested before.

A call to Stuberd was not immediately returned. Police released him on....

The post went live on the Courant's website at 3:07 p.m. By midnight that night, it had more than 12,000 shares on Facebook and more than 775,000 views, making it one of the most popular articles of the year for the Courant.

The story also had over 2,000 comments. They included:

• *"What a idiot. At a strip club and he thinks he's Lancelot. Lock him up and throw away the key for not only being violent but justifying it."*

• *"Forget getting arrested, he should get a medal! No man should ever strike a woman. A real-life Lancelot indeed!"*

• *"Three-inch pumps, huh? Guess he left Excalibur at home."*

And on and on they went.

Monday morning, Jude Young, an editor for The Huffington Post who was from Connecticut, saw the post appear in his newsfeed. Immediately, he told the executive editor and they aggregated the post from the Courant.

Next followed Yahoo. And BuzzFeed. And then Vox

wrote how the whole case was a reminder about how women are so unfairly treated in this world.

And on and on they went. Some of the headlines:

Knight In Shining Armor Valiantly Defends
Exotic Dancer – With A Shoe

Lancelot Is Real After All.
Just Ask The Guy Who Hit A Stripper

Is This Strip Club Assailant
A 'Modern-Day Lancelot'
Or An Old-School Chauvinist?

Domestic Violence, Strip Clubs, And Why
The 'Modern-Day Lancelot' Represents
Everything Wrong With Today's America

Soon, it found its way on television. The late-night shows led their monologues with it. The early-morning shows had coffee-table discussions about it. What kept it going was the fact that it split people right down the middle – some thought Berith should be let free for beating up a guy who was beating up a woman, while others thought he was a sketchy drunk guy alone at a strip club who liked to fight.

Then came the social media push via the hashtag, #moderndaylancelot, where people did unremarkable things and declared themselves a #moderndaylancelot.

Some examples:

• *Just put the shopping cart in the cart return place instead of just leaving it near my spot like I always do.*

#moderndaylancelot

> • *Let my gf control the remote tonight and didn't complain once about it. #moderndaylancelot*

> • *Held a fart through all of dinner with my in-laws. #moderndaylancelot*

And on and on it went. Throughout the whole thing, Marcus never returned a reporter's call, never wanted to discuss what happened that night publicly.

Berith did a few interviews, including one for the radio and another video interview for a morning television spot. Each time, he was adamant that he did nothing wrong, saying that perhaps he was hyperbolic when he declared himself a "modern-day Lancelot" but his reasoning was sound.

Meanwhile, Berith was arraigned that Monday and his first court date was set for August 17. However, Berith's lawyer managed to keep pushing it back, which turned out to be good news.

New London, Connecticut
Sunday, July 21, 2012; 9:34 p.m.

Why was I such an idiot?

"Real-life Lancelot?" Was I kidding? Why did I go to the strip club? Why did those fucking cops arrest me? Why would I be protective of a stripper who will probably just find a new guy to beat her anyway?

And then, I would remember what I did in the parking garage. How I smashed those cars. And that would make me feel so bad I couldn't even muster enthusiasm to be upset about everything else that had happened after.

On Sunday, when *The Day* ran a brief article about

me getting into that fight, the paper's front-page story was about how 13 cars in a downtown parking garage had been smashed by someone with a baseball bat. People in their 60s and 70s were quoted as saying they didn't feel safe and they now wanted to move out of New London.

They said they'd lived in the city their whole lives and actively tried to make it a better place, and it had great sentimental value to them, yet they were going to have to leave. After all, many assumed it was the work of a gang.

What if some of those older people were outside when the attack happened – would the gang have attacked them as well?

The whole article made me feel like shit.

Meanwhile, I had to deal with nonstop phone calls, a never-ending news cycle and all the negatives overnight Internet infamy brings a person. The first day, I had to delete my Facebook page because I got so many messages. The second day, we had to delete the Berith Construction Facebook page because it got so many comments on it.

And the reporters wouldn't stop calling. Somehow – I found out later police accidentally put my cellphone number on the police report they sent to reporters – they knew how to reach me and they all wanted to do an interview with me.

Oh boy, did they want that interview.

Some of them I would answer and would actually give them an interview, for no other reason because they were nice enough and seemed like they were just doing their jobs. Plus, sometimes I would read a post or a comment and I would get so pissed off, I couldn't take it and I'd take the next call.

All that did is further the story another day, lead to even

more calls, and keep me as the butt of the late-night jokes.

The worst part was seeing my father the Monday after my arrest. He didn't use the Internet, so he found out about it when he saw it in the newspaper, just a brief that morning. Soon after, he realized how big the story had become from friends and family, and I could tell he didn't know how to handle it.

For his part, he didn't say much. Asked me about the legal costs and all that and said I could take time off if I needed it; asked a bit whether the lawyer thought I would get in any real trouble with it.

I told him the lawyer said he probably could get me off with a slap on the wrist, although all the publicity wasn't helping my case. The lawyer said normally someone like me with no record would plead down to a misdemeanor and do some community service. But now the press was involved and there was a chance the prosecutor might want some attention out of this, and that wouldn't be a good thing.

But it wasn't really what my father said. It's what he didn't say. We worked together that week – thank God we already had a job, because there was no chance of getting a client that week – in almost complete silence.

At the time, I wished he had yelled at me or at least talked about it or something. But I felt so shitty about smashing up all those cars, maybe that silence was good, because I felt so depressed anyway.

Looking back, if he had really yelled at me, I probably would have had a breakdown.

My sister called me on Tuesday after she saw what a huge shit show the whole thing had become. She tried to laugh about it and loosen me up, but I was so damn depressed I got off the phone, quick.

Some of my friends reached out. I ignored all of their texts and calls – most of them were jokes to lighten me up – except from Tom. I talked to him for about an hour or so, rambling on about what an asshole I was and how I probably screwed up the business my dad had spent his lifetime building.

I didn't tell him about the cars I smashed up, though – didn't tell anyone about that. That would be my secret, the one I'd keep to the grave.

The following weekend was fun. I got out of work at 5 on Friday, grabbed dinner at McDonald's on the way home and got a six-pack of beer. I ate my burger and drank the six beers and watched boring movies all night, and pretty much repeated the same activities all throughout Saturday.

Early Sunday morning, I went for a run just to get outside of the damn house. But I just felt like everyone was looking at me, judging me, thinking what a jerk I was.

"Modern-Day Lancelot," he calls himself, they'd think to themselves. "What a fucking jerk," they'd think to themselves.

So I went back home, showered and went back to more eating, watching TV and taking care of myself whenever the self-hate in my head got too loud. Just a sad, lonely 27-year-old idiot who ruins people's cars for no damn reason and creates an imaginary attachment to a stripper.

What a guy.

By Sunday night, I was sitting on my red chair, sort of watching some sci-fi movie on my TV, wallowing in my own self-pity. Normally, I wasn't one to wallow, but I was so fucked I couldn't think of any way out of it.

That's when my phone rang. It was a phone number I didn't recognize with a 401 area code, which was Rhode Island. Probably just another reporter.

I let it go to voicemail, and the person left a message. Figured I'd check it.

"Hey, Dan – this is Nikki. Well, Jen, really, you know me as Nikki *(nervous laughter)*. I got your number from a friend of a friend. Um, anyway, I just sort of wanted to talk to you for a second. We haven't had a chance to talk since that night. Just call me back on this number, it should be on your cellphone."

I walked into the kitchen, grabbed a bottle of Patron tequila I had in the freezer and took a long chug. Then I walked back into the room and called her back.

"Hello?"

"Uh, hi, this is Dan."

"Oh my God, thank you so much for calling! You probably think I'm such a stalker."

"No, seriously, it's fine. I'm good. What's up?"

"It's just – it's just I just wanted to thank you for what you did the other night. It really – it was really brave, I guess, that's all. Really romantic *(nervous laughter)*. No, honestly, I was hoping to thank you or something."

"Well, honestly, you don't have to thank me. I'm sorry you got punched."

"No, seriously, I want to. In person."

"In person?"

"Yeah, like tonight actually, I'm in the area. I was hoping to buy you dinner."

"Well, I already ate."

"Can I buy you a drink?"

"Um, yeah, okay, I guess. You want to meet somewhere?"

"Let me meet you at your house. We can go out somewhere. I saw in the paper it was 30 Montauk, right?"

"Ha, that's right. When will you be here?"

"Actually – I'm sort of outside now."

"Ha-ha, seriously? I'm beginning to think you are a bit of a stalker."

She laughed nervously. "Shut up! Come on, come outside and we'll grab a drink. Know a good place?"

"I do actually, it has a good view of the water."

"Okay, perfect. See you in a second."

We had sex that night in my bed, the first time I had gotten laid in nearly two years. I was nervous a bit about it, to be perfectly honest with you, but it was good, hard sex.

After, we were lying in bed, about to go to sleep.

"My modern-day Lancelot," Nikki said, chuckling.

"Oh, fuck you," I said, and hit her with a pillow.

And, with that, we started in on round two.

Part IV: A Night in Jahannam

"Go to Heaven for the climate, Hell for the company."
–Mark Twain

New London, Connecticut
Thursday, October 18, 2012; 4:33 p.m.

>*>I have a surprise waiting for you when you get home (:*

>*<Oh you didn't have to do that*

>*>It's not every day my little sex god turns 28 (:*

>*<What do you mean by little?*

>*>lol big in the important places*

>*<Speaking of him, Sir Francis Drake is excited to see you*

>*<That's what the special surprise entails (:*

>*>Can't wait baby. Be home soon*

It was a crisp, cool fall day, the weather dropping from its noon high to a piercing 47 degrees. The sun had put in its 11 hours or so of work and was heading back home, as were we, happy with the four first-story walls we put up.

It was funny, all the publicity actually led to some phone calls for business, with people really believing I was a "modern-day Lancelot."

It got us a job – building a 2,300-square-foot house in New London – that my dad was hoping to clear a solid 18 percent on, even after paying our salaries.

Not so bad.

We even hired someone for the first time since the housing crash, a black guy named Chuck. He was lazy, didn't know much and wasn't particularly interested in learning much, but he showed up for work each day on time, so he stayed around.

The media coverage had all but faded away. My court date continued to get pushed back because my lawyer purposely wanted to wait until the last of the publicity evaporated and the prosecutor would see this case as just another file, instead of a chance to become an overnight celebrity. Sure, the local papers would cover it – the sentencing, at the very least – and it might get a few mentions by the online aggregators, but overall it would probably be pretty silent from here on out.

My lawyer said I had a legitimate case since I truly did act to protect Jen. Marcus would be screwed – mostly for hitting Jen, and for all his other crimes – and would probably have to spend time in jail. But Marcus probably never imagined a world where he wouldn't have to spend at least a little bit of time in jail, so it wasn't really too big of a deal, I thought to myself.

Either way, there were bigger things on my mind, anyway, all regarding the stripper I just texted. Jen – aka Nikki – and I had become quite the item since we first screwed in July, and yet I knew there was some trouble brewing.

Within two weeks, she was staying over six days a week, giving me the wildest sex of my life each time. Every day I'd come home, still smelling of sawdust, and she'd have me sit on my red couch and grab a beer. Then she would go to work on "Sir Francis Drake" (more on that later) until I was up to getting my hips involved, and we'd retire to the bedroom.

Sounds perfect, right? That was the problem. 'Twas a little too perfect, if you asked me, and I remembered something my old buddy Derek used to say – a girl who cares so much about what other people think about her to the point that she makes a great first impression is likely a crazy person. Bat-shit, out-of-her-mind crazy, and best avoided at all costs.

And I saw all those signs. Her father was the proto-typical alcohol abuser who spent his nights chugging Bud-weiser and beating down his wife and Jen. She said he never touched her sexually, but who knows, I tried not to think about that.

Jen's mom, Ann, was the classic excuse-making vic-tim. Ever afraid of angering her husband or losing Jen as a daughter, she pretended everything was fine, as if the neigh-borhood didn't notice the bruises on her face or hear her screams at around 10 each night. She felt so guilty about everything that happened to Jen in her childhood she began acting as a servant to her daughter, as well, and Jen hated her for it.

When Jen turned 18, she left home, never to return again. Her father had since died – massive heart attack from eating like shit and drinking like a fish his whole life – leav-ing Jen's mother to spend her time in and out of rehab, try-ing to kick an addiction to Vicodin that didn't seem to want to go away.

At first, Jen worked as a bartender and probably shacked up with any man who would have her, despite her obvious beauty. When she turned 21, she made friends with a stripper, who talked to her about all the money she could make showing those perfect cans of hers on stage.

When she was 22, she began taking her shirt off and rubbing her privates against any man who had some dispos-able income and the desire to escape whatever life he was living. It was profitable, as she made $600-$800 a night, with some particularly successful shifts earning her five (mostly) untaxed digits.

And now she was 24, sans Marcus, essentially living

at my house. And as hard as she tried to keep me, her crazy began seeping through the cracks, and I was growing ever more concerned.

Perhaps the best example of this happened two weeks before, when I went out for a night with my buddy Tom. It was two guys hanging out at Buffalo Bills with no other intentions aside from eating Buffalo wings, watching sports and having our typical philosophical conversations.

The first hour of the night went fine, although Jen was texting me about every four minutes. Nothing accusatory or anything like that, at least overtly, just texts saying how much she missed me and asking what we were doing.

Tom made a joke about it and I began to feel a bit whipped, so I told her I just wanted to hang with him for a bit and I wasn't going to check my phone. She seemed cool with that at first, but about three minutes later my phone died.

Unbeknownst to me, over the next two hours, while my phone was dead, she sent 34 texts, called me three times and left two desperate voicemails. I found out about this only when I finally got home, and she was parked in my driveway, crying.

"You fucking asshole!" she said. "What if I was dead! Do you have any idea how hard I tried to get a hold of you?"

"Alright, alright, take it easy, my phone died," I said.

"I don't believe you, you fucking asshole!"

"Here, here, look," I said, pulling the phone out of my black jeans, showing her it was indeed dead. "You can see for yourself."

With that, she hugged me, and I could feel all of her muscles relax. The crying didn't stop.

"Alright, take it easy, let's go inside," I said, as I escorted her into my New London home.

"Okay, sounds good," she replied, and kissed me.

I should have know right there and then she was nuts, she was crazy, that bad things were happening. But it was a night of particularly kinky sex, which gave me precious little time for reflection.

Anyway, she was now waiting at my house, and while I was excited for yet another night of enthralling fornication, I knew keeping her around was a bad idea. Like, to the point I could almost guarantee it would end in disaster.

I never told my father or anyone, aside from Tom, I was dating her, for that exact reason. Well, that and the fact she was a stripper.

And yet, "Sir Francis Drake" was winning out. So I drove home, curious what she had in store for him.

4:45 p.m.

"Stop right there!"

I had just opened the door to my home, my shirt and beard still covered with sawdust, the bottom of my right thumb covered in oil from the nail gun. Briefly shocked, it took me a second to realize what was standing before me.

"Holy shit," I said.

I stared, mouth open, at Jen and a fellow stripper she was friendly with, Tabitha, who were both wearing black panties, skin-tight "police shirts" that barely covered their breasts, black cop hats and aviators. Jen was holding a plastic gun.

"Hold it right there. We need to question you."

I erupted in laughter. Jen, trying to play the part of tough cop, broke the fourth wall and joined in. Tabitha just smiled, looking a bit uncomfortable.

"What, you don't like it?" she said, smiling and suddenly insecure.

"Are you kidding me? I love it!"

"Good," she said, breaking out into laughter. "Although your night is just beginning."

The two girls came up to me and I grabbed Jen and kissed her, hard, while Tabitha began kissing my neck.

"I've heard so much about Sir Francis," said Tabitha, a skinny blonde who was optimistically marginally attractive, but certainly a welcome addition nonetheless. "Can't wait to meet him."

"Oh, I should really shower," I said, as the two girls began kissing my neck and rubbing my shoulders. "I'm a mess."

"We can't wait any longer for the Drake," Jen said.

A brief second to explain. You're probably wondering how my penis got the nickname "Sir Francis Drake," obviously after the great Englishman who sailed around the world stealing from the Spanish and starting the legend that pirates bury their own treasure.

You see, one thing Jen loved was reading, particularly about English history. Don't ask me why, but she loved reading about the kings and the queens and the many revolts to overthrow them, with one of her favorite books being a profile of Sir Francis Drake.

To Jen, Drake was perhaps the most interesting man who ever lived, yet there were few other books about him and he was never featured in more popular media, i.e., TV and movies. This amazed her, considering his history, and she always pointed out that there were two biopics for Steve Prefontaine yet nothing about Drake.

When we started dating, I admitted to my relative sexual inexperience, only bedding a few women in my time before her. But she loved my penis, particularly its width, and couldn't believe it hadn't been shared more in this world (if this was true or if she was just saying this as another insecurity-fueled effort to keep her around, I wasn't sure).

Hence, my penis was the "Sir Francis Drake" of penises, fantastically entertaining but criminally under-promoted. Needless to say, I didn't exactly mind the nickname.

Anyway, back to the impending threesome. I won't bore you with the details, but the long and short of it was I banged them both, twice. Then, and only then, did I take my well-deserved shower.

7:34 p.m.

It was the birthday that kept on giving, as Jen bought me pizza and wings. The three of us watched a rom-com on TV while eating, mostly in silence.

"So, do guys what to go out for a drink or something?" I asked once the movie went to commercial.

"I would like to," Tabitha said, rather unexpectedly.

"Sure, anything you want, babe," Jen said. "Maybe we can go out for a little bit and come back for round three."

Now, I was not a man who had been in a lot of relationships, nor a man who had dealt with the crazy female all too often. That said, even I knew this threesome would be a once-in-a-very-long while sort of thing, if not perhaps a once-in-a-lifetime event, because I knew Jen would likely become jealous from the whole affair and not want another woman around Sir Francis.

So when she offered her plan for the evening, I thought it was a pretty damn good idea, particularly the latter half of it.

"That sounds great," I said. "Why don't you two get ready."

The girls left my light blue living room and went into the spare bedroom off my kitchen I hardly used that Jen had adopted as her dressing room. Sitting there, eating my last slice of pizza, I began to think about things.

I began to think about what a lucky guy I was. Sure, I was embarrassed by some short-lived publicity thanks to a stupid fight at a strip club, but I just got to have a threesome because of it.

And then I began to think about whether I would ever seriously consider dating Jen, or would ever introduce her to my dad and Amanda. She'd probably have to stop stripping, even though I couldn't argue with the money and didn't really know what else she could do. Probably waitress, I'm sure, and still do okay.

She was crazy, she'd probably spend a lot of money, she was incredibly insecure, incredibly clingy, but she was hot. And she was nice enough, if not a bit strange. I didn't love her, it wasn't anything like that. But she was certainly better than the alternative – loneliness.

Actually, that's underselling her. She was kind of hysterical. And I liked the fact she read so much – I don't know, made her unique from the regular girls. And she truly had a good heart, and I legitimately cared about her.

Oh well, probably shouldn't make those decisions right after a threesome, as they probably skewed to the positive. Tonight was the beginning of my 28th year on earth, I had two girls who were willing to have sex with me at the same time, and I was going to enjoy it.

The two girls came back. Jen looked ridiculously sexy, wearing a drooping purple blouse, a white sweater, tight blue jeans and her brown hair down to her shoulders. Even Tabitha looked good under all her paint, wearing a green sweater and tight white jeans.

"Where do you want to go?" I asked. "Figure something basic for a couple of drinks, not too crazy or anything."

"How about Sunsets in Niantic, soak up that beautiful view of the water?" Jen said.

"It's night. The only real view is the lights of Millstone," I said.

"Well, it's still nice. I'd like to go."

"Tabitha?"

"Sounds good to me."

"Then let's hit the road."

And into my truck we went.

Waterford/New London area, Connecticut
9:07 p.m.

Marcus Stuberd was driving around in his truck with a girl named Sasha, reflecting on what a shitty past few months he just had.

As Stuberd would tell his friends, "Some white cock-sucking bitch is going around, calling himself the modern-day motherfucking Lancelot, all because he cheap-shot me with a pair of fuck-me boots when I was in the middle of resolving a dispute with my woman. And now that woman is running around with that white cocksucker."

In case his subtlety was lost on you, Marcus didn't appreciate that very much.

He'd spent the past few months as an Internet pariah, getting bashed by talking heads of all colors and bents for being "just another black eye for the black race, just one more idiot we have to overcome as a people," as one black commenter put it. Dan the fucking white man was being lauded by at least half the people who talked about him, but everyone with a camera or a blog universally agreed Marcus was just another street thug.

Never mind that this white man's country made him sling crack, made him angry, made him the person he was, Marcus thought to himself. They are trashing a monster they created, ultimately trashing a part of themselves, he said.

He hated Berith. He hated that bitch, the stripper. She should have just shut the fuck up when he was trying to make his point, and none of this would have ever happened, Marcus thought.

And his business was broke. It's pretty hard to get inventory when you're the most hated man on the Internet. No drug supplier wanted to deal with that kind of public-ity. He tried everything to get around it – had his boys buy it secretly on his behalf, would buy huge quantities and assume all the risk – but no matter what he did, his supply began to dry up.

Not that it really mattered. He was expected in court on Tuesday for all his charges – both the assault and the drug charges from before – and his lawyer was crystal-clear with him. It was likely going to be jail, probably at least a year.

All because of that fucking white boy and that stupid stripper bitch. Oh well, fuck it, he was going to have one more weekend before he'd be put in some white man's cell, and he was going to enjoy it.

"Yo, let's get some chicken wings," Sasha said. "I like those ones at Buffalo Bills."

Marcus and "one of his bitches," as he so affectionately called them, were in his red Ford F250 that he'd been leasing for the past 16 months. Marcus was wearing a blue button-down shirt, faded blue jeans and a Celtics hat with a straight brim that was tilted slightly to the side; Sasha was wearing a slutty white tank top, a jean jacket and tight blue jeans.

Her jeans showed off her ass – her giant, black ass. Although she was only about 5'2", it was the biggest round ass Marcus had ever seen on a girl, and he loved to fuck with it.

About an hour before, he did just that, taking her doggy style in his New London apartment. Since, they had driven off to a quiet place in the woods to smoke a joint, and now they were just cruising around Waterford and New London, looking for something to do.

"I got four days left as a free man," Marcus said. "I don't want to spend one of them at Buffalo Bills watching some fat white boys suck chicken off the bones."

"Alright, alright, you don't have to get so angry about it," Sasha said in her lazy voice, her eyes closing as she said it, as if it required all her effort. "Where do you want to go, baby?"

"Let's go someplace different, someplace nice, where

people aren't covered in Buffalo sauce," he said.

"How about Sunsets? That's a nice little place on the water."

"It's too cold to sit outside."

"So? We can still see it from the windows. Plus, they got some good goddamn food."

"Yo, chill about the food, aight?"

"You ain't going to feed me, baby?" Sasha said, rubbing Marcus's lean yet muscular leg.

"Alright, I'll feed you. Let's go to Sunsets."

Five minutes later, they were there. Dan, Tabitha and Jen were already inside, sitting at the bar.

Niantic, Connecticut
9:21 p.m.

"Well, well, well, if it ain't Sir Camelot himself."

"Actually, it's Lancelot."

"Oh, we got ourselves one smart motherfucker, who knows his Arthurian lore," Marcus said. "And look at who he's sitting with, miss chickenhead herself."

"Bro, seriously, why don't you just move on."

"Move on? Move on? To where, the troll bridge, where some knight's foe like myself belongs? Pretty hard to move on when you're facing time in prison, all because of your stupid white ass."

"From what the lawyers said, it looked like you were headed there already."

Marcus had walked into the bar and immediately spotted Berith, with Jen to his right. Tabitha was next to her, but Marcus didn't know her and figured she was just another white girl trying to get a beer.

Marcus wasted no time confronting Dan, who was wearing a black T-shirt, blue jeans, a blue hoodie and sneakers so old they were ripping apart along the seams. White boy doesn't even know how to dress, Marcus thought to himself.

"So, my lady, how's this white boy measure up to me?" Marcus asked from his position about 6 feet from Berith and company. "Once I was done with you, and this cracker came next, it probably felt like a miner walking into a coal mine."

With that, Berith stood up himself and squared up to Marcus, the men now just 3 feet apart. As Dan spoke, he walked even closer to Marcus.

"Why don't you just leave us alone," he said, the last word spoken but a few inches from Marcus's face.

"Why don't you just meet me outside," he replied.

"Haven't we gotten enough trouble already doing this," Jen said, now standing herself. "Do you guys want to make international headlines again?"

Sasha laughed and said, "Look at the little white bitch, all scared of a little tussle."

Tabitha stayed sitting and sipped her drink, watching the situation unfold like it was on playing on the TV screen above the bar. She could see that Sasha's comment took all the restraint out of Jen, and there was now no holding back these two men from a fight.

Tabitha took another sip of her wine.

"You know what, that's not a bad idea," Dan said. "Maybe we should take this little conversation outside."

The bar had probably 70 people in it all told, with the vast majority now staring at these two men. Marcus was the taller of the two and more cut, but Dan had a wider build, with a barrel chest and thick, if largely shapeless, arms.

Frankly, it was a fight between blue-collar muscles and street-smart slyness. It captured the imagination of the crowd, and when the two men and three women went outside, nearly everyone at the bar went to the window for a view.

Yes, three women, as Tabitha couldn't help herself and tagged along. Despite fucking just one of its participants, she didn't care who won the bout – she just wanted it to be an entertaining one.

Once they got outside, with the crowd plastered against the window, Dan and Marcus removed their jackets and gave them to their respective love interests. Then they squared up again in the cold fall night, their noses a mere 3 inches apart.

Sunset's outdoor lighting for its patio was good, but just behind its reach was a thick curtain of darkness. Both men could see their breath.

"I'm going to fuck you up, you little cocksucker," Marcus said. "You fucked me over, you fucked my business over and you fucked my girl. Now, I'm going to fuck you up, you little white bitch."

"Bring it," Dan answered.

With that, Marcus threw a punch, which Dan easily blocked by grabbing his arm. Using it, he threw the black man to the concrete ground, put his knee into Marcus's shoulder, and started pulling back on the arm.

"Who's the little bitch now," Dan shouted while tugging back on Marcus's arm, surprised how easy it had been. "Who's the little bitch now!"

"Fuck you, you – ahhhhh!" Marcus shouted in pain,

with his knees on the cement patio, as Dan pulled back hard on his arm. "Ahhh, you motherfucker, you're going to break my goddamn arm!"

"You're right, I am you going to break your arm, you piece of shit, until you say it. Say you're a little bitch and you're not going to ever bother me or my girl ever again."

Sasha stood watching with her mouth open in disbelief, amazed at what was happening. She thought for sure her man would take down this white boy in a few seconds and they'd get some chicken wings.

Jen was surprised, too, at what just went down, seeing Marcus scream in pain like the little bitch she thought he was. In that moment, she'd never been more turned on by Dan, watching him dominate another man like that.

Tabitha, like Sasha, thought Marcus would easily win. Dan's pretty sexy, turning that big man into a little bitch within a few seconds, she thought.

She also thought it was kind of cold outside. She hoped they would finish up fast so she could go back in to her wine.

It was the last thought Tabitha ever had, aside from a brief moment of shock. Suddenly, a bullet hit her in the shoulder, passing through the other side, and she looked down in horror at the destruction it caused. Before she could even voice a scream, a second bullet ran through her chest, pierced her heart and ended her 21 years on Earth.

Sasha gasped. Jen began screaming uncontrollably before a bullet flew through her neck, ending her 24-year existence.

With that, Dan let Marcus go and the two men stared in disbelief. A duo, both Arabians, had emerged from the darkness, with AK-47s pointed right at the Americans.

One of the two – the one who shot both girls – was massively overweight and was wearing a dark blue collared shirt, a blue jacket and jeans he barely fit into. He looked completely ignorant of the fact that he just killed two people – his face a blank stare, looking for direction at what to do next.

The other, a 5'9" man in his late 20s with short hair and a build similar to Dan's, was also wearing a dark blue collared shirt, a lighter blue jacket, blue jeans and, strangest of all, a captain's hat. The man, despite not once shooting the AK-47 he was carrying, looked quite the opposite of his rotund friend: He was shaking and his hand went to his face twice, out of anxiety.

"Everyone inside," the man in the captain's hat said, entirely too loudly. "Now."

Everyone listened.

Thursday, October 18, 2012
Niantic, Connecticut; 9:38 p.m.

It had been a weird few months, knowing I was going to die. The only real question was how many people I was going to take with me.

I really began to hate the Americans during my time underwater. Their idiotic obsessions with everything stupid, and yet their government acted like they knew best. Their fat, disgusting bellies. Their annoying children. Their general ignorance to what their leaders do to us.

I especially hated their president, Samuel Rivera. So high and mighty. Proclaimed so "cool." So allegedly charismatic, so caring, as he dropped bombs from unmanned drones and killed thousands of our innocent people.

You know he won a Nobel Peace Prize? For what exactly, I'm not sure. Murdering thousands of people? Trying to run other countries' governments from his safe little spot tucked away in Washington?

I would kill him, no question about it. After all, if he killed me, he'd probably win another peace prize. Yet if I killed him, I'd be forever be known as one of the world's great villains.

I hated him. I hated his army, which killed so many of our people and – worst than that – was so intent on telling everyone else what to do.

And yet, despite all that, I couldn't justify murdering a bunch of innocent people.

It wasn't so much the act, although that was horrific enough. It was more that I questioned what the point was. Even if I killed 40 of the most overweight, most ignorant, most useless Americans, 80 more would pop up in their place. And it would completely undermine anything we were trying to say.

It was weird, though – those logical thoughts seemed be trumped by the basic movement of things. I can't explain it, really, other than it felt like I was on a conveyer belt, being slowly pushed to my destiny. Sure, I was complaining loudly about where I was going, but I was going forward nonetheless.

Enough of all the meta-analysis, though. I'm sure you've had enough of that. You are probably wondering how I wound up in Niantic, Connecticut, wearing a captain's hat, holding a machine gun.

Well, it all started around 6:30 that morning...

Long Island Sound
Thursday, October 18, 2012; around 6:30 a.m.

My five months underwater were about to end. The Russian sub was rising upward, just off the coast of "Rhode Island" – I never heard of it before – and we were about to be released.

The only problem was I still didn't have a plan.

Well, I had the basics of a plan. I knew I was going to send Raja off with a machine gun and tell him to cause chaos about 20 miles from where we planned to land. I figured he'd cause a distraction that would let us sneak in undetected, with the local police stretched thin. At least for a bit.

In reality, I knew what I was doing: essentially, telling Raja to kill as many Americans as possible, and sentencing him to his own death. The last part didn't bother me so much – Raja was a particularly brainless psychopath, and I was convinced the world would be better off without him.

The former bothered me quite a bit. I handled that part beautifully, though, by refusing to think about it.

That would leave myself, Ahmad and the Masih brothers to capture some hostages and get our message out.

Realistically, I knew we were going to die, but my hope was that we'd live long enough to get what we had to say on TV. From there, I'm sure it would go viral, and our message would serve as inspiration to our soldiers overseas and perhaps even change a few minds.

Alright, that's far-fetched – it certainly wouldn't change any American minds. But it would prove the allegedly great country isn't as mighty as it proclaims, and hopefully lead to a revolution that would end with their pesky CIA and military out of our lands. Yes, we would serve as liberators. And fearless ones at that.

"So we are about to surface," Captain Pavel Emin said as he entered our tiny quarters. "I'm going to give you guys a raft, lifejackets, street clothes, an AK-47 each, a pistol each and some rations. From there, you guys are on your own."

"You are going to dump us off in the middle of who-knows-where, with machine guns, and think we are possibly going to land on shore?" I asked.

"Listen, we didn't pick this spot because it was good for you," he said. "The Coast Guard is based here and a Navy base is here. We picked it because that Navy base gets a lot of subs and the Coast Guard also brings in a lot of ships, so if someone happened to stumble across a nuclear submarine, it wouldn't raise much suspicion. We picked it for us, not for you."

"Great," I said. "You went through all this trouble to pick us up, and now you are going to sentence us to die. How are we possibly going to get ashore? I'm one of the most wanted men in America!"

"First, you aren't one of the most wanted men in America anymore, at least to the general public, because everyone thinks you're dead," Pavel said. "Additionally, most Americans aren't going to remember you anyway. I doubt you'll be recognized."

"I think five Arabs with machine guns floating in a raft might raise suspicion, whether we are recognized or not."

"Akil – not my problem. There's a bunch of commercial and recreational vessels around, though. Here's my suggestion: Take one of them and hide your men in there."

"Oh, okay, now I have to commandeer a ship. What's

the chances of doing that without being detected?"

All of a sudden, I heard a crash above us and then the unmistakable sound of thousands of gallons of salt water rushing off the top of our hull.

"Good news, we just surfaced," Pavel said, slapping me on the shoulder. "You seem like a smart guy. I'm sure you'll think of something."

"Thanks a lot," I said, but by the time I finished speaking, he had already walked out of the room.

8:03 a.m.

Five dudes floating in the middle of Long Island Sound on a hexagonal red raft, all wearing the same blue polo, blue jacket and blue jeans. And armed to the teeth.

In some ways, it was kind of peaceful. The ocean and the air were quiet as we gently bobbed up and down in the water. Perhaps if I weren't facing imminent death, I could have found it relaxing.

"Hide the machine guns, guys, will you," I told the crew as Caleb and Hassan fooled around with theirs. "Let's try not to raise too much suspicion."

"Oh yeah, we aren't going to raise any suspicion, the five of us floating around in a raft all wearing the same outfit," Ahmad said.

"Just listen to me and we'll be fine," I said. "We just need someone to jump in."

"Throw Ahmad in, he looks like he'll float easy enough," Caleb said, snickering.

"Hate to say it, but that's actually not a bad idea," I said. "Ahmad, jump in."

"I'm not jumping in that water," he said, and that was the end of that.

"I'll jump in," Raja said, as he raised his arm like a doofus.

"Alright, Raja, you win," I said. "They gave us wet suits. Put yours on, put your clothes over it, and plunge, my friend."

Raja nodded in agreement, as he always did. "Should I bring my gun with me?" he asked, holding his pistol in the air.

Ahmad let out a snort of laughter. "The water will destroy the gun," I said in the nicest tone possible. He was about to jump in the water for me, after all.

Raja put on his wet suit and put his clothes over it, as he was told. "Here I go," he said, and in he went.

8:44 a.m.

Sure, Raja had his wetsuit. But he still looked pretty cold to me.

The 23-year-old was shivering in the water on the beautiful fall day – no clouds in the sky, temperature around 57 or so – just waiting for the signal. Luckily, about 45 minutes after he jumped in, it came.

Here's one thing I've learned about Americans: They all think they are superheroes forced into living a quiet life, waiting for their real moment to come.

And when it does inevitably come, nothing is going to stop them from seizing it.

I suppose it's a good thing. After all, it is a philosophy rooted in optimism (arrogance perhaps, as well, but optimism is at the heart of it). Other countries, people don't dream so big, are more content with the day-to-day whatever. But in America, everyone is Batman; everyone is only one moment away from being seen as the country's next great hero.

I took advantage of that.

It was a 30-foot white ship that found us, with a white awning over the captain's spot and an American flag on its rear blowing in the wind. Behind the wheel was a tanned, gray-haired man in his 50s or so, his wife bundled in L.L. Bean sitting behind him.

Of course, the man was wearing a captain's hat, which only confirmed my theory that he thought he was a superhero. The minute he came into view, Raja began screaming, and the fearless captain revved his engine.

Just as I predicted.

By the time he reached us, Ahmad had pulled his gun out. He wanted to shoot the two people right there, and truthfully it wasn't the worst idea. But I didn't think they deserved to die, and there was no way I could justify it.

So instead, we merely switched places, the man and the woman both in shock as we kept our guns locked on them. I took his captain's hat – I sort of liked it – but left him with his cooler, which contained wine, cheese, crackers and some overpriced sausage.

As predicted, the man never called in with his radio before rushing to save us, as he was too eager to play hero. That was perfect, as it meant we wouldn't have to deal with any distress call or police on the lookout for the boat.

We wished him well, took off on his boat and left the couple with a lifelong story about that beautiful day in October they spent helplessly floating in a raft. All told, hospitable people, those two.

10:23 a.m.

We beached the boat off of a wooded shoreline, put our weapons in a big black duffle bag, waded to shore and ate the first of our rations. I had no idea where I was.

Oh well, we'd figure it out. No need to get too pessimistic on your last day alive.

I was tempted to have some fun. Get a steak for lunch. Talk to some women. Rent an expensive car. But I knew there was a good chance that if people saw me, they'd recognize me and I'd be caught.

And all this would all be for naught.

At the very least, even if they didn't recognize me, people would be suspicious of five Arabians wearing the same basic outfit carrying around a giant duffel bag. No, we would wait here until nightfall, and then make our move.

2:23 p.m.

It had been a fun four hours.

After we landed, we walked for about a half-mile into the woods, until we found a nice little clearing and made camp.

Hassan and Caleb dragged over some logs for us to sit on. Raja got some wood for kindling. And Ahmad, bless his soul, actually lit a fire using two sticks (who knew!), providing some extra warmth on the fall day.

After that, we just sat around the flames, laughing

hysterically at each other's jokes and telling each other our most embarrassing secrets. We shared our stories about the women we loved, the weird sex we had, and all the crazy things we ever did that we hoped nobody ever found out about.

Even Caleb and Hassan, so craven normally, seemed to not have a care in the world. And they were even getting along! I guess knowing you are going to die brings people together.

Throughout the conversation, the fire crackled on, with the five of us taking turns throwing in wood.

As far as details, Raja pretended he had lots of sex – until we called him on it. After some badgering, he finally said he'd never gotten laid, an unsurprising admission that was met with howling laughter from the four of us.

Caleb and Hassan had particularly strange tales. Apparently, they both dated the same girl at the same time for nine months. Eventually, she broke up with both of them, unable to handle their jealousy anymore.

I figured I probably had the most experience. After all, by the end of my reign, I was the leader of an entire sect and a bit of a local celebrity. That came with some benefits, and even when that didn't work, I would just buy it.

Ahmad, though, had me beat, although he went broke doing it. Apparently just about every dollar that man made went to a whorehouse, as he told story after story of one paid encounter after another.

"Here's the thing, though," said Ahmad, who had to be about 38 or so. "None of them ever looked at me. No matter what stories I told them, no matter how much I paid them, when we had sex, they never looked at me. Always stared at the ceiling, waiting for me to finish, and I'd go as quickly as I could."

It wasn't completely surprising. Ahmad had to be 75 pounds overweight, at least. But even beyond that, he was an ugly man, with scars on his cheeks where acne used to be, eyes too close together, and a protruding forehead that made him look downright prehistoric.

"I think that's part of the reason I kept going," he said. "Figured one of them would be able to stand the sight of me. Finally, one of them did."

"So why didn't you keep going to her?" I asked.

"I did. She worked at a place in Mana, where I was stationed for about nine months, and I would go see her every chance I had. Probably three or four times a week. She even began to give me discounts, and I'd take her out to dinner after, and we'd enjoy the night together."

"She wasn't beautiful, but she had great curves and these beautiful, full lips. I loved those lips. And, most of all, every time we had sex, she would stare right into my eyes, giving me a big smile with those beautiful lips of hers."

"Bet that's not the only thing she did with those lips," Caleb said, which was met with the hearty laughter that had dominated the day.

Ahmad even joined in.

"You're right," he said. "She knew how to use them. But I kept wanting to ask her out, kept wanting to see her as something other than just a whore. But I was too scared, too worried she'd say no and I'd lose those eyes staring at me forever, and I'd be forced back to an endless succession of head-turning women."

"Did you ever do it?" I asked.

"Well, one night, while I was still in Mana, we got bombed by the Americans. A drone. Four men who I slept right next to died. The only thing that kept me alive was I happened to be up making something to eat when the bomb dropped."

That caused everyone to erupt in laughter. "No surprise there," Hassan said, smiling.

"How can I argue?" Ahmad said, patting his belly. "But after that, I figured, fuck it. Truth is, even if she said no, I'd probably be dead soon enough. So I figured I didn't have much to lose."

"What did she say?" I asked.

"She said yes," Ahmad said, grinning from ear to ear, the happiest I'd ever seen him. "She said yes. And we were together for four beautiful months."

"What happened?" Caleb asked.

"Well, our unit moved to another house – actually, it was more like a shack – just outside of Mana," Ahmad said. "And I didn't really like her coming there. We had never been attacked there once, did a good job of keeping a low profile, but you never know."

"Anyway, it happened to be my birthday, and she wanted to surprise me at the house," Ahmad said. "Just as she reached the place, an American and Afghani mixed unit ambushed us, and she was shot in the head during the fire-fight. They must have followed her to the spot."

Suddenly, all the happiness around the campfire evaporated, and we all went quiet. Yet Ahmad seemed oddly at peace with it, or perhaps he was still just numb.

"After that, I didn't really care about much anymore," Ahmad said. "And I'm certainly not going to give a fuck about any American tonight, or even if I make it or not."

"You are going to make it, my friend," I said, putting my hand on his shoulder. "And we'll make the Americans pay."

After that, we were quiet for a few minutes. During that time of silence, I figured I'd do my best to deliver on the second part of my promise to Ahmad, at the very least.

The fire crackled on.

5:32 p.m.

As the sun set and the temperature began to drop, we made our way out of the woods, and to our Maker. I was with Raja, who almost assuredly knew he was about to die.

We were walking through piles of dead leaves, crackling with every step.

"Raja, be safe out there," I said, right before we reached the road. "And you know, man, I love you."

I grabbed his shoulder, gave him a good shake, and patted him on the back. He smiled.

"Thanks Akil," he said as he dragged his legs through the layers of brown and orange leaves that covered the ground. "This should be good, anyway. I'll get all over Facebook, I'm sure."

He laughed nervously.

"Facebook?" I said, smiling. "Facebook – of course."

"What do you mean, of course?"

"Raja, you just gave me the secret to the whole thing. This won't be as hard as I thought."

He smiled. "Good luck," he said, and we hugged. He then went around to the other three men; each of them wished him luck and hugged him, and he turned to leave.

In that moment, I wanted to stop him and say something else, but I didn't really know what to do. Or what to say.

So I let him go. I really did care about him, even if he was a brain-dead psychopath.

But he made his choice, he knew what he was facing. And I couldn't think about him anyway. I had my own problems.

Still, despite all the justification, it would have been nice to say something profound in that moment. Nothing came to me.

After watching Raja walk off, I grabbed the captain's hat that I had shoved in my back pocket earlier and put it on my head. It was showtime.

"Facebook," I muttered to myself as I walked to the road with my three remaining soldiers. "Why didn't I think of that?"

Niantic, Connecticut
Thursday, October 18, 2012; 9:50 p.m.

One thought kept running over and over in my head as I stood in disbelief on that concrete patio outside of Sunsets: *I'm going to kill that motherfucker.*

Well, technically speaking, there were two motherfuckers. One was a fat fuck who had to be about 40 and ugly as hell. The other was the obvious leader of the pair, some Arab about my age wearing a ridiculous captain's hat.

"Who the fuck are you?" I said.

"Do you want to die?" the man in the captain's hat said,

still shaking. I didn't respond. Our eyes met.

"Get inside," the man yelled. "Now!"

I thought about charging him right there, I really did. But, before I could, Marcus grabbed my shoulder.

"Chill, bro," he said to me quietly. "Let's just do what he said."

So I did, and followed Marcus back into the restaurant. I figured it would be empty, with all the people running out after the murders, but I was wrong. Two other Arabs – brothers, they looked like, in their early 20s and with wispy beads – had their machine guns out and the 70 or so people at Sunsets were on their knees.

"Everyone," the Arab in the captain's hat said after Marcus and I filed into the room and went down to our knees as well. "Listen up, I'm going to make this easy to understand. If you do exactly what I say, and cause no trouble, you will all make it out of this place alive."

Sunsets truly was a beautiful place to get a drink. Outside was classic wood siding, painted white, with a blue-black roof and a beautiful concrete patio that had a perfect view of the Niantic River.

The inside had all wood floors and a giant, Mahogany bar, with chrome bar rails running down the middle of it. All told, they must have had nearly 30 beers on draft, with a crab, a Rastafarian, an apple tree and a dozen other pieces of art serving as taps.

The walls were painted an Atlantic blue and were lined with lobster pots and water-painted pictures of nautical scenes. Directly behind the bar was a giant iron anchor, attached to the wall with four massive struts.

Of course, the beauty was a bit lost in that moment,

considering the bar was filled with terrified 20-somethings kneeling on the ground. And four Arabians holding machine guns, ensuring everyone stayed that way.

"Who is the fucker?" I whispered to Marcus, the two of us kneeling about 3 feet to the left of the bar.

"You don't know?" he said. "That's Akil Dhakir, one of the most wanted terrorists in the world. I thought they caught him; he must have escaped in the whole Cuba thing and no one said anything. Anyway, that's one bad motherfucker."

"Alright, dude, I know who he is, I thought he was dead," I said. "You think he's going to kill us?"

"He's a fucking terrorist," Marcus said. "Of course he's going to kill us. That's what terrorists do, they kill people."

"Then why did you listen to him?"

"What are you two talking about?" Akil said, walking over to us. "I just said if everyone does exactly what they are told and was quiet, you'll make it out of here alive. And you couldn't follow that for a second."

"You're a terrorist, you are going to kill us," I said. "Why would we listen to you?"

"Let me ask you a question," Akil said. "If I kill all of you, how long will it take for the police to kill me?"

"About four seconds," I said.

"Exactly," Akil said. "But if you are alive, and I have you as hostages, they can't just run in and murder us. So our interests our intertwined. That's what you should listen to me."

"Fine."

"Good. Now shut the fuck up."

"Now, listen everybody, you are probably wondering who I am," Akil said, addressing the terrified room. "My name is Akil Dhakir, and I was at one time one of the most wanted 'terrorists' in the world. They called me a terrorist despite the fact I never killed anyone other than soldiers from foreign lands trying to take over our country. I was called a terrorist because I was an Afghan; if I was an American, you'd call me a hero."

"You just killed two innocent people a second ago," Marcus said.

"Well, really, my friend Ahmad did, but that's a fair point," Akil answered. "So that makes two innocent people I'm responsible for killing. Your country, meanwhile, has killed hundreds of thousands of innocent people in my country, and some of them were my closest friends."

The restaurant was silent.

"So that's who I am – now, what I'm doing here. It is simple. As I told the bearded gentleman, I need you as hostages. That's it. Once your role is up, I'll let you go and you can be free. I'm going to make a quick video and send it out to the world. That's it."

"That's bullshit," I shouted. "You are going to kill all of us."

Suddenly, Ahmad shot his machine gun at an overweight 22-year-old girl wearing a slutty halter top and tight white jeans, hitting her in the knee. Immediately, she began to wail in pain, and a puddle of blood began to pool on the wood floor directly below her.

Akil and Ahmad began screaming at each other in Arabic, and it looked like Akil was livid that Ahmad shot her. After about a minute of arguing, Ahmad relented.

Meanwhile, some of the girl's friends ran over as her cries of pain rang throughout the restaurant. One of them took off a jacket and wrapped it tightly around her leg, which seemed to dull her pain a bit.

"Listen," Akil shouted in English, his body trembling, after he had finished arguing with Ahmad. "Fact is, if you don't listen, we are going to shoot someone else. So, you with the beard, you can know perfectly well that it was your own stubborn insubordination that just got that girl shot."

"I wasn't me, you fucker, it was that fat fuck who pulled the trigger," I shouted back angrily.

Nearly the whole rest of the restaurant hushed me at once. "Shut up," Marcus said to me under his breath. "You are going to get someone else shot."

"Fine, go ahead, make your stupid fucking video," I said to Akil. "I won't say a peep."

"Now, I need something from one of you," Akil said, still shaking. "Who has an iPhone?"

The restaurant was silent.

"I said, who has an iPhone?" Akil said. "If I don't hear from anybody within the next 30 seconds, I'm going to shoot another person."

Marcus jumped up. "I have an iPhone," he said, pulling it out of his pocket.

"Thank you," Akil said, cautiously taking it from him. "You are the only sensible one in here, talking down your bearded friend over there and actually listening to me."

9:53 p.m.

I can't believe that cracker brought me into this, Marcus thought to himself as he kneeled back down on the hardwood floor. I'm going to fucking die tonight, he thought.

245

Caleb and Ahmad had their guns out as they patrolled the back of the restaurant, ready to shoot whoever moved. Meanwhile, Hassan was about 6 feet away from me in this beautiful American restaurant, iPhone in hand, videotaping my every word.

"Hello, I am Akil Dhakir," I said to my eventual audience. "I'm sure many of you are surprised to see me. Your government made quite the big deal when I was captured and then said I was murdered. Once again, your government has lied to you. Truth is, both the Cubans and the Russians helped me get out of your fancy prison in Guantanamo back in the spring, although the Russians wouldn't be too happy if I told you that."

"Anyway, as you see, I've since landed in a town called Niantic and have 70 American hostages. And I hear the newspapers spewing their ink already, the crazy Muslim and his friends are about to commit another unforgivable tragedy, which only the white knight American military can stop."

"And, you know what, in that very narrow view, perhaps they are right."

Hassan slowly scanned the restaurant with the iPhone, showing the world a room full of hostages. They all were still, kneeling on the floor, too frightened too move.

This is going well, I thought to myself as I took a deep breath. I just need to get this next part right.

"But let me ask you something. Today, I have 70 hostages in this bar that I have complete control over. If they don't do as I want, I'll kill them. If they say something I don't like, I'll kill them. This evil man from another land has taken complete control of their lives, and we all agree, for them it's a dystopia."

"If one of these people were to rise up against me, would they be seen as a vigilante? As a terrorist? As a threat that needs to be stomped out, no matter how many civilians are killed along the way?"

"Of course not. They would be seen as a hero, as a liberator, as someone who stands up against the force that unfairly subjugates them."

"And yet, that happens in my country every single day. Men from a world away, with no care or worry about our well-being, seek to control us. They kill our leaders, bribe the ones who survive, and attempt to brainwash our people. If we step out of line, if a group disagrees, we are viewed as unstable terrorists who are smeared by the press and murdered by whatever fancy new toy your government decides to use next."

"And for what? Why has our independence been taken away, our morals challenged, our government perverted? Surely, there's some noble cause, some worthy outcome that perhaps doesn't justify the means, but at least rationalizes them."

"I could only wish. Arabia has been destroyed from the outside for the manifestation of evil itself – the dark, thick liquid that lives beneath our sands. A long while back, the grandson of an imperialistic leader decided that dark liquid was the key to America's fate, and they would destroy whoever got in its way."

"Since then, it's been 60 years of murder, of destruction, of American dick-waving just so you can have oil. Oil!

And why do you need this oil? So you can live your vapid, pathetic, materialistic lives without the slightest bit of adversity. You choose Barbie dolls for your children and breast implants for your mistresses over the lives of millions of good, hardworking Arabians."

"Oh, and how you justify it. 'Those Arabians, they hate women,' you say, as you beat your wives and fondle your daughters. 'Those Arabians, their beliefs are archaic and violent,' as you bomb those who pose no true threat. 'Did you see what they did to us,' you say, as you ignore the blood covering all of your hands."

"We know why you can get away with it. Because we are brown. And we talk a little different. And our religious book is slightly different than yours. It's been going on since the beginning of time – wars fought over resources, under the thin veil of religion or a flag, justified by superficial differences."

"So I ask you, Americans, you alleged rugged, John Wayne types, what should I do? What would you do? Return to your country? Let a government continue to control your people, bombing whichever one of us makes them uncomfortable? Listen to a people who love to tell every other country in the world how to live, while they allow every possible perversion in theirs?"

"You wouldn't, and nor shall I. I will not walk back to the sand-filled jail you've created for me, a broken and beaten man. Chances are, I will die tonight. But you will understand my pain. You will understand what you and your leaders have done to us."

"Tonight, you will stop seeing us as the evil your media makes us to be. Instead, you'll see us as we really are: as the brothers you have mercilessly strangled for the past 60 years."

The speech was going well, I thought to myself. All I had to do now was wrap up the video and have Hassan send it to a friend in Kabul. From there, that friend would post it online, and it would spread quickly throughout Facebook.

I figured within a few hours, it would get a few hundred million views.

At the very least, it would serve as a complete embarrassment to the American government and proof of their lies. And I knew it would help recruit millions to our cause, and perhaps even force the Western world to take a more humanitarian approach in dealing with the Arabian one.

Or so I thought.

9:57 p.m.

As Akil was giving his speech, Marcus turned to me.

"We have to kill that motherfucker," he whispered.

We were probably 10 feet away from the guy holding the iPhone, who had his back to us. Akil was 6 feet past him, intently staring at the camera. Meanwhile, Ahmad and the other Arab were watching us all like hawks, AK-47s in hand.

"How are we going to do that?" I whispered back. "They'll shoot us before we get off the ground."

"They aren't prepared for guys like us," Marcus said, looking determined. "We'll catch them off guard."

"Bro, he's only making a video," I said. As I did, Ahmad looked right at us and glared. I shut my mouth.

We waited about another 30 seconds, for Ahmad to look elsewhere. Marcus met my eyes again, bulged his eyes out at me and pointed his eyebrows at Akil.

Throughout my life, I always felt like a frog, sitting on a lily pad, too scared to leap. Either the pond was too dark. Or the shore was too far away. Or whatever.

So I just kept floating around on my lily pad day after day, doing just enough to stay alive, without ever really making a decision. About anything. My feet were wet, there was barely enough food; but I was too much of a pussy to do anything about it.

Well, I was tired of it. I wanted solid ground under my feet so bad, I couldn't take it anymore.

In that moment, in that beautiful Niantic restaurant, I finally leapt.

Niantic, Connecticut
October 18, 2012; 10:01 p.m.

I'll never forget my last minute.

As I was speaking, suddenly I saw a flicker out of the corner of my eye. Before I could turn to it fully, I heard Ahmad's shots fire out.

The black man fell down, dead. The white man took one in the ass, but kept running, clotheslining Hassan in the back of the head.

And then he reached me.

At that point, the rest of the crowd joined in. Caleb and Ahmad were shooting wildly as everyone in the restaurant struggled to bring them down. Another few seconds, and I knew they'd be dead.

I should have taken the American. He was about my build, perhaps an inch taller, but he didn't go through what I went through. He didn't spend five years living in a cave. Or six months getting tortured by the Pakistanis and then the Americans. Or nearly half-a-year living in a sub underwater.

He was just another vapid, empty American with too much freedom and not enough to do. He had never killed a man, never lived with a constant threat of death, never saw one of his friends get blown up in front of him.

But I didn't take him. Before I could even react, he smashed me in the face, his adrenaline fueling the punch. Next thing I knew, he was on top of me, throwing an avalanche of fists.

It didn't hurt. In fact, for a moment there, it felt like I left my physical body completely behind, my soul looking over the Picasso that used to be my face.

And then I traveled. Through time and space. Next thing I knew, I was sitting around the kitchen table of the shitty two-room shack in Zhari where I grew up, looking at my dad.

The room looked more modest than it ever had, but it was warm. Welcoming. My father's face was morose.

We talked.

"How did I get here, dad? Why didn't I just listen to you?"

"Son, since you were 3 years old, I knew you'd never listen to me," my father answered. Although he looked old, his face was smooth, as if every care and wrinkle had faded away.

He spoke calmly. "I knew you'd eventually run off and join the army. It was just the way you were, an anger inside of you, and there wasn't any stopping it."

"Why do we hate, dad? Why do we kill? Why did I kill?"

"I don't know son, I really don't," he said slowly. "You think you get wiser as you age, understand things better, but you don't. I still can't figure that out. Just the way we are, I guess."

"Am I a bad person, dad?"

"I don't know that one either, son. Only you can answer that."

"I should have stayed with you, dad, I should have."

"There's no point in worrying about what happened before. What's done is done. All you can do is focus on what's left."

"I love you dad," I said, tears running down my cheeks.

"I love you too, son," he said. We both stood up and, for the first time in our lives, hugged.

Just as with Raja earlier, I wished there was more to say, something more profound. But that was it, just a man and his son, enjoying one last moment together.

And then everything went black.

Part V: Cognitive Dissonance

*"Nowhere else in history has there ever been
a flag that stands for the right to burn itself.
This is the fractal of our flag.
It stands for the right to destroy itself."*
– Ken Kesey

Washington, D.C.
Friday, October 26, 2012; 3:34 p.m.

"Ladies and gentlemen, today we are surrounded by heroes."

President Samuel Rivera was standing at the podium, wearing a deep blue suit, a solid red tie and an American flag lapel just above his heart. He wasn't a particularly tall man – only about 5'8" – but his dark hair, dark eyes and deep, penetrating voice, along with his spontaneous fits of passion, made him a man who commanded all the attention in whatever room he went in.

I was standing behind him, wearing a black suit and blue tie, unable to sit down thanks to the bullet in my ass.

"Many times in our nation's history, we've been tested. We were tested during the winter of 1778, 20 miles northwest of Philadelphia. We were tested in the summer in 1863, in the foothills of Pennsylvania. We were tested in the late fall of 1941 in our westernmost state, again on that terrible day in November in Dallas in 1963, and that time when it seemed like the world was ending before our very eyes on that horrifying September morning."

"Time and time again, we've been tested, our freedom challenged, our ideals attacked. And time and time again, we've withstood the onslaught and struck back with unyielding force. Time and time again, we have prevailed."

The small crowd applauded as the cameras snapped and the reporters took notes.

"Eight days ago, we were challenged again. It was in a place we'd never expect, a small town on the coast of the Long Island Sound, two hours west of New York and two hours south of Boston. That night, evil men ascended from hell itself and tried to tear apart the fabric of our very nation."

"And again, our nation stood strong."

The crowd roared.

We were all in the iconic East Room of the White House. The reporters and families were sitting in steel padded chairs on the room's hardwood floors directly in front of the president. Behind the president were most of the people who survived at Sunsets that night, sitting in padded steel chairs of their own.

The room was painted a fading white, with mustard-colored curtains covering each window and a giant gold chandelier hovering just above the world's most powerful man.

"Here's what our enemies continually refuse to understand. We will not quit. We cannot quit. Because ultimately our ideals of peace and freedom will never flinch to ideals based in hate and violence."

"These people behind me today, they embody that spirit. Eight days ago, when it would have been so easy for them to give up, to allow the personification of evil to have its way, they fought back. They showed again that our nation is not defined by boundaries or by a shared ethnicity, but a shared idea. And they showed that idea is stronger than any terrorist plot."

More applause.

"Of course, this day isn't just about proving something all of us already knew was true. It is also about the 43 great Americans we lost at the hands of evil, a sacrifice we shall never forget."

"Let's have a moment of silence for those brave souls who gave their lives for this nation we hold so dear."

Everyone in the audience, myself included, dropped their heads. After roughly a minute, Rivera was talking again, his eyes lit with passion.

"It's a shame that there are still people in this world who kill, who murder for no other reason but they can, and no amount of my own rationality can account for that. It is only because of the bravery of the people around me they don't triumph."

More silence.

"There are two people here today that I would specifically like to call out. One of them is present, the other is not. I'll start with the latter."

"According to the firsthand accounts of the people sitting behind me, 26-year-old Marcus Stuberd was particularly brave that day. He, along with a second fellow I'm about to name, stood up to the men who waged war against innocent, unarmed Americans."

"In fact, I'm told that when Marcus charged at a man so evil I won't dignify him by saying his name, it ignited the revolt against the group of terrorists that ultimately overtook them. Marcus's bravery shall never be forgotten."

"I have no doubt that he is watching down on us today in his well-deserved place in heaven. But here to represent him is his mother, Luticia Stuberd, and his brother, Alexander Stuberd. Can you two please stand in recognition of Marcus."

The two stood, with Alexander looking down and holding back tears while Luticia let hers flow freely down her face. The audience – including myself and the people sitting around me – gave the grieving family thunderous applause, which only meant more tears for Ms. Stuberd.

After about three minutes, the crowd sat down. "I love you, Luticia," a black woman shouted, and the crowd cheered again.

"To show our appreciation to Marcus for his extreme courage, he will posthumously receive the Presidential Medal of Freedom," Rivera said, and again the crowd burst out in applause.

After about another minute, Rivera started up again. "As mentioned, there's a second man I'd like to mention, a man who we have the pleasure of being joined by today. Dan Berith, would you please come over here."

I was standing but a few feet away from the president, so I just took two strides to meet him. He turned to me and shook my hand as the crowd again stood and erupted in applause.

The scene brought me to tears

As we shook hands, Rivera grabbed my shoulder and came close to me. "Congratulations, you truly are a modern Lancelot," he whispered into my ear, which caused me to briefly break out in laughter.

Then he returned to his spot behind the podium, as I remained standing just to his right.

"This man, 28-year-old Daniel Oliver Berith, I'm told never accepted imprisonment. He refused to bow, continued to fight, and ultimately pinned down and killed a man who likely would have shot dozens of innocent Americans."

The audience clapped.

"That night, this man, Daniel Oliver Berith, was the personification of everything America believes in. He, ladies and gentleman, is a true hero, and he deserves all the acclaim America can give to him."

Again, the audience applauded vigorously. In the front row, I saw both my father and sister were crying.

"Like Marcus, Mr. Berith will receive the Presidential Medal of Freedom, the highest award a civilian can receive. And even that doesn't feel like enough."

President Rivera turned to me. "I think I speak for the nation, Dan, when I say thank you very much."

Another roar from the standing crowd, this one louder than any of the rest.

Again, I burst into tears. I've never felt so much emotion in my life, even when my mother died.

Rivera quieted the crowd and began again. "Of course, those two men weren't the only heroes that night. The people sitting around me all charged and overthrew their enemies. Despite five of the people around them being shot and killed in the revolt, they continued and overthrew those evil men. Let's hear it for them."

Another burst of applause, with family members of all ages shouting how proud they were of their sister, son, mother, nephew, father.

"And there were the police in Groton, Connecticut, who mercifully took out another terrorist sent to kill as many of our countrymen as he could. Unfortunately, it wasn't before the deaths of 48 unarmed and defenseless Americans. We are having a ceremony to honor the Groton Police on Monday, but I wanted to take a minute to honor them now, as well, along with the brave American civilians who didn't deserve to die."

Another applause from the audience.

"Before we go and let these heroes back to their families, there's something I want to say to the people in this world who wish harm upon this nation," Rivera said, his voice becoming more intense. "I hope you remember what happened eight days ago, when a militia of highly-trained, highly-motivated and well-armed terrorists attacked a group of unarmed, unsuspecting civilians."

"Despite all the odds stacked in their favor, the terrorists were overthrown. The mission was unsuccessful."

"I'm not sure how many more times America is going to have to prove itself. I'm not sure how many more innocent people will have to die. I wish it were none. I hope and pray this is it, this really is the last time, and we never have to deal with this sort of unprovoked attack ever again."

"And I say to you, the terrorists watching today, why? You will not win. No matter how well you think the odds are stacked in your favor, no matter how genius you think your plan is, you will not break us. Every time you attack, we grow stronger. Every time you strike, we strike bad harder. From a practical standpoint, there is absolutely no justifying ever attacking us ever again."

"But rather than come at it with that approach, I'll go with another. What's the motive for attacking us? We mean no harm. We wish to trade, to share our resources with you, to become partners with you, to share this gem of a planet together, in peace."

"If we continue to fight each other, to preach killing, we'll never progress. But I know all of us are better than that, and for evidence, I point to the success of this very country. Here, every ethnicity in the world lives in relative peace, each with an opportunity for a good job and the freedom to worship who they please and to vote for whoever they want."

"Stop fighting against that. Embrace it. We all become stronger when we hold hands instead of trading fists. We are lucky enough to live on the only planet in our universe that we know of that can sustain life – why can't we make the most of it?"

The audience applauded.

"In the meantime, we shall stand guard. We shall be more prepared than ever for your attacks. But truly, what we'll hope for is that will never have to use our defenses. What we'll hope for is peace."

"Thank you all, particularly the people behind me, who were so brave when our nation needed them most. God bless all of you and God bless America."

With that, the audience erupted in applause one more time, and a nation began to heal.

Or at least that's how the history books told it.

Washington, D.C.
Friday, October 26, 2012; 5:07 p.m.

"Come in, Mr. Berith."

"Please, Mr. President, call me Dan."

"Well, then, call me Sam."

The leader of the free world smiled behind his giant oak desk in the Oval Office. The Mexican-American – the first minority ever elected to the world's highest office – had shed his jacket since his speech and was now sipping what appeared to be a glass of whiskey on the rocks.

His desk was a giant oak monstrosity, with two flags

behind either end of it. There were two Secret Service agents in the room, both wearing black suits, both frowning.

It was intimidating.

"Surprised to see the president drink," Sam said, breaking the tension with a smile, as I took a stood across from his desk.

"A little," I admitted.

He laughed. "It's a Friday for me, just like it is for everyone else. Of course, you could use a drink more than I. Would you like something?"

"Uh, sure, that would be great."

"What would you like?"

"Whatever you're having."

"Johnny Walker Blue for the young man, then. Only the best for a hero."

Sam winked at me. One of the Secret Service agents in the room poured a drink and brought it over to me, which I took politely and sipped cautiously. Sam indicated for me to sit down, but I pointed to my ass, and he laughed a bit.

"Oh yeah, I forgot about that," he said, smiling. "Hope it heals up."

"Thanks," I responded. "I can sit on it a bit, but it starts to hurt after awhile."

The president broke his smile to let out a breath.

"Son, do you know why I called you in here?" Sam asked. He was only 47, a bit young to be calling me son, but I suppose the president of the United States can call you whatever he wants.

Even if you didn't vote for him.

"I'm assuming it's got something to do with last Thursday."

The president burst out in pleasant laughter. "You're an intelligent man, Mr. Berith."

I tried to smile, but my lips quickly returned to the frown that had possessed my face since Akil Dhakir entered my life, and I looked down.

A few people who were in Sunsets that night didn't attend the president's speech, and I couldn't say I blamed them. The reason they gave publicly was that they were recovering medically, but it was all above the neck, where no surgeon's scalpel could touch.

I myself hadn't really slept since that night either, reimagining myself slamming the head of Akil again and again into the ground. I did it far past his death, to the point that his skull was reduced to a jigsaw puzzle, with half the pieces covering my shirt.

But that wasn't the worst part. It was all the questions. Did Akil actually have a point? Would I think the same way, if I were him? Why did Marcus die, instead of me? How did I possibly survive? Is there a bigger point, or are we all just complex proteins holding on for dear life as our planet spins on its axis at 25,000 miles per hour?

And why the fuck did the president's speech 90 minutes ago really piss me off?

Sam read all of it within me, without me having to say a word. I suppose that's the sort of quality that gets someone elected president.

"You don't feel too good about your Medal of Freedom, do you?" Sam said.

"Not really," I said, my eyes pointed at the floor as I said it, only to flash them briefly at the president.

"You know, sometimes it seems like the dead have it

easier," he answered. "They don't have all the questions that you're dealing with right now. Your friend Marcus, for example, hardly a pillar of society. And yet he no longer has to think about any of that stuff: his place in the world, what it means to be a good person, did he do the right thing. He's just dead. And a hero. He doesn't have to worry about anything ever again."

The president took a sip of his whiskey and looked over at me, seeing a man staring at him intently. He went on.

"Living is hard. It's really, really hard. It's hard on me every day with all the decisions I have to make; I'm sure it's been hard on you all these years, and this incident might only make it harder."

"You see, sometimes I wonder if we became too evolved for our own good. Why go beyond just what is necessary to get food, reproduce, protect. All that extra brainpower only serves to drive us crazy, to make us constantly question things that no other living creature on this earth would ever question."

"Do you know a lion, when he takes over a pride, kills all the children within it? That way, only his genetic makeup moves on, and his mates' time isn't wasted on offspring that isn't his. Think the lion feels bad about that? Hell no."

"It would be easier to be the lion. It would be easier not to feel any guilt for the men you killed and help kill. But you know where the lion lives? Well, some live in cages we built for them for our amusement. Others live in the wild, but only because we allow them to live there."

"If we wanted to, we could wipe out every lion on the face of the earth. But we don't. The lions would do that to us, if they could, but they can't, because we're smarter than them. Because we are in control, the world is a more peaceful place, where lions are still allowed to live."

Not completely following his point but engrossed with his passion, I continued to stare intently at the president. Until that point, he was turned sideways to me, the common position for a man pontificating.

But now, he turned his swivel chair 30 degrees or so, making his shoulders square with mine. He leaned his head forward and began to talk, this time more intensely.

"The man you killed last Thursday and the people they represent are lions. They will kill us any chance they get, for no other reason because they can. We are generous to allow them to roam this earth, make some money off their oil-filled reserve, but make no mistake – they are not the same species as you or I. They are savages, created by hell itself to overtake everything we hold dear."

"I wish it weren't so. I thought for many years they weren't lions, they were people like you and I, who could be dealt with peacefully. But it just isn't in their blood. They are violent, angry people who want to kill us, and the only solution is big guns pointed at their direction."

I was shocked at what I was hearing.

"I don't think they are lions, sir. I just think some of them have too much fire in their blood, and don't like what we do."

The president laughed. "You know, I'm glad you said that. If you hadn't, I'd actually be a little worried about you. But let me show you something."

"Eric," the president said to one of the Secret Service agents in the room, the one who didn't make my drink. "Grab that file over there," the president said as he pointed to a built-in bookcase that, low and behold, had a manila folder on one of its selves.

Eric the Secret Service agent walked over and grabbed it. The president stood up from behind his desk, walked over to me while taking the folder from the suited man, and plopped it down on the oak I was standing just behind.

"Open it," he said.

I did. The first document that appeared was an 8-by-11-inch photo of a woman holding a baby, but both were missing their heads.

"This photo was taken just outside of Herat, Afghanistan, just the other day. As you can see, it's a woman and her newborn child, sans their heads. Do you know why they don't have their heads?"

I said nothing, still shocked by the brutality of the photo.

"The reason was this woman had an affair on her husband, her husband who regularly beat her. So you think the husband chopped off the head, right?"

Again, I said nothing.

"If only we could be so lucky. When the husband found out, he told the local head of the Taliban village there. And he, with the blessing of his peers, chopped the heads off the mother and the baby, declaring them an affront to Allah."

I continued to stare blankly at the photo in disbelief.

"Go on, look through some more photos," Sam said.

I did, and there were at least a dozen more like the first. Mothers and children, decapitated.

"All of these, each and every one, were from the decree of a Taliban court. See why I used the lion as a metaphor? These men, they too kill the young who do not belong to them. In fact, they are worse than the lion, because they kill the mothers as well."

Sam grabbed me by the shoulder and stared into my eyes, his face but a foot from mine.

"Imagine if these people had real power? Could you imagine what they would do? Do you still think you did the wrong thing or your country is somehow immoral, compared to this?"

"I don't know," I said weakly. "I'm not so sure Akil was much different than me."

"A humanitarian to the core," Sam said, as he slapped me on the back. "Enough talking shop. Let's enjoy our drink, and I'll send you on our way."

We spent the next 15 minutes or so chatting idly – Sam was a sports fan too, although he liked the Heat and the Marlins – and then we shook hands and I left the Oval Office. The whole time, though, all I could think about were Marcus and myself, and how maybe we had too much fire in our blood, too.

5:37 p.m.

I walked out of the office and was greeted by Amanda and my father, who were impatiently sitting on an uncomfortable-looking red couch just outside the door.

"How was he?" Amanda asked as she leaned in to hug me.

"It was fine," I said dismissively.

"Come on, you aren't going to give me any details?"

"I said it was fine!"

"You seriously just met the president and you aren't

going to say anything more than 'it's fine'?"

"Okay, honey," my father butted in, "he said it's fine. Let's leave it at that."

We began walking out of the White House in silence. When we made our way through two big oak doors to the great outdoors, twilight and 53-degree temperatures greeted us.

"Say, how do you guys feel about steaks tonight, my treat," my father said.

"Sounds real good dad, real good," I answered.

"Yeah, maybe Dan can finally tell us how the president was," my sister said as I playfully pushed her away.

We'd probably get to the restaurant at 6:30 or so, which meant we'd probably get back to the hotel around 8, I thought to myself. Which probably meant I'd likely have the whole night to myself, the last night we'd have in D.C.

I should probably live it up, I thought to myself, as we felt the crisp fall air. And, even more than that, I really wanted to take my mind off the president.

That asshole president.

Maybe there are some good strip clubs in the area, I thought, as I exited the home of our nation's leader. There's got to be, with all these politicians around, I figured.

Yeah, that should make for a good time. Just a lion, out to roam about the town.

THE END

A Note from the Author

I wrote this book on nights and weekends over the course of a year, from February of 2015 to February of 2016. I did it having no idea how successful it might be or if anyone would buy it, because I believed there was a story inside of me that I had to get out.

I self-published this book because I didn't want to go through the bureaucracy of a publishing house. Instead, I just wanted to give you the story inside of me as straight as I could, with as little filter as possible.

I have no real marketing budget to advertise this book and little idea of how to do that anyway. But, if you enjoyed it, I ask you to tell your friends and family and to post about it on your social media pages, as I'd like other people to enjoy it too.

Thank you, as I can't tell you how much I appreciate you taking the time to read this book. I sincerely hope it was worth it.

Paul Petrone
Tuesday, Feb. 2, 2016
Waterford, Connecticut

DanBerithLions@gmail.com